SONS OF ANARCHY™

Also by Christopher Golden

Snowblind

Father Gaetano's Puppet Catechism
(with Mike Mignola)

Joe Golem and the Drowning City
(with Mike Mignola)

21st Century Dead

The Monster's Corner

The New Dead

SONS OF ANARCHY™

BRATVA

~~~

CHRISTOPHER GOLDEN

From the mind of executive producer
KURT SUTTER

St. Martin's Griffin
New York

SONS OF ANARCHY™ & © 2014 Twentieth Century Fox Film Corporation and Bluebush Productions, LLC. All rights reserved. Printed in the United States of America. For information, address St. Martin's Press, 175 Fifth Avenue, New York, N.Y. 10010.

www.stmartins.com

Designed by Kathryn Parise

The Library of Congress has cataloged the hardcover edition as follows:

Golden, Christopher.
    Sons of Anarchy : Bratva / Christopher Golden. — First U.S. edition.
        p. cm.
    ISBN 978-1-250-06083-9 (hardcover)
    ISBN 978-1-4668-6659-1 (e-book)
    1. Motorcycle clubs—California—Fiction. 2. Motorcycle gangs—California—
Fiction. I. Sons of Anarchy (Television program) II. Title.
    PS3557.O35927S635 2014
    813'.54—dc23

                                                                    2014026971

ISBN 978-1-250-07695-3 (trade paperback)

Our books may be purchased in bulk for promotional, educational, or business use. Please contact your local bookseller or the Macmillan Corporate and Premium Sales Department at (800) 221-7945, extension 5442, or by e-mail at MacmillanSpecialMarkets@macmillan.com.

First St. Martin's Griffin Edition: November 2015

10 9 8 7 6 5 4 3 2 1

SONS OF ANARCHY ™

1

Jax Teller liked peace and quiet as much as the next guy, but he'd learned the hard way never to trust them. He'd spent his whole life as part of the Sons of Anarchy motorcycle club—first as the son of its founder, then as a member, and now as vice president of its original charter—and he didn't know any other way to live. Even when the club wasn't in the midst of trouble, there was usually some brewing.

Not today.

Just to have something to do, Jax reeled in his line, checked his bait, and then cast it back into the deep, churning river.

"Nothing biting," he said, just to say something.

Opie Winston sat six feet away, broad back against a rock formation and a beer in his hand. Shortly after they'd come down to the river, Opie had driven a black plastic tube into the soft, damp soil of the riverbank, cast out his line, and slid the handle of his fishing pole into the tube. It wasn't fishing so much as drinking beer and shooting the occasional glance at the line to see if anything might be tugging at it.

Jax thought he was begging for the fishing pole to get dragged into the river—exactly what would happen if a decent-sized steelhead decided to take the bait—but Opie looked too relaxed for him to bring it up. In truth, the arrival of a thieving steelhead didn't seem very likely, considering that there had been two nibbles on Opie's line in nearly three hours and that he had only bothered to reel it in a few times. His focus had been on emptying the cooler of beer they'd lugged down from the cabin.

Jax rose to fetch a fresh beer, doing his share to help lighten the cooler for the return trip. He propped his fishing rod in the crook of his arm to open the beer and took a long gulp.

Opie stretched and rotated his head, and the bones in his neck popped loudly. "Either the fish are getting smarter or they can sense how unmotivated we are," he said.

"Speak for yourself, Op. I'm motivated."

"Then you're doing it wrong," Opie said. "Fishing's a state of mind, Jax. It's Zen. If you wanted to finish the day with something to eat, we should've gone hunting like I suggested."

Jax settled himself at the base of a massive tree whose thick roots had been exposed by decades of erosion. When the river ran low enough for the ground between the roots to dry out, it made the perfect seat.

"Hunting's too much work," he said. "We came up here to clear our heads."

"Then why are you bitching about the fish not biting?"

Jax drained a third of his beer. "Things get quiet, I squirm a little. Need to break the silence."

He drew back on his fishing pole a bit to see if there was anything dragging on the line, but it moved easily, not even the ghost of a nibble. When he realized Opie hadn't replied, he turned to find his best friend studying him curiously.

"What?" Jax asked, not bothering to hide the edge in his voice.

"How many days do you think you'd have to be up here before you could stop worrying about all the other shit?"

Jax sipped his beer. "Not sure I can count that high, brother."

They fell quiet again, only the sounds of the river and the rustle of the wind in the trees to disturb the silence. Opie had suggested the trip the day before, and Jax had surprised himself by agreeing. They'd thrown beer and bait and a single bag of groceries into the back of Opie's truck and made the drive up to the cabin. The place had been a private retreat for the club since the days of the First Nine, back when Jax's and Opie's fathers and guys like Clay Morrow and Lenny the Pimp had been laying the groundwork for what would become SAMCRO—Sons of Anarchy Motorcycle Club Redwood Original.

As kids, Jax and Opie had run wild in the woods around the cabin, fished and swum in the river, and drunk beers they'd stolen from their dads. John Teller and Piney Winston had made their sons drink those beers until they threw it all up—a biker's lesson. Sitting in the cradle of those old tree roots and watching the river flow by, Jax felt haunted by those days. They hadn't come up to the cabin on anything but business in years, and now he struggled with the weight of his responsibilities to Tara, to his sons, and to the club. Coming up here with Opie had seemed like a good idea, and he'd enjoyed just *breathing* for once, but he could feel hooks set deep in his flesh, dragging him home.

He and half the club had survived months in prison and upheaval in their relationships with the Real IRA and the Russian mafia—the Bratva. Jax had been shivved in Stockton Penitentiary on orders from the Bratva's chief, Viktor Putlova. SAMCRO had managed to broker a peace with the Russians that lasted long enough for Jax and the other club members who'd been sent up with him to get back on the street. SAMCRO had broken that peace at Opie's wedding to Lyla. Putlova and his muscle were all dead, and the Sons had struck a new deal with the Mexicans—the Galindo cartel—and bought themselves a moment to breathe.

Jax and Tara had gotten engaged and announced it to the club. All should've been right with the world—he told himself this trip to the cabin, a sort of mini bachelor party, was proof of that—but the engagement had only deepened the fault line that splintered Jax himself in two. There was the man he wanted to be, and then there was the man he'd been raised to be. SAMCRO's business had always been illegal guns and now it included drugs, and he'd promised Tara he had a plan to get himself—and his sons—away from the club and the dangers that came along with it.

He'd promised. And he'd meant it.

Sometimes, though, promises turned to quicksand.

Opie's line twitched, bobbed, and then bent. Jax called his name, put aside his beer, and pushed himself up from the cradling tree roots, but Opie was already in motion. He'd seemed to be half-dozing a second before, but now he hurtled toward his fishing pole and grabbed hold just as it began to tilt and slide up out of the tube. Jax dropped his own fishing pole into the tube, thinking he might need to help.

"Son of a bitch!" Opie growled, whipping the pole back to set the hook in the mouth of whatever fish had been dumb enough to take bait that had been sitting in the river for three quarters of an hour.

Opie had a few inches and at least thirty pounds on Jax. With his beard and grim eyes, he looked intimidating, like the kind of man who would break a musician's wrists for playing the wrong song—which he'd actually done.

He looked ridiculous reeling in that fish. Jax couldn't help laughing.

"Guess you met your match," he said, trotting back to fetch his beer. He stood on the riverbank and watched Opie dip the fishing pole toward the water and then jerk it back again, reeling quickly each time he did so.

Opie turned to sneer at him, but he couldn't maintain the anger and started laughing instead. He took a step toward Jax and the fishing line snapped, twanging as it ribboned back toward them like a spiderweb in a breeze.

"Fuck it," Opie said.He hurled the fishing pole into the river, drew his gun, and fired off half a dozen shots in the general direction of the fish. As the echo of gunfire died away, the two of them stood and stared at the fishing pole as it bobbed along for a few seconds longer and then slid below the current.

"That's one way to fish," Jax said with a grin.

Opie turned to gaze downriver, brow furrowed.

Jax wasn't grinning anymore. "What's up?"

"That fishing pole was my old man's."

Jax glanced at the pole he'd brought down from the cabin. They'd gotten the rods and reels from a dusty closet. Most of them were rusty, and Jax had chosen the one that seemed the least deteriorated. If one of the fishing poles at the cabin had belonged to his own father, John Teller, he wouldn't have been able to pick it out from the others. But Piney was alive, and he felt bad about the loss.

Half a dozen smart-ass remarks came to mind. Jax gave voice to none of them. Instead, he picked up his own fishing pole and began to reel in the line.

Opie gathered up the empty beer bottles and piled them into the cooler. In an alley back in Charming, they might not have bothered.

"Looks like you needed to get out of Charming more than I did," Jax said. Opie hefted the cooler. "I'm not the one who just got out of Stockton."

Jax put on a smile. "I'm fine, Op. Like you said, I'm *out*. Now I'm engaged, and you're a newlywed. The club's put its house in order. Cash is flowing again. Things are good."

Opie gave a soft laugh, but without a trace of humor.

"That's what worries me," he said, and started trudging back up through the woods toward the cabin.

"How does that make sense?" Jax asked, falling in step beside him. "We in some kind of trouble you're not telling me about?"

Opie smiled grimly. "Trouble's always on the way, Jax. What worries me is times like this. Times when we don't know which direction it's gonna hit us from."

His words lingered in Jax's head as the two men reached the cabin and prepared to head back to Charming. It bothered Jax how much Opie's thoughts about trouble seemed to echo his own, like they were swimming in an ocean of it, just waiting for the next big wave.

Neither of them could have predicted how soon the next wave of trouble would hit or whom they'd find drowning in it.

2

They'd just come off the wooded road onto the long, faded, two-lane road that ran parallel to Route 99 for a dozen or so miles on the way to Charming and Lodi. Opie was behind the wheel, and Jax had been digging through the stack of old CDs on the floor. He'd chosen *Drunken Lullabies,* by Flogging Molly, because the head-banging title track always wormed its way inside his skull and made him think of Ireland and his father, two topics that, when considered together, always pissed him off and yet somehow amped up his mood.

He turned to peer out the window at a dusty vineyard that had seen better days. In the rearview mirror he caught a glimpse of a black Humvee coming up behind them, moving fast.

"Be happy, brother," Jax said, popping open the glove compartment and retrieving the Glock 17 that had been waiting there. "At least you know what direction the trouble's coming from."

Opie glanced in the mirror. "Shit. Feds, you think?"

"Just drive," Jax told him. "If it's feds, I won't need this."

He jacked the slide, slamming a round into the gun's chamber. Jax had a feeling this wasn't feds.

Opie floored it, the truck jumping forward with a roar. The gap separating them from the Humvee opened up for a second or two, and then the monstrous black vehicle began closing again. Jax tightened his grip on the Glock and glanced to the left, across the two-lane road and the span of grass and trees and scrub that separated it from Highway 99. "Cut across," Jax said.

Opie shot him a quick, hard look. "Serious?"

A hundred yards ahead, the ground between the side road and the highway flattened out, and old, worn tracks showed that others had driven across it in the past. A white box truck rumbled toward them from the other direction.

"Right after the truck," Opie said. "Hang on to something."

Jax watched the box truck coming along the two-lane road, counting seconds in his head. The Humvee's engine roared, and it bumped the pickup. Opie and Jax jerked in their seats, rattled by the impact.

"Guess that rules out the feds," Jax said, bracing himself against the dash with his free hand.

Opie didn't reply. Jaw tight, he watched the box truck, his knuckles white on the steering wheel, ready to swerve left, tap the brakes, and shoot across the open ground between the faded side road and Highway 99.

The white box truck swerved first—across the lane in front of them.

A setup.

"Son of a—" Jax managed before Opie cut left as planned, tires skidding.

Their pickup slammed sidelong into the box truck, but Opie hit the gas, gunning it for the break in the trees—that tire-worn gap that would put them on Highway 99, give them room to run, put some other vehicles into the mix.

The Humvee hit them broadside, shattering windows and caving in Opie's door. The engine screamed under duress as the Humvee slammed them sideways and Opie's pickup skidded along the road and off the shoulder. They missed the gap. The Humvee kept pushing, and they hit a stand of old pine trees with a jerk that bounced Jax's skull off the passenger-side window. His grip on the gun loosened, but only for a second.

"Down!" he shouted.

Opie ducked his head. Jax grabbed his shoulder to be sure, steadied his hand, and fired through the shattered driver's side window, blowing out the Humvee's windshield. The Humvee's driver reversed, tires spinning as the vehicle withdrew; then it skidded to a halt, and the doors popped open.

Jax knew he ought to be moving, but he wanted to see what they were up against. If they were dealing with a rival club, like the Niners or Mayans, the assholes would have been on motorcycles. *Must be a different breed of assholes,* he thought.

"Cartel?" Opie asked, twisted in his seat and rooting in the back for the shotgun there.

"We're solid with Galindo," Jax said, frowning.

"Is anyone ever solid with the damn cartel?"

The question went unanswered. The men piling out of the Humvee and the white box truck were pale and dressed in blacks and grays, all of them carrying guns. These weren't cartel hitters, and they sure as hell weren't part of Lin's Crew. Jax might've thought them Real IRA, but he didn't recognize a man among them.

"Russians," Opie said.

Jax grunted. "Let's move."

They piled out the passenger door, using Opie's pickup as cover. Jax's boots hit the ground, and he ducked behind the truck's bed, gun raised. His temples throbbed with rage, but he pushed the anger away, forcing himself to think. A quick glance over the truck bed showed the Russians fanning out, guns trained on the pickup but not firing yet.

Of course they're Russians. How could he have thought anything else? Their dour Slavic countenances were unmistakable. Pale killers, there for vengeance for Putlova's murder.

That's why they aren't shooting yet, he thought. Putlova's whole crew were dead and the Russians had no one who could confirm that SAMCRO was behind it.

"They want us alive," Jax muttered.

Opie had his back to the truck, shotgun primed. "They got a funny way of showing it."

Jax exhaled. The Russians might want them alive for the moment, but that wouldn't last. Whoever had ordered this move would be reluctant to expose himself to any unnecessary public risk. Jax and Opie would be tossed in the back of the box truck, driven to wherever the boss might be, questioned, and then very likely executed. It would be hard to convince the Bratva that SAMCRO hadn't killed Putlova and his buddies . . . mainly because they had.

"Mr. Teller!" one of the Russians shouted, his accent thick. "You and your friend throw out your guns and come out where we can talk."

"We can hear you just fine from here!" Opie shouted back.

Jax couldn't help the hint of a smile.

"This isn't how you want this to go down!" Jax told them, risking a glance over the top of the pickup's bed. The Russians hadn't come any closer, nor did anyone open fire.

"You need to come with us. This is to be a private conversation," the Russian said, "and this is a very public place."

Jax looked at Opie, then over at the cars passing on Highway 99. A black Mercedes slowed down—a driver rubbernecking, thinking he'd seen an accident—and Jax realized the clock was ticking. Cops would be on the way. He glanced at the pine trees behind them.

"You're too quiet, Mr. Teller!" the Russian shouted. "But we will catch up to you, and then there will be bullets. I imagine you'd prefer to keep bullets out of this."

Opie frowned at Jax. "Gotta buy some time," he rasped quietly.

Jax nodded. Every option he considered seemed to lead to only two possible results: die or survive and end up back in prison. They could claim self-defense if they shot these bastards, but possessing the guns they would use to defend themselves might be enough to flush his parole down the toilet. His mind reeled, trying to puzzle his way out of it.

Ticktock, pass the time, keep them talking.

"Who sent you?" he called. "Might make our decision easier if we knew who we were dealing with."

"Your only decision is bullets or no bullets," the Russian said, his accent somehow growing thicker.

The wind picked up. If there were any birds in the trees, they'd fallen silent.

Off to Jax's left, a man in a gray suit sidestepped into view, edging over with his gun raised, trying to get a clean shot behind the pickup. Jax whipped around and took aim.

"Back the hell off!" he roared. "Or the decision is made!"

The man did not move, but neither did he shoot. He kept his gun trained on Jax, who glanced at Opie and wondered how many seconds they had before another Russian moved into view on that side of the pickup. They hadn't had a long list of choices to begin with, but the list was getting shorter with every passing second.

"Jax," Opie muttered.

The Russian called his name. "Time is running out. In moments, the decision will be taken from you. My men have witnessed the opportunities I gave you. My employer won't blame me if you die here on the side of the road. Your children will cry for you, Mr. Teller, but I will sleep well tonight."

Jax stopped breathing. Anger blinded him for a second or two as images of his boys, Thomas and Abel, swam into his head.

"I will count to five," the Russian said. "One—"

The countdown narrowed their options to only one. Jax glanced at Opie, found his friend already looking back at him, dark anger in Opie's eyes that matched Jax's own.

"Two," the Russian said.

Opie helped keep him focused, keep him grounded. They had been best friends so long that Opie understood him better than anyone. When Jax has lost his brother and later his father . . . and when Opie's first wife, Donna, had been killed . . . they had relied on each other. Hell, they'd always relied on each other.

"Three."

"I've got the asshole to your left," Opie whispered.

Jax took a breath, relaxed his grip on the Glock, then popped up from behind the pickup's bed. In one smooth motion, he took aim at the Russian who'd just brought his children into the conversation and shot him twice in the chest. One of the bullets punched all the way through, fanning bright crimson blood onto the grass behind him.

Simultaneously, Opie stepped back from the pickup, leveled the shotgun behind Jax, and blasted the guy who'd come around the side. The Russian blew backward through the mist of his own blood. The boom rattled Jax's brains as he ducked behind the pickup again, but then he and Opie were both running into the copse of pine trees. The Russians opened fire, and the pickup rocked with scores of gunshots that plinked metal and shattered glass. By then, Jax and Opie were in the midst of the trees, and Jax had begun to count the seconds in his head. How many until they caught up? How far to the highway, running at this angle through the trees?

Opie crashed between two pines, and Jax raced to catch up.

"We need a ride!" Opie said.

The clamor had died down behind them, but Jax knew that didn't mean the Russians were departing. They would be in pursuit. He glimpsed Highway 99 through the trees, spotted an eighteen-wheeler, a whining Suzuki motorcycle, its rider all in vivid blue, and a couple of cars racing in either direction. Their best hope was to force someone to stop—no one would willingly pull over for a couple of shaggy guys in biker cuts. Might be they had to jack a car.

And I end up right back in Stockton.

Shit. Whatever they were going to do, it would have to happen here. Their only real choice was to outlast the Russians, stay alive until the cops showed up, and then leave it to the lawyer.

Across this section of Highway 99, the trees were thicker. They could get lost in there, at least for a while, maybe long enough to call the clubhouse and get Juice or Phil to come and pick them up before the cops tracked them down.

A way out, maybe.

A bullet grazed Jax's right shoulder, and he swore as he stumbled. He dodged left and kept running, the skin on his back prickling with the sensation that every inch was a possible target. Opie'd heard him grunt when the bullet tagged him. He turned toward Jax.

"Keep moving!" Jax snapped, and Opie didn't need to be told twice.

Bullets zipped by, punching the air and shaking tree branches. They broke from the edge of the pine grove twenty feet from the shoulder of Highway 99. A big rig thundered past, sucking gravel and someone's discarded McDonald's burger wrapper into its wake. A bullet hit the truck's broad side. Another took out a window in a Mustang racing along the northbound side of the highway, and the car slammed on its brakes.

Jax thought they might just have found themselves a ride.

Heads low, he and Opie hurtled into the road.

Amidst gunfire and the blare of car horns, they reached the median strip that divided the highway, only to hear tires skidding behind them and voices shouting loudly in Russian. Jax spun, ducking behind the guardrail at the median, and took aim with the Glock as a silver Lexus skidded to a halt on the grassy shoulder they had just vacated.

"What the hell?" Opie said, dropping down beside him.

A guy in an old Volvo shouted and honked as he drove by, maybe not noticing the guns. Opie racked another round in the shotgun's chamber, and he and Jax both stared at the Lexus. More Russians poured out—no mistaking those icy eyes and granite features—but instead of opening fire on Jax and Opie, they turned their weapons on the men now emerging from the pine grove.

"Check it out," Opie said, and gestured back to the cut-through between the side road and highway—the gap where they had left Opie's pickup.

A black Escalade raced along the same dirt track and slid to a halt at the edge of the highway, and more armed men jumped out.

Another big rig roared by. Jax closed his eyes and turned away as grit pelted his face. When it had passed and he turned to look again, the gunfire had ceased entirely. Russian voices rose in warning and anger as the newcomers took aim at the men from the Humvee and the white box truck. The two groups barked challenges at one another, and a huge, bearded man who'd climbed from the Escalade came forward. The man had presence, and the body language of both groups changed as he started shouting at them all.

"The boss?" Opie asked.

Jax nodded. "*Someone's* boss."

The bearded man smoothed his tailored charcoal suit and gestured southward. Jax frowned, wondering what he might be telling the other Russians, but then he heard sirens in the distance and got the gist.

"We gotta go," Opie said, starting to turn. They needed to be in the woods on the other side of the highway and hidden deeply before the cops arrived.

Jax stayed to watch the Russians, who had all begun to retreat. Sensing his hesitation, Opie waited as well. The first group kept their guns out as they backed awkwardly into the pine grove, then turned and hurried back through the trees to their vehicles. Three of the newcomers kept their weapons trained on the fleeing group as the rest climbed back into the Lexus and the Escalade. In moments, all four vehicles were pulling away.

The sirens grew louder, but with the open highway, Jax thought the police could still be miles away.

Maybe.

"Come on," he said, leaping the guardrail and running back the way they'd come. He wished he could toss the Glock away but knew how foolish that would be, with his prints all over it and the cops certain to search the pine grove.

A car swerved to avoid killing Opie, the driver laying on the horn.

The two of them ran through the trees, Jax gambling that none of the Russians were suicidal enough to have stayed behind to finish the job when the others had taken off and the sirens were growing louder.

Opie's pickup remained where they'd left it, jammed against a couple of pine trees, most of the windows blown out. The engine choked a bit as Opie turned the key in the ignition, but then it growled to life, and he threw it into drive, pulled back onto the side road, and hit the gas. They were headed away from the sirens, but Jax was sure cops would be coming the other way. No way they could stay out in the open with windows blown out. "There!" Jax said, pointing to a narrow, tree-lined street on the right.

Opie spun the wheel, and the pickup groaned and slewed in gravel as they turned onto the back road. In seconds, they were out of sight of Highway 99, driving a curving lane that climbed gently into the same hills they had left behind such a short time ago.

Two miles up that lane, they found an old logging road that had been transformed into a hiking trail. Opie drove down it until they reached an unfamiliar leg of what Jax assumed was the river they'd fished in that morning.

Opie backed the truck up to the water, where they wiped down their guns and hurled them as far out into the river as they could. Only then did Jax take out his cell phone and call the clubhouse. Chucky answered but put Bobby on the phone as soon as he heard the urgency and anger in Jax's voice.

When Jax ended the call, phone clutched in his hand, he turned to Opie. "Only thing we can do now is wait."

Opie nodded toward the hiking trail. "You think we oughta wait up that way, in case the cops get here before Juice does?"

Jax took a deep breath and then nodded as he exhaled, trying to make sense of the shitstorm they had just been through.

"What was that?" Opie asked as they started walking up the trail.

"You asking me why we're still alive?"

"I'm asking why double the Russians didn't mean double the bullets headed our way."

"That first bunch wanted us dead because they think we killed Putlova," Jax said. "Maybe the second bunch didn't like Putlova as much as the other guys did. Maybe we did those guys a favor."

"I thought we had solved our Russian problem," Opie said, his boots scuffing the ground as he walked. "At least for a while."

"It's a tough economy, Op. A job opens up, every asshole and his brother rushes in to try to fill it."

"So what do we do about it?"

Jax smiled. "If we're smart enough, we steer clear and hope the morons kill each other."

3

John Carney saw the redhead coming from fifty yards away. Not that he was a perv or anything. Hell, he hadn't been on the prowl for twenty years, not even after his wife, Theresa, had left him back in '04. Carney'd had a girlfriend or three, but always someone he'd met through friends. No online dating for him, and he certainly wasn't going to pick up women in bars.

Bars were off-limits if he wanted to keep his fifteen-year chip in his pocket. Sober life might get boring at times, but boring was preferable to dead.

The Summerlin Gun Show had seen a dip in business the past few years, but he continued to set up out of loyalty to Oscar Temple, the fellow who'd run the thing from the beginning. This year Carney's loyalty had paid off—the first two days of the Summerlin show had brought booming business. Americans had been growing paranoid about their right to bear arms being curtailed or taken away entirely, and any time that happened, business picked up. Nothing helped gun sales like talk of gun control.

They were in an open field on Oscar Temple's ranch, just at the western edge of Summerlin proper, spitting distance from Red Rock Canyon in one direction, and not too far a drive from downtown Las Vegas in the other. Ground zero for tourists and easy enough to find for gun enthusiasts.

The redhead didn't look like your typical gun enthusiast. And now that she'd come a little closer, he realized she wasn't precisely a redhead. More of a strawberry-blonde. Lovely hue.

She moved through the crowd like a shark, barely browsing the tables and tents as she studied the faces of the dealers more closely than she did the weapons they had for sale. Sunshine turned her hair into a reddish-gold halo. Her bottle-green tank top and tight, faded jeans showed off a shapely figure, but Carney noticed the confidence and determination in her walk more than the fullness of her breasts or the swing of her hips. At fifty-five, he certainly wasn't beyond appreciating a lady's attributes, but he'd always appreciated a formidable woman—even if she looked like she was barely more than a girl.

The strawberry-blonde stopped at Hal Burlingame's table, rapped on top of a glass case to get the old man's attention, and cocked her hip as she asked him a question. Her smile was a mask of sweetness that appeared only as he turned toward her and vanished just as quickly when she had her answer.

Burlingame turned and pointed to the rows of gun dealers.

Only when the strawberry-blonde turned and spotted Carney—and smiled that same masquerade grin—did he realize Burlingame was pointing at him.

He frowned in puzzlement as the young woman strode toward him. Customers were perusing his wares, and a guy who'd been asking him why he didn't have a Barrett M82 .50 caliber sniper rifle for sale had started complaining about the government's infringing on his rights, but Carney ignored them all.

The cute little thing sauntered up to him, but the saunter didn't fool him. This wasn't a girl who sauntered.

She turned her right hand into a finger pistol, and pointed at him as if she might shoot him with it.

"You'd be John Carney?" she said.

Even in those four simple words, he heard the Irish accent, and it took him back. His parents had been from Carrickfergus, just up the coast from Belfast, and he still had a bit of a brogue himself.

"I'd be him, yes. What can I do for you, miss?"

Lass, he told himself. If he still had any of the old Irish left in him, he'd have called her lass.

Her smile was deadlier than any of the guns at his table.

"Mr. Carney, a friend told me that you could help me, and I surely hope he was right. A lot's ridin' on it."

For the first time, Carney noticed the two men moving through the crowd behind her, cruising without shopping, just as she had done. They were hard men, almost as young as the Irish lass, with flinty eyes and thin lines for mouths. *Cops?* he wondered. *Or the opposite?*

The urge to warn her bubbled up in his chest, but then he saw that she'd noticed him looking past her—seen the flash of alarm on his features— and seemed unconcerned.

So they were with her.

His brow furrowed. Whatever this girl was, she carried trouble with her. She carried the charm and the painful beauty of his heritage on her every word, and he knew right then that she wasn't worth it.

But he nodded anyway. "I'll see what I can do."

She looked around in a way that made it clear she hoped to speak to him without being overheard. The jackass looking for a .50 caliber sniper rifle had wandered away, mumbling, and so Carney led her to the back of his booth, the rear corner of one of his tables.

"I'm told you can introduce me to Oscar Temple," she said.

Her pale skin shone brightly in the sun, and the light splash of freckles across her nose only added to her beauty. But when she mentioned Oscar, he saw the hard set of her jaw, and the confidence in her eyes slipped just like the mask of her smile, revealing fear and desperation. The mask returned an instant later, but Carney had seen behind it.

"What's your name, love?" he asked.

"Caitlin Dunphy," she said, in a tone that told him she was lying and that she didn't care if he knew it.

Carney swallowed hard and glanced around, worried now about who might be watching. Even the flinty-eyed men who were obviously her backup were not openly looking at them. *Don't do it*, he told himself. *You're legit, John. Pure legit.*

If Caitlin Dunphy wanted his introduction to Oscar Temple, there would be nothing legal about whatever conversation followed. He ought to stay far, far away, tell the girl he couldn't help her.

But Oscar had been very good to him over the years, and he'd want whatever business the girl was bringing his way.

And, God help him, John Carney had never been able to say no to an Irish girl.

Even in its early days, the city of Charming, California, had been uniquely suited to become home base for a motorcycle club. Most locales would have been less hospitable, troubled by the reputation biker gangs had for chaos, violence, and criminal pursuits. Once upon a time, gold rushers had settled into agriculture and the lumber business, founding a small community based on true pioneer spirit. After the San Francisco earthquake, scores of city folk relocated in search of a simpler lifestyle, but it wasn't until the end of World War II that these different factions melded together and built a piece of true Americana.

The people of Charming had two philosophies. One was, *Live and let live,* reflecting the pioneer spirit of the original settlers. The other was, *Don't shit where you eat.* Maybe not in those words, but with the same effect. Charming did not like chain stores or shopping malls. Most of the real estate developments were homegrown—their investors from Charming—and most of the businesses downtown were mom-and-pop operations. Through the tumultuous second half of the twentieth century, Charming had changed very little, and that was just how folks liked it.

SAMCRO had been in town for more than thirty years, running Teller-Morrow Automotive Repair nearly as long. The original partners in the business—John Teller and Clay Morrow—had been two of SAMCRO's First Nine, and when the Sons of Anarchy became involved with the illegal gun trade, T-M was the legitimate front for those operations. For years the chief of police, Wayne Unser, had looked the other way, and the locals considered the club upstanding members of the community.

That had been getting harder and harder over the past couple of years. Chief Unser had retired, and the entire Charming Police Department had been eliminated, with local law enforcement falling to the county sheriff. Now SAMCRO had gotten involved in the drug trade, and its relationship with Charming had begun to unravel. As president of SAMCRO, Clay Morrow had been grasping at the frayed strips of that unraveling bond, but for every one he managed to tie back down, two more tore loose.

It had really begun to piss him off.

Clay sat at the head of the enormous conference table in the Chapel.

Chain-link fence topped with barbed wire ran the perimeter of the auto-repair yard's property. In the middle of the yard were the garage, office, and clubhouse. With the bloody-scythed reaper carved into its meeting table, the Chapel was the beating heart of SAMCRO, and by extension every Sons of Anarchy charter in the world.

"Where's Juice?" Clay asked, shooting a dark look at Bobby Munson, the rotund, bearded, graying Elvis impersonator who had become the conscience of the club. For years, Clay had considered Bobby one of his greatest assets, had trusted him for his cool head and his ability to see all sides of an argument. Recently, those same traits had become inconvenient for Clay, and now he felt the urge to blame Bobby for everything.

"You saw the damage to Opie's truck," Bobby said. "Juice is figuring out the repairs, making sure the guys know—"

The Chapel's door opened, and Juice ducked his head in. He gave the same shy, apologetic smile that seemed a fixture on his face and slipped inside, closing the door behind him.

"Sorry," he said, rubbing a hand over the bristle of his buzz-cropped Mohawk and the tattoos on either side of it.

To Clay's left, Jax straightened up and nodded at Juice. "Sit down."

Clay cast a sidelong glance at Jax, saying nothing. The boy had been feeling his oats lately, developing the swagger of a man who thought he ought to be holding the gavel instead of wearing the vice president patch. But Clay had calmed things down between him and Jax after they'd gotten out of Stockton, made a side deal that would ease Jax's way out the door when the time came, and had paved the way for SAMCRO to get into business with the Galindo cartel. The kid would be out of his way soon enough.

Still, Clay didn't want Jax getting too comfortable giving orders.

"All right, let's figure this shit out," Clay said.

He gripped the gavel, clenching his jaw at the stabbing pain in his arthritic hand, and banged on the table to bring the meeting to order. All eyes were on him, and he took a moment to survey the club members seated around the room. Jax and the sergeant-at-arms, Tig Traeger. Bobby and the Scottish-born Chibs Telford. Opie and Juice. Happy and Kozik, both of whom had patched back in from other charters. Miles, who'd been patched in as a full member while half of the club had been in Stockton.

Opposite Clay, at the far end of the table, sat Piney Winston. One of the three living member of the First Nine, Piney had cofounded SAM-CRO with John Teller and had been the one who'd sponsored Clay at the beginning. Now the old man sat with his oxygen tubes up his nose and his watery eyes and gazed at Clay with seemingly constant doubt and disapproval.

Jax getting cocky was something Clay figured he could deal with . . . but Piney had started to become a problem.

"Short and sweet, now," Clay said. "Jax?"

The VP glanced around the table. "You've all heard parts of this already. Me and Opie were on our way back from the cabin. Humvee hit us from behind. A truck boxed us in, drove us off the road. One look at Opie's truck should give you an idea how that went."

"You're still breathing, Jackie," Chibs said. "That's a piece of luck."

"Any landing you can walk away from, right?" Kozik added.

Tig leaned over the table, eyes narrowed. "We're talking about Russians, yeah? Looking for payback for us taking out Putlova and his girlfriends?"

Opie gave a nod. "What we figured. They wanted us alive, though. At least long enough to bring us to whoever gave them the order."

"We didn't play along," Jax said. "The shooting started, and then the other Russians showed up."

"What other Russians?" Piney rasped. He'd been frowning from the moment the gavel had gone down, but for once Clay didn't blame him.

Opie could take care of himself, but no father wanted to hear about Russian Mafia shooting at his son.

Jax and Opie told the rest of the story, trading off details. There wasn't much to tell. A couple of minutes later, the table fell silent for several seconds, until Jax turned expectantly to Clay. Exactly what Clay had been waiting for—that moment when Jax acknowledged who held the gavel.

"This stays at the table," Clay said. "I know you all thought we'd settled our Russian problem for a while. So did I. Now it looks like the Russians may be having a turf war."

"Do we bring Galindo up to speed?" Jax asked, scratching thoughtfully at the blond scrub of his beard.

"On what?" Clay said, scanning the table to make sure they all understood his reply. "We don't know shit at this point. Chibs, if this is gun-trade business, could be our friends in Belfast heard something."

Chibs had been born in Scotland but grown up in Belfast and had done stints with the British Army and the RIRA before some ugliness forced him to leave Belfast. He still had enemies in Ireland, but the old connections remained in place—unpleasant as they could be.

"I'll reach out to Connor Malone," Chibs said. "See what he knows."

"We should talk to Lin, too," Bobby said, that perpetually worried look on his face. "If the Russians are making a new play, could be Lin and his crew already know."

"I'll give Lin a call," Jax said, nodding.

"Do it," Clay instructed. "Report back."

He glanced around the room. The Chapel was sacrosanct, everything discussed at the table considered private unless it was voted otherwise.

"These assholes may be nothing to worry about," he said. "A bunch of Bratva dogs fighting over table scraps, hoping their masters in Moscow notice and carve them off a bigger piece. They keep shooting each other, that oughta distract them from worrying about who put Putlova in the ground. Just the same, keep your eyes open, watch each other's backs until we figure out who's giving the orders on either side."

Clay scanned their faces again, making sure nobody else felt the need to weigh in.

"All right, then," he said, banging the gavel. "Adjourned."

Jax left the others in the clubhouse and went outside, swinging the heavy door shut behind him. The air grew close when they were in church, jammed in that meeting room. There were a lot of guys, now, and that was good—it made the club strong.

As he strode to his bike, he dug into his pocket and tugged out his cell phone. Calling Lin might be a waste of time—the Russians wouldn't have asked permission from the Chinese before they started their civil war—but it was possible Lin had heard something. If the Russians killed each other off, that was all for the better, but Jax worried about collateral damage.

He reached out to Lin.

Footfalls scuffed the parking lot behind him and Jax turned, still skittish from the attack that morning. He must have looked ready to fight, because Chucky held up his hands—what was left of them—in immediate surrender, just to make sure Jax knew he wasn't a threat.

As if Chucky Marstein could ever have been a threat.

"Whoa, Jax. It's just Chucky."

"You think I wouldn't recognize you?"

Always nervous, the bald, goateed little guy seemed more agitated than usual. "No, no. I thought maybe you'd gone, ya know, rabid or something."

Jax cupped the phone in his hand. "You came out here for a reason."

"Sorry, yeah." Chucky rolled his eyes at his forgetfulness. "You've got a call in the office. Lady sounds pretty upset. Urgent-like."

A frown creased Jax's brow as he started walking toward the office. "You get a name?"

"No," Chucky said, catching up to him, "but if it helps, she's got some kinda accent. English, I think. Maybe Irish."

Jax slid his phone into the inside pocket of his cut, Chucky completely forgotten. He stepped into the shade of the office and saw the phone on the desk, old-fashioned corkscrew cord all tangled. His mother, Gemma, had inherited his father's share of Teller-Morrow, and most days she could be found in the office. Jax was grateful she wasn't there now or she would have been the one to answer the phone. During his time in Belfast many years past, JT had gotten involved with a woman named Maureen Ashby. Jax had a half-sister whose existence he'd only discovered when he'd made his own trip to Belfast. Any woman with an Irish accent calling the office of Teller-Morrow and getting Gemma on the phone would not be well received.

Jax picked up the phone. "Hello?"

"Can you talk, Jax? I didn't know who else to call."

Maureen was a woman with sharp edges, but he'd gotten along with her well enough while in Belfast. She reminded him of his own mother, though Gemma would have crucified him if he'd ever said it aloud.

Hearing Maureen sound this desperate and afraid made Jax very nervous.

"What's up?" He glanced back at Chucky, alarm bells going off in his head. Only one thing could have made Maureen Ashby lose her cool. "Something happen with Trinity?"

"Girl's gone missing," Maureen said. "Off the radar. I've left her twenty messages. Haven't heard from her in more than two weeks and now—"

"What do you mean, two weeks? She lives with you."

"Not for months she hasn't."

"Hang on," Jax said, growing more frustrated than worried. He turned and ushered Chucky from the office. When the little guy had gone, he sat down at the desk. "Start from the beginning."

"There's no beginnin', Jax. She's off with them Russians, and I figure if anyone can find her, it's you."

Jax pushed a hand through a thick scruff of his blond hair. "What Russians?"

Given the events of the day, just asking the question made him nauseated.

"Five months ago, it was. A whole Russian delegation shows up—Mafia bastards—wantin' to do business with Brogan, Dooley, and Roarke—"

"The Russians didn't come to Belfast uninvited," Jax interrupted.

"Do I bloody care if they were invited?" Maureen snapped. "They were here doin' business, that's all I know. Roarke had a friend among them, as much as Roarke has friends."

A dreadful calm settled over Jax, the same feeling that always descended on him when things took an ugly turn. It felt like sinking into quicksand and simply throwing his hands up, letting it drag him down, knowing that once it had swallowed him, things would only get worse.

The Irish Kings—the ruling council of the Real IRA—had entertained a visit from some faction of the Bratva. It made a sick kind of sense. Jimmy O'Phelan had been the RIRA's man in California, handling the illegal gun business and the relationship with SAMCRO. He'd tried to cut SAMCRO out by directly approaching the Russians, but he'd gone completely rogue, making a mess big enough that the Kings not only gave their blessing for him to be killed . . . they rewarded SAMCRO for carrying out the hit.

Now, if Maureen knew what she was talking about, the Russians had made an appeal to the Kings after Jimmy O had been killed. Jax needed to know more—needed to know how that visit had gone and what it meant for the relationship between SAMCRO and the Irish—but Maureen hadn't called to talk business or the politics of criminal enterprises.

"One of the Russians—a strong-arm fella named Oleg Voloshin—he followed Trinity like he was in orbit around her."

"You think he took her?" Jax asked, grip tightening on the phone.

"I know he did, Jax. Trinity fell for Oleg. She thinks she's in love with him . . . and if I'm honest, I didn't mind so much. I've loved my share o' men who didn't exactly follow the letter of the law, and Oleg—he's a sweet lad for a hired gun. Trinity went off with him about four months ago, but she kept in touch, called me regular until a couple of weeks ago. I haven't heard a whisper from her, and it's got me scared out of my wits."

Jax leaned back in the chair, staring at the office door Chucky had left open—staring at nothing.

"Listen," Maureen went on, "I know there're other things we need to be talkin' about, but right now—"

"You're worried," he interrupted. "I'm worried myself. But getting out of the country'd be next to impossible for me right now. Going to Russia—"

"Who said anything about Russia?"

"I thought Trinity went back with Oleg."

"She left with him, yeah, but your sister's not in Russia. She's in America. Last I knew, she was in Nevada."

Jax spun toward the desk, digging up a pencil and a sheet of paper.

"Anything else you can tell me about where Trinity's been staying, or about this Oleg guy or his people?" he asked.

Maureen rattled off what she knew, which was precious little, and Jax scrawled down anything that sounded promising—which wasn't much. Only when he hung up the phone did he sense the presence of someone else behind him.

He turned to see his mother, Gemma, staring at him with a familiar, disgusted curl to her lips.

Gemma sneered. "You've got to be shitting me."

4

Caitlin Dunphy had been stabbed to death by her boy-friend after she'd found him in a pub with another girl. Hurt and humiliated, Caitlin had confronted him and then left the pub in tears, after which the girl he'd been chatting up had given him a further dressing-down and poured a beer over his head. The boyfriend, Tim Kelley, had stalked back to Caitlin's flat with more alcohol fueling him than a drunken sailor would've thought wise. Tim and Caitlin had argued, and then they'd fought, fists flying. Like any good Irish girl, she'd given as good as she'd gotten . . . right up until he grabbed a kitchen knife and stabbed her in the throat.

Trinity had loved dear Caitlin. They'd been at school together as girls and spent plenty of nights together at the pub, as well as mornings on a run in the park. Once they'd even been in jail together, and the less said about that, the better. Trinity had been unable to cry at Caitlin's funeral, rage obliterating her grief, desperate to get her fingers around the handle of a knife and give Tim Kelley what he had coming. Less than a month later, the bastard was done for, but it hadn't been Trinity who'd killed him.

She'd regretted that for years. Always would. Trinity Ashby had spent her life on the fringes of a violent world, but she'd never been a criminal herself, and she certainly wasn't a killer. She would've made an exception for Tim Kelley.

For Caitlin Dunphy.

When John Carney had asked her name, Caitlin's had popped out. It shamed her now to think of it.

Too late to turn back now, she thought.

In so many ways.

The Summerlin Gun Show wrapped up in the late afternoon, but the breakdown took a while. Trinity had a hell of a time keeping Oleg and the other guys from getting impatient while they waited, never mind that the four of them just standing around together—this Irish girl and a trio of grim Russian guys, all edgy and paranoid—was going to draw some unwanted attention, even in the waning hours of a gun show. She'd sent Gavril and Feliks off on a drive, while she and Oleg had alternated between perusing the sellers' booths, listening to the musical act performing at the east end of the show, and visiting the big silver Airstream trailer that had been converted into a mobile cantina and snack shop.

Their kettle corn had been delicious.

Now, with the gun show over and the sun swiftly sinking behind the red mountains in the west, they drove along the dirt road leading up to the main house on Oscar Temple's ranch. There were fences everywhere, but their focus was on security. They spotted a couple of guards and at least three cameras, which made Oleg and the guys nervous. They were following the battered old Ford pickup with the heavy cab on the back that John Carney used to bring his wares to gun shows, and Carney had called ahead.

They were *expected*.

Trinity had to wonder, though, just what it was that Oscar Temple might be expecting. Carney must have given him the basics, but would a man like Temple react poorly to scuffed-up, stone-faced men with Russian accents? If she'd learned anything about Americans, she thought he might.

"Let me do the talkin'," Trinity said from the backseat.

Gavril was at the wheel, with Oleg in the passenger seat and Feliks in the back, beside Trinity. They all scowled at her, even the man with whom she'd fallen in love.

"It's possible you have said that once or twice already," Oleg said.

Trinity narrowed her eyes, pushed herself up between the seats, and made sure he was looking her in the eye.

"I'll say it a thousand times if that's what it takes to get through your thick Russian skulls."

Oleg's grin stretched the thin white scar that ran along his jaw from chin to earlobe. The tattoos on the back of his neck and along his arms were somehow cruel and beautiful at the same time. He had high cheekbones and a small mouth and the narrow eyes of a man who might like to hurt you. The stubble on his shaved scalp did nothing to alleviate such concerns, but Trinity knew better. She'd felt his touch and seen the hunger for her in his eyes. Oleg would never hurt her, except perhaps by dying for her, and she wanted to do everything in her power to prevent that.

Gavril drove. Always. Ugly and dark-eyed, he had a face that looked as if he'd been in a thousand fights and lost them all.

Feliks was the quiet one. Six and a half feet tall, he had built himself into a wall of muscle. Trinity had the feeling that most fights with Feliks ended before they began, with his opponent pissing himself before a punch could be thrown.

"You talk to us like children," Gavril said. "I crushed the throat of a man who spoke to me like that."

Trinity smiled and sat back in her seat. "You're not the first man to hint he'd like to kill me. I believed the other guy more."

"One of us loves you, Irish," Gavril muttered, huge hands tight on the wheel. "But it isn't me."

Oleg glanced into the backseat again, one eyebrow raised. Gavril might be a killer, but the two men were like brothers, and he would never hurt the woman Oleg loved. Feliks kept silent, as always, but he rolled his eyes just a bit to indicate that he also thought Gavril's threats were hollow.

The huge, rambling ranch house grew larger ahead of them. Trinity saw Carney's brake lights go on, and then Gavril hit the brake. The tires of their black Mercedes kicked up a cloud of dust, and they waited for it to clear before opening the doors. The Bratva had taught her not to expose herself anywhere she didn't have a clear view of her surroundings.

Trinity climbed out of the car and slammed the rear door. The Mercedes ticked as the engine cooled. She'd suggested they steal something a little less Russian Mafia–cliché than a black European sedan, but Gavril insisted that they had standards. Oleg had swapped out the plates with those from an old Volkswagen Rabbit. Nobody would be catching up with them tonight, at least.

Oleg and Feliks emerged from the car a few seconds behind her. Gavril waited behind the wheel, right hand no doubt on the ignition. They had no key, but getting the engine running would take the man half a second. He'd done this once or twice before.

Carney stepped out of his pickup and put his hands to the small of his back the way aging men always did. He stretched and then ambled toward them, more cowboy now than the Irish boy he'd been raised.

"Miss Dunphy," he said.

She wanted to tell him her real name, but she could not. Oleg might decide that information was worth killing him for.

"I ought to tell you now," Carney went on, "I'm not real comfortable with this."

Feliks dropped his hand back a bit, the better to reach for the gun tucked into his rear waistband if he had the need.

Oleg seemed about to open his mouth and reveal his accent, but Trinity shot him a look that made him as silent as Feliks.

"There's nothin' for you to be uncomfortable about, Mr. Carney," she said. "You're introducin' an old friend to a new one, that's all. If you'd rather not stick around after the introductions are made, nobody here will hold it against you."

Carney shifted awkwardly and glanced up at the house. "Oscar might."

The friend in Belfast who'd given her Carney's name had told her that the man had been on the straight and narrow path for many years. His discomfort at being involved with anything outside the law seemed genuine enough, but he'd agreed to bring them here, and once involved, it wasn't the sort of thing he could easily walk away from.

Carney seemed to recognize this truth a second or two after Trinity had. He sighed with a let's-get-on-with-it expression and headed for the sprawling ranch house's front door with Trinity, Oleg, and Feliks in tow. Gavril remained behind the wheel of the Mercedes until the door opened and a bearded man in a rust-colored sport coat beckoned for them to come inside.

At the door, Carney greeted the bearded man whose name seemed to be Aaron. Aaron Something didn't bother to introduce himself to his employer's guests. Trinity would have taken him for a fool with his crisp new blue jeans and unscuffed, pointed-toe cowboy boots, but she saw the slight bulge of a weapon beneath his sport coat and a dark intelligence that glittered in his eyes like tiny burning coals. This man was more than a thug.

Aaron led them into a foyer and gestured toward a small table beneath a coat rack. "Leave your guns right here. They'll be waiting for you on the way out."

A ripple of unease went through them all. Trinity shot Oleg a dark look and he nodded, watching Aaron carefully as he drew the pistol out of his rear waistband and set it on the table. Gavril and Feliks followed suit.

"What about you?" the man asked, turning to Trinity.

"I'm just here to talk," she said. "I don't even like guns."

He studied her a moment, taking in her jeans and boots and the thin cotton sweater she wore. Aaron was trying to figure her out, what she might be doing with these men, and Trinity could tell he hadn't managed it yet. Neither had she.

"Strange company you keep, if that's the case," he said.

"No argument from me."

He gestured for them to move deeper into the house. "Mr. Temple is waiting for you in the kitchen."

"The kitchen?" Trinity echoed.

No one said a word. Carney followed Aaron, and she and her Russian boys were obliged to go along. At first it seemed odd to her that the man would welcome them in his kitchen instead of a study or sitting room, but of course the kitchen was more intimate, more personal . . . and somehow more hospitable. Meant to create the illusion that they were all friends and could speak their minds.

They found Oscar Temple chopping vegetables at the granite-topped center island. He wore a big Colt pistol on his hip like a marshal in the Old West, the leather belt and holster as oiled and supple as a young boy's precious baseball mitt. A pot simmered on the fancy stove, and Trinity's stomach growled at the wonderful aroma that filled the room.

"Hello, John," Temple said warmly. "And hello to your friends."

"Evening, Oscar," Carney replied.

Temple glanced at the window over the sink. "Is it evening already? Well, she sure snuck up on us, didn't she?"

On a second cutting board was a whole chicken that he'd stripped, the meat stacked on a plate. Once he'd put the meat and vegetables back into the spicy broth that simmered on the stove, he'd have quite a stew.

"Smells good, doesn't it, Miss . . . ," Temple said, glancing her way.

"Dunphy," Trinity said. "Caitlin Dunphy."

Temple wiped his hands on a dishrag and greeted her with a handshake. He'd zeroed in on her—maybe Carney had told him up front that she'd do the talking—and he didn't bother to offer his hand to any of her companions. Trinity had a moment of total panic as she realized that, instead of being just Oleg's girlfriend, she had taken part in a criminal endeavor, working with the Russian Mafia.

Lord, what am I doing? she thought, unable to take a breath.

Then she glanced at Oleg and remembered the answer. *Staying alive. Keeping Oleg alive.* This was her family now.

Light footsteps came from another corridor at the far side of the kitchen, and they all glanced over to see a brunette woman step in. Tanned and weathered, she wore her own variation on Aaron's sport coat, complete with the bulge of a handgun. How many were there? Trinity wondered.

"Antoinette, there you are!" Temple said happily. "Could you give Miss Dunphy a pat-down, please? When you're done, Aaron can do the same for her friends."

"They left their guns at the door," Trinity said. "And I'm not armed."

"Could be that's true," Temple said. "But Antoinette is searching you for cameras or listening devices . . ."

He paused, studying Oleg before moving on to Gavril.

"Though, judging by your companions, I'm certain you're on the up-and-up. Our federal friends are never quite this convincing," he said, finishing with Feliks. "Russian, aren't you?"

Trinity had told them to keep quiet, and they heeded her advice, saying nothing.

Temple glanced at her, reached up, and tapped the back of his own neck. "The tattoos, my dear."

She glanced at Oleg, thinking of the crude images in the flesh at the back of his neck, remembering the times she had stroked that skin.

"Russian gulag is the only place you get something like that," Temple said. "Do they still call them that, gulags? Or are they just prisons now?"

Gavril inched toward him, menace rolling off him in waves. "Do you have issue with Russians? A rule, maybe? You don't do business with us?"

Trinity wanted to cuff him around the head but didn't let her irritation show.

Oscar Temple held his hands wide to show they were all friends. "Not at all, *tovarisch*. Politics ain't my game. I'm a businessman. Anyone willing to pay me in U.S. currency is American enough for me."

Gavril nodded, perhaps reconsidering his decision to speak up. He glanced at Oleg and Trinity. Feliks had hung back, staying as close to Temple's mustachioed bodyguard as possible.

"Go on and pat me down, then, Antoinette," Trinity said, hoping she sounded friendlier than she felt.

The woman went about the task thoroughly enough that Trinity figured it qualified as her first girl-on-girl experience. When Antoinette finished, she retreated into the hallway from which she'd appeared, and it was Aaron's turn to pat down the Russians. Oleg and the boys shifted uncomfortably as Aaron took his time.

"What about the old man?" Aaron asked, nodding toward Carney.

Temple smiled beatifically. "You armed, John?"

Carney frowned. " 'Course I am. I've got that old Beretta you gave me when I turned seventy."

"I wouldn't have it any other way," Temple said.

Aaron shrugged. "All right, then. No wire, and no other guns. But that one has a knife," he said, pointing at Oleg.

Temple smiled that devilish grin. " 'Course he does." He glanced at Oleg. "You look like a knife man, Ivan."

Oleg chuckled softly.

Temple's mask slipped a moment. "I say something funny?"

"Nobody calls us Ivan anymore. Ronald Reagan has been out of office for a long time," Oleg said.

Trinity sighed. Okay, Temple was an asshole, but when you wanted something from an asshole, you had to let him peacock around acting like King Shit. She glanced at Carney, who stood only a couple of feet from her. The old man looked nervous as hell.

"You're in my house," Temple warned. He rested his right palm on the gun handle jutting from the holster on his right hip. "I guess I'll call you whatever I want, particularly since you didn't offer up your names."

Carney took a step away from Trinity, marking himself out as separate from her and her friends.

"Listen, I did my part," he said, his voice a tired rasp. "I made the introductions. But you're all a little too wound up for me, so I'm gonna be on my way."

Trinity's skin rippled with gooseflesh as if a malign presence had just entered the room. She didn't believe in evil spirits the way her grandmother always had, but she certainly believed that bad intentions carried a weight, an aura that could be felt.

"You sit tight a second, Carney," Temple said. "You brought these folks here."

"Can we get down to business?" Trinity asked, raising her hands in supplication. "All we want is a fair price, and we've heard you're a man who deals fair."

Temple exhaled. He glanced at Aaron, who seemed to deflate a bit, and most of the tension drained out of the room. Oleg and Gavril relaxed visibly, but Feliks didn't move any farther away from Aaron.

"What are you looking for exactly?" Temple asked.

Carney hummed to himself, looking at the floor, pretending he wasn't involved in an illegal gun deal.

"MAC-10s. Tec-9s," Oleg said. "Mix and match. We need a dozen, plus twenty handguns. Hollow-tip rounds, if you can get them."

Temple whistled appreciatively as he scraped chopped vegetables onto a plate and walked over to the simmering pot. "You guys have quite a Christmas list. That's a lot of guns just for the four of you."

No one said a word. Temple dumped the vegetables into his stew and then went back for the big plate of chicken.

"I can get them," he went on.

Antoinette stepped back into the kitchen. Temple glanced at her, and the woman gave a tiny tilt of the head.

Trinity didn't like that head tilt, or the way the left side of Temple's mouth lifted in an almost imperceptible smirk. Something had just passed between Antoinette and her employer, and Trinity ran back through the past couple of minutes in her head, trying to figure out what she had missed.

"How soon can you have 'em?" she asked, as if she hadn't felt the change in the room.

Temple scraped the chicken into the pot and then adjusted the level of the flame.

"Something's got me wondering," he said. "Not that it's any of my business, but I'm curious what sort of shitstorm you're all in that you've got to come to me. Let's face it, most of the guns ghosting their way up and down the west coast of this country came through Irish or Russian hands at some point, so why not go to your own people for this?"

Trinity felt cold. "Like you said, Mr. Temple. It's not your business."

The smarmy, condescending look returned to Temple's face. The bastard had snake's eyes and a predator's smile.

Antoinette's pocket buzzed once. The kitchen had fallen silent except for the hum of the refrigerator and the tick of the clock, and the buzz was loud enough that everyone in the room glanced over at her.

Everyone except Oscar Temple.

Trinity stared. Why wouldn't Temple react to the buzz of Antoinette's phone, the sound of a text message coming in? Unless he'd been expecting the sound—waiting for it. Suddenly all the talk made sense, as did the way Antoinette had slipped out of the room.

Swearing under her breath, Trinity darted left, slipped behind John Carney, reached up under the back of his jacket and drew the gun the old man kept holstered there. Antoinette barked a warning even as Carney cried out in protest, but she nudged the old man aside and leveled the gun at Oscar Temple.

Aaron swore and reached inside his jacket for the pistol holstered at his armpit. Feliks was in motion as he drew the gun, ripping it from his grasp and then slapping him so hard that Aaron crashed into the wall and slid down to one knee, shaking his head to try to clear it. Feliks followed him, cracked the gun across the bridge of Aaron's nose, smashing cartilage. Temple seemed too calm. Antoinette went for her own gun, but the rancher gestured for her to be still.

"Son of a bitch," Aaron growled, starting to rise as he wiped at the crimson flooding from his nose.

"No, stay there," Temple instructed, sneering at the man who'd been his bodyguard. Trinity had the feeling he was fired.

Oleg and Gavril were staring at Trinity like she'd lost her mind. Maybe she had. Paranoia could be an insidious thing—she'd seen it in others, but never in the mirror.

With his mustache and his brand-new, fake-cowboy clothes, Aaron looked ridiculous there on the floor, like a 1970s porn star past his prime. All the threat had hissed out of him like helium from a punctured balloon.

"Want to explain yourself, girl?" Temple asked.

Trinity ignored him.

Feliks handed the bodyguard's gun to Oleg, then darted back along the corridor to retrieve their guns from the table in the foyer. Seconds later he reappeared and gave Gavril back his own pistol.

"I trusted you," Carney said, staring at Trinity.

"Wasn't us you shouldn't have trusted," she replied, hating the weight of the old man's gun in her hand and the way her skin prickled with awareness of what a bullet could do.

"Antoinette," she said, making her way around Temple while keeping him in her sights. "Take the mobile phone out of your pocket."

The darkly tanned woman fished out her cell and handed it over. Trinity made sure Oleg and the others were covering Temple and his sidekicks and flipped open the cell phone. The text had come from a local phone number—no contact name—and consisted of four words. *Stall. Fifteen minutes out.*

Trinity read the text aloud.

"Shit!" Oleg muttered, glancing at Gavril. "Krupin?"

The name made Antoinette flinch. Trinity felt her stomach lurch. She pointed the gun at Antoinette's skull, pressed it into her dark hair, and *nudged,* wondering when she had become so hard. All her life she'd had this sort of violence around her, but most of the time she'd been inside a kind of protective bubble. Never a part of the violence.

Now she jabbed Antoinette's skull with the gun barrel again. "Who sent that text? Who's on the way?"

Carney let out a shuddering breath. "I'm sorry . . . I can't be here. I've got to go."

He started toward the corridor, jittery and shaking his head. Feliks moved to block his path, and Aaron used the distraction, lunging to his feet and crashing into Feliks, trying to strip the weapon from his hand.

Trinity swore, an instant of panic freezing her in place.

Oleg opened fire on Temple, who dropped behind the kitchen island as he drew his gun. Gavril faded left, trying to get a clear shot.

Antoinette grabbed Trinity's wrist, twisting to throw off her aim. Trinity pulled the trigger, and a bullet punched the ceiling, raining plaster down on them. Antoinette drove her fist into Trinity's kidney and then into her armpit, tried to take Carney's gun from her. *No, no, no.* Her thoughts whirled, heart pounding. It was all falling apart.

The bitch grabbed her face and pushed her backward, slammed her into a rack of cabinets, rattling dishes inside. Antoinette slammed her head twice more, fighting for the gun, and Trinity lost her grip. She felt it as her fingers opened, knew what it meant—that any second the woman would put a bullet in her, and she would die. They would all die. Oleg would die, and she couldn't have that.

Gunshots boomed in the kitchen.

Trinity spun away from her. Smelled the spices from Temple's delicious stew. Grabbed the handles on the big pot with both hands and flung the simmering, burning broth into Antoinette's face.

Her skin steaming and bubbling, the woman screamed and dropped the gun. Trinity dove for it. Her fingers closed around the cool metal, and she rolled into a sitting position and took aim at Oscar Temple's back. He was hiding behind the kitchen island, but she was on *his* side, nothing to protect him from her.

Temple didn't hesitate. He started to turn.

Trinity pulled the trigger twice and missed both times. The shots made him flinch, made him draw back as splinters flew out of the kitchen island. The flinch cost him a vital second or two, and then Gavril was there. He shot Temple in the forehead, snapping his head back as blood and brain matter sprayed the cabinets behind him. Gavril shot the old man in the chest as he collapsed.

Antoinette kept screaming. Her face and eyes were raw-red and covered in broth as she lunged for Trinity. Oleg shot her—in the head. The bullet went in through her temple and never emerged.

A pause. A breath. Even the clock and fridge seemed to have fallen silent in that moment between moments, and then one more shot rang out.

Aaron struggled to free himself from beneath Feliks, who had just gone hideously limp. The broken-nosed bodyguard pushed out from under the huge Russian. Blood poured out of a hole in Feliks's neck like it might never stop. Shaking, Aaron tried to bring his recovered gun up to defend himself but Oleg reached him, kicked him in the face, and then did it again. Aaron howled as his shattered nose was pummeled, mashed bloody against his face. Trinity thought she heard his cheekbone crack.

"Shoot him!" Gavril roared. "He killed Feliks! Put *all* the bullets in him!"

"No!" Oleg snapped. He kicked Aaron again. "On your feet, *khuy!*"

Aaron staggered as he rose, one hand against the wall to keep from collapsing. Feliks had hurt him badly, but now Feliks was dead. Trinity hated it all, but she wouldn't lie to herself. Aaron deserved whatever Oleg and Gavril did to him. They had come here to make a fair deal, and they'd been betrayed.

Oleg had a fistful of Aaron's hair and jammed the barrel of his gun against the bodyguard's gore-streaked throat.

"You know where the guns are in this house," Oleg said. "Tell me no, and I shoot you in the leg. Then I stomp your balls until they burst."

Trinity's stomach roiled.

"You're gonna kill me," Aaron said, his voice trembling.

"It's what happens when you're on the wrong side," Oleg said, jamming the gun barrel harder against his throat. "But you take us to the guns right now, not another word from you, and you die with both balls and both eyes still where they belong. No pain. One bullet. Quick."

Aaron deflated, all hope leaving him, and nodded once. He started toward the back corridor where Antoinette had gone to make her call.

"We've got maybe ten minutes," Gavril said. "Less if anyone heard gunshots."

Against the wall, John Carney shifted and let out a small sob. Trinity, Oleg, and Gavril all turned to look at him. Broken and shaking, he stood there crying old man's tears.

"Gavril," Oleg said.

Trinity knew the tone, knew what it meant.

"No," she said.

Oleg frowned, glancing at her, his gun now aimed at Aaron's back. "*Trinity.*"

Letting the old man's gun hang by her side, Trinity walked over to Carney and stood in front of him. She didn't look at him, afraid to meet his eyes.

"This man did nothin' wrong. He'd put this life behind him till we asked him to do us this favor. I'll not allow you to kill him for it."

Oleg hesitated. Lips pressed together in a white line, he thought it over, but Trinity knew how it would end. The brutality he'd threatened Aaron with . . . he'd have done it all but gotten no joy from it. Violence was a tool for Oleg, but he didn't have a killer's heart, and he believed in people reaping what they'd sown.

He gestured toward Carney. "Go and sit at the table. You'll leave when *we* do."

Silently, Carney went to the little round table in the kitchen, dragging out a chair.

Aaron started to turn, maybe to make a fight of it again. Oleg struck him in the temple with the gun.

"Walk."

The bodyguard walked the first of his final steps. Oleg and Gavril followed.

Trinity knew they could have used her help to carry the guns they were about to steal, but she pulled out a chair and sat down across the table from red-faced John Carney. He wiped his tears and looked at her with doubtful eyes.

Carney glanced over at the corpses of Temple and Antoinette, and his expression darkened. She thought for a moment that she saw in him the hard man he'd once been.

"Oscar dealt the cards, lass," Carney said. "He used to say, 'The house always wins,' but he was a fool to think it. Sometimes the house loses. Sometimes the cards go the other way, and the house gets burned to the ground."

5

Jax held his son Thomas in his arms and pressed his nose against the boy's head. Thomas wasn't a baby anymore, but his head still had that baby smell, reminding Jax of his most important role. His sons were his world, his reason for breathing. People talked about the measure of a man, but to any man with children, the only real measure was in the eyes of his kids. If someday they learned the things he had done for the club, for brotherhood, and to try to build the future he wanted for them . . . he hoped they would understand why. But the more time passed, the more he realized that giving them that future mattered more than them forgiving him for what he had to do to get them there.

Laughter and the sound of splashing came from the bathroom. He kissed Thomas on the head and nudged the door open. Tara Knowles knelt beside the tub, washing the hair of Jax's older son, Abel. They both looked up at him—his old lady and his boy—and their smiles tugged at him. Abel's hair was full of suds, and Tara had been sculpting it into strange curls and waves, showing Abel in a hand mirror.

"Hello, Daddy," Tara said.

Abel tried to throw a handful of soap bubbles at him but they didn't go far.

"I'm headed out," Jax told her.

Tara stood and reached for Thomas, who stretched out his arms for his mother. Jax kissed the boy's head and handed him over. Tara smiled again, and it lit up her angular features. Her face could turn a man to stone if Tara was displeased with him, but she had a dark beauty that made him reach up and trace the contours of her face.

"Be safe," Tara said, kissing him even as she took Thomas in her arms. "You come back to me."

"Don't I always?" he asked with a grin.

"If you know what's good for you."

The lightness of the conversation hid a darkness beneath it. Tara didn't want him to go—not with just Chibs and Opie to back him up—but she wouldn't tell him to stay, either. Jax had not shared the details with her, only that Trinity was in danger.

Tara had wrapped her arms around him, pressed her body against his to remind him what he would be missing while he was gone, and knitted her brows as she stared into his eyes.

You have to go, she'd said. *I love you for that. But you never knew she existed until half a year ago. Don't die for her.*

He didn't plan to, but they both knew the risk was there. For everyone, yeah . . . and moreso for the people in their world. The life they'd chosen meant he was sticking his head in the lion's mouth on a regular basis. One of these days, the jaws were gonna chomp.

Jax went to the tub and splashed Abel, who kicked and splashed him back. He kissed Tara and Thomas again, then turned and left without looking back. He picked up a small bag by the door—just a change of clothes and a few things—and went out, closing the door behind him.

Chibs and Opie were little more than shadows in the driveway as Jax stepped outside. Their bikes were familiar silhouettes, comforting ghosts awaiting new life.

Opie lit a cigarette, the flame momentarily illuminating his face. Jax approached them as the moon slid out from behind a scrim of clouds.

"You set?" Opie asked.

Jax went to his bike. "She understands."

Opie shook his head, reminding Jax of a bear. "Wish Lyla did. Maybe Tara can talk to her."

"I'm sure she would if you want."

Opie exhaled cigarette smoke. "She's gonna have to get used to it. She thinks we're going to end up in Vegas with a roomful of whores."

Chibs stepped between them, threw an arm around each of them, and grinned the devil-may-care grin that always seemed to lift the spirits of his brethren.

"We get this sorted out, maybe we save that bit for the return trip," he said.

Opie smiled, took another drag on his cigarette, then dropped it to the pavement to grind it out. At some unconscious signal, the three of them moved toward their bikes. Jax had the sack with his gear slung over his shoulder, and now he slipped the second strap over his other shoulder. He wore a leather vest similar to his cut, but this one had no markings—no patches or symbols of any kind. Chibs wore a threadbare old denim jacket with an olive drab T-shirt beneath it. Opie had a plain navy sweatshirt with its sleeves pushed up to his elbows. Without their cuts—with no link to the club—he thought they all looked naked.

"You sure this is the right move, Jackie?" Chibs asked, smoothing his goatee as he sat astride his Harley-Davidson Dyna Street Bob. "Traveling without showing our colors?"

Jax nodded. "We can't pick sides till we know which side tried to kill us."

"Clay seemed pretty unhappy about it," Opie noted, reaching for the handlebars.

The plan had not pleased Clay—that was certain. He didn't like the idea of the club being three men down for days, didn't like them going out essentially undercover, and most of all, didn't like the fact that he couldn't control whatever unfolded in Nevada. If it had only been about Trinity, Jax figured Clay would have bitched even more, but he at least acknowledged that the trip ought to help give them a better idea of what the hell the Russians were up to.

"Clay knows it can't be avoided," Jax said.

Chibs kicked his bike to roaring life. Jax was about to follow suit when headlights washed the driveway in yellow gloom, and he turned to see his mother pull up in her black Cadillac XLR-V. She left the big vehicle idling at the edge of the property and climbed out, slamming the door before striding across the yard toward them.

"Boys," she said, her voice almost lost beneath the growl of Chibs's engine.

Opie and Chibs both nodded at her. Opie might have said her name, but Jax was barely paying attention. He sat on his Harley, one hand on the throttle.

"You didn't have to come see us off," he said.

Her lips pursed in something like a scowl. "I came to see my grandsons."

Gemma Teller-Morrow looked damn good for her age. Her brown hair had blond highlights and auburn streaks. She had a hell of a figure and enough of the beauty of the girl she'd once been that much younger men would look at her twice—and maybe keep looking—until her eyes drew their attention. Once they looked her in the eye, most guys turned away, unprepared for a woman so in charge of every moment of her existence. She worked hard to keep hidden the never-healing wounds that life had given her. Jax had seen them, though. He knew them well.

He also knew that those wounds made her more formidable instead of less. Gemma had raised him by example. No one understood her as well as Jax did, not even Clay. She knew why he had to go to Nevada and wouldn't stand in the way, as much as she hated it.

Gemma kissed him on the cheek, took his forearm, and squeezed once, not at all gently.

"Don't take stupid risks for Maureen Ashby's little bitch."

Jax shook his head. "I'll see you in a few days, Mom."

Gemma walked off, her heels clicking on the driveway as she approached the front door. Tara would not be happy to see her, but Jax couldn't run interference any longer. They had to get on the road. He kicked the Harley to life and felt immediately at ease. On the back of that bike, engine snarling, road unfurling beneath him . . . that was where he belonged.

Jax rode out of the driveway with Opie and Chibs in his wake.

Just one stop to make before they headed to Nevada.

Connor Malone had never liked his office. It was the place where he was most vulnerable. At his desk, he felt that at any minute law enforcement might break down the door and arrest him. He never answered the phone without his skin prickling with paranoia that his conversations were being overheard.

Instead, he took most meetings in pubs and diners, at dog parks and boxing clubs . . . even in a run-down barn on an Indian reservation. He'd read somewhere that a man who courted trouble couldn't be surprised when it followed him home.

Ah, wee Connor . . . ye're nervous by nature, his ma had always told him.

And yet somehow, as nervous as he was, Connor had worked his way up in the Irish Republican Army to become right-hand man to Gaalan O'Shay, who ran the RIRA's operations on the west coast of the United States. Should have made him nervous as hell, but it was never the work itself that unsettled Connor—it was the knowledge of how quickly it could all go tits up, landing him in prison or with a bullet in his back.

Lately he'd been more anxious than ever. The illegal gun trade was enough risk, but now their arrangements with the Sons of Anarchy involved the Galindo cartel, which meant drugs. American culture's love of guns was romantic, which meant many citizens would rather look the other way than worry about illegal guns. But Americans' love for drugs was more like carnal lust, and they were ashamed of their addictions and more eager to point a finger.

The word had come from Belfast—the deal had gone through. Gaalan didn't trust Jax Teller, thought of him as volatile—unpredictable—as much for his temper as for the streak of righteousness that went through the younger man. Connor liked Jax well enough, but Clay Morrow had always been easier to read. Clay's motivations were clearer, not muddied up by doubt or moral hesitation.

Jax Teller had called an hour earlier, and Connor suggested they meet in a booth at the White Horse Diner, a spot just off the highway in Morada, not far from Charming. Connor liked the place because they served breakfast twenty-four hours a day and because the tired truckers and exhausted parents and manic children never gave him a second look, no matter whom he might be meeting.

He shoveled forkfuls of southwestern omelet into his mouth and kept glancing at the door. He'd chosen a booth at the back out of reflex, though he'd have preferred to sit by the window. He didn't expect the Sons of Anarchy to come riding up to the plateglass window at the front of a diner and open fire—they might be lunatics, but they weren't stupid—still, caution was a good habit. The sort of thing that kept a nervous Irishman alive.

He took a bite of toast, a sip of tea, and then glanced up to see Jax and Chibs moving toward him through the diner. Connor frowned at their attire—strange to see them without their cuts—but the absence of the familiar SAMCRO vests served to make them less conspicuous, which pleased him.

"Connor," Jax said as he slipped into the booth, "thanks for coming out."

"It sounded important," Connor replied.

Chibs glanced around, eyes seeking trouble, then slid into the booth beside Jax. "Hello, Con."

"Filip," Connor replied with a nod.

Chibs glanced at the meal on the table with an expression that was not quite a smile—more like a memory surfacing. "Breakfast three meals a day."

"My doctor advises against it," Connor replied. "We're not as young as we used to be. But I spoil myself now and again. You gonna order something?"

Connor asked as he put a forkful of omelet into his mouth.

"Tempting as it looks, I just have a question for you," Jax replied.

"One question? You couldn't have asked over the phone?"

Chibs shot him a withering glance. "No."

Connor understood. Jax wanted to look him in the eye while asking. It troubled Connor to think they viewed him as someone so easy to read. Maybe it was true—maybe he was a bad liar. He promised himself he'd work on that.

"So ask," Connor said.

Jax rested his hands on the cracked linoleum tabletop. "Where do things stand between your bosses and the Russians?"

Connor could hear his mother's voice in his head again, reminding him what a nervous child he'd been.

"I'm not sure what you're askin'."

"Bullshit," Chibs muttered, brows knitted in consternation. "Don't piss about, Con. We haven't the time."

Intense as they were, unpredictable as ever, these guys wouldn't do anything to upset their arrangement with the RIRA. Connor knew that, just as he knew they wouldn't risk violence in the middle of a diner when there were small children just two tables away.

He knew that, but he didn't *know* it.

One of these days, that uncertainty—the fury simmering inside Jax Teller—was going to get a lot of people killed. Connor didn't plan to be one of them.

"As far as I know," he said, "there are no ties between us and them. Not now."

Jax leaned over the table, brows rising, blue eyes fiercely intent. "A bunch of Russians forced me and Opie off the road, tried to kill us in broad daylight. A second group showed up and drove 'em off. They're killing each other, Connor, and they're doing it on American streets with illegal guns. This conflict is gonna be bad for business, ours and yours. So maybe rethink your answer. I know the Russians sent a delegation to Belfast a while ago. I wanna know if anything came of it. I've got two factions shooting at each other and at members of my club. I wanna know which side the Irish are on."

Connor took a deep breath. On his plate, the remnants of his omelet were beginning to get cold, but he'd lost his appetite.

"If this comes up later," he said, "you and I never had this conversation."

Jax nodded. "Agreed."

Chibs gave a small nod as well, prompting Connor to forge ahead.

"Bratva went to Belfast lookin' for a deal. You've got that right," Connor said. "From what I hear, they were on the verge of something that might've proved inconvenient for you lads, but when word reached Roarke that the Bratva had splintered, that ended it. Belfast won't get involved with the Bratva until the power struggle's over and the dust has settled."

Jax narrowed his eyes unhappily. He glanced at Chibs and then cocked his head as he looked back at Connor.

"Thanks for that. All I wanted to know," he said. "Shit was happening back then, kind of chaotic, so I understand Roarke and the others considering alternatives. But the arrangement between Belfast and SAMCRO is solid now. If the Russians come back to try again once their situation stabilizes, that door is closed."

Connor scratched the stubble on his chin. "You askin' me or tellin' me?"

"I'm saying our arrangement is clear," Jax replied. "If the subject comes up, you make sure you let Roarke and the others know."

"I can't do that, Jax."

Chibs had his fists on the table. They tightened as if he wanted very much to use them. "Why not?"

Connor dropped his fork onto his plate and sat back. "I already told you, Filip . . . as far as anyone else knows, this conversation never happened."

He turned to signal the waitress for a coffee refill. When he looked back, Jax and Chibs were leaving. They didn't bother to say good-bye, and Connor was just happy to see them go. He picked up a half-eaten slice of toast and took a bite, erasing the past few minutes from his mind.

6

Moccasin Road ran east to west across the northern edge of Greater Las Vegas, mostly through gray-brown scrubland with more cactuses than houses. At its western end, the hills of Red Rock Canyon rose upward, changing the view from isolated alien landscape to something approaching true beauty. Jackrabbit Ridge was the sort of lost and lonely road that Hollywood had taught Trinity to expect to find all over Nevada, dusty and lined with prickly brush. When she'd first come to Nevada she had been disappointed to find it much more civilized than she had anticipated, but in recent weeks she'd learned just how much of the state remained wild and inhospitable. Las Vegas might be close enough to show its garish lights at night, but out here they might as well have been lost in the desert.

Jackrabbit Ridge had a handful of houses along it, mostly occupied by people who wanted to stay off the grid and away from the prying eyes of the federal government. They drove pickups and American-made SUVs festooned with flags and testimonials to their love of hunting and guns in general. Farther toward the national park there were side streets whose signs had long since been knocked down or stolen, so she did not know their names. There were some homes similar to the ones on the main road—although just thinking of Jackrabbit Ridge as a main road gave it far too much credit—but there were also two startlingly suburban-looking developments of single-family homes. Some of them were occupied, others abandoned or never sold, and more than one had been left half-built when the local economy proved unable to support middle-class dreams on Jackrabbit Ridge.

Trinity glanced out the window. They'd ridden in silence, she in the passenger seat and Oleg behind the wheel. Gavril had gotten in back and spent most of the ride with his head leaning against the window, striking the glass every time they hit a bump or a pothole. The air inside the car felt haunted by the unspoken awareness of the dead man in the trunk. Feliks had been their friend—to Oleg and Gavril he had been close to a brother—and they could smell his blood in the car, slipping up through the air vents somehow or just seeping through the backseat.

Numb, Trinity put a hand on Oleg's thigh just to tell him he wasn't alone. He didn't pull away, and that was good. These men were supposed to be cold. In the past, when she'd implied that Oleg might be allowed to have emotions, that he didn't have to be the hard-edged thug that Kirill Sokolov and the others wanted him to be, he had pulled away from her. She knew his heart—knew without a shred of doubt that he had a soul and a conscience—but she also knew that the Bratva was his life, his world, and his brotherhood. It was all he knew, and he measured himself by how much his brothers needed him.

"I'm sorry," she said.

In the backseat, Gavril's head banged the window. They hadn't hit a bump or a pothole.

Outside the car, the moon and stars made a ghost land of the desert, and Trinity thought that was only right. It felt to her that they were all ghosts out here, that there was no real difference between the living and the dead.

Pretty soon that might not be far from the truth.

They hit a bump and something rattled in the trunk. The corpse of their friend wasn't the only thing back there. They had the guns.

Trinity would have thought the price they'd paid for those guns was too high, except without them they would all have been dead soon enough. Now, with the weapons and ammunition they'd taken from Oscar Temple, they had a chance.

In the distance, she could see what remained of Storyland. Built in the 1980s, it had been a minor amusement park aimed at small children, full of shoddy attractions based on fairy tales and nursery rhymes. Mother Goose and Hansel and Gretel figured prominently, and, from what Trinity had learned, the attractions had included a track for antique cars, spinning teacups, a flying carpet ride, and other rides that would be eclipsed by even the least sophisticated modern theme park . . . all of this a relatively short drive from downtown Las Vegas.

The headlights picked out the shape of the Wonderland Hotel. Oleg tapped the brake and guided the car around the back of the building. The Wonderland had one tall wing and one short one, which met at the two-story lobby structure. Another section of the hotel stuck out the back in a T shape, which allowed for the rooms along the rear leg of the T to be invisible from the few cars that made their way along Jackrabbit Ridge.

Gravel crunched beneath the tires as they pulled up in the midst of the five other vehicles parked there.

The door to one of the abandoned hotel's rooms opened, and Kirill emerged with a pistol and a bottle of beer. Perhaps forty-five years old, Kirill had skin so leathery that its lines seemed more like scars. He kept his remaining hair buzzed tight to his scalp, and he had icy, blue-white eyes that never smiled, even when he himself might laugh. Louis Drinkwater—who'd told Trinity everything she knew about the area—was a local real estate agent who owed Kirill Sokolov many favors and owed the Bratva tens of thousands of dollars. He'd given them the keys to the Wonderland Hotel. Sokolov didn't trust Louis, but Trinity did. The real estate man had more than his share of sorrow, but he didn't strike her as a coward.

Still, they kept watch. Someone would have been on guard in the front, hiding behind darkened windows. Kirill would have known they were coming, but still he had the gun. It was impossible to be too careful.

They should have been more careful with Oscar Temple.

Kirill watched them as they climbed from the car, his brow furrowed. He said something in Russian. Trinity heard Feliks's name and knew what he was asking.

"In the trunk," Oleg replied.

Kirill swore and cast his beer aside, striding toward the car as Oleg went around to the back, keys in hand. Trinity refused to look, marching toward the room she and Oleg had been sharing. She halted before she reached it and forced herself to turn and watch as they opened the car trunk and Kirill clapped his hands to the sides of his skull.

Grieving for his brother.

No one brought up the fact that they'd managed to get the guns. It was important—it might give them the edge they needed to survive, maybe even win—but Kirill Sokolov didn't care about guns just then. He leaned against the car, lay his head back, and stared at the stars.

Trinity wasn't close enough to see if he cried.

The Wonderland Hotel had been their refuge for weeks, but none of them had expected to be buried there.

On long rides, Jax couldn't help thinking about his little brother Tommy. With the sky spreading out in front of him and the road whipping by beneath him, he could hear Tommy's laughter. There'd been many times when Jax, six years older, had been appointed guardian and protector for his brother while JT had worked on restoring a vintage Harley he'd picked up somewhere.

Gemma would be making dinner. Jax would take Tommy out to the small yard or to the concrete basketball square next door, the one with the dingy, torn net hanging from the hoop . . . and they'd run. They never had a destination, the Teller boys—they just ran. From the time Tommy could walk, they would run together. Sometimes they would put out their arms and *fly* together, or pretend they were astride a Harley when they were far too young to ride. By the time Jax turned eleven, his urgency had faded a little and Tommy tended to take the lead, even though he was only five years old.

At six, Tommy had died of a congenital heart defect. It was the family flaw—Gemma had it, too.

Jax didn't do a lot of running these days—not unless there was trouble. But on these long rides, he remembered what it had felt like to fly with his little brother. Those memories should have caused him pain, made him grieve, but instead they made him happy. For a little while, Tommy was with him again. He wondered if his sons, Abel and Thomas—named after an uncle he'd never known—would run together. Jax hoped that they would.

Three headlights cut the darkness out on that ribbon of highway. Jax,

Opie, and Chibs had been riding for a couple of hours already, and they wound along two-lane blacktop that curved through pine forests, up hills, and into canyons. Later, they would ride through desolate badlands that had a rugged beauty all their own, but long after dark in the middle of a workweek, these roads could be just as desolate. Quiet and peaceful.

He felt the weight of the gun at the small of his back and knew that quiet and peaceful were good. Less chance of trouble.

Opie rode on his left and Chibs on his right. When a car or truck appeared coming the other direction, Opie dropped behind them, but vehicles had been few and far between for the past three quarters of an hour or so. Opie had been his best friend pretty much all his life. He had a gentle soul and a savage heart, able to find mercy where others could not and to be merciless when a line had been crossed. Jax worried about Opie—the loss of his first wife had broken something inside him—but when shit turned ugly, there was no one he'd rather have at his back. Chibs had survived ugliness and tragedy, too. A son of a bitch named Jimmy O had given him the scars on his face, stolen away his wife and daughter, and made it impossible for him to stay in Ireland and keep drawing breath. Jimmy O was dead now, but somehow betrayal had made Chibs understand loyalty better than anyone else.

Jax had unwavering faith in both men. Out here, flying, these guys were his brothers now. He trusted them with his life.

Kirill asked Trinity to say a prayer over his brother's grave. They stood there, nineteen Russian men and this one Irish girl—no longer such a girl—and lowered their heads. In the moonlight, the dirt on the arms and faces of those who'd dug the grave made them look like orphans out of some grim, modern Charles Dickens tale. They didn't have much use for God. They were gunmen and leg breakers. Since the moment Oleg had begun introducing Trinity around to his Bratva when they'd been in Belfast, she had tried very hard not to wonder what their worst crimes might have been. Drug smuggling, certainly. Murder? Some of them, she was sure. They were hard men, and some of them seemed like cruel men, but to Oleg they were family, and if she wanted him, she knew that they were part of the package.

Quietly, her voice carrying in the reverent hush that the small hours always created, she said the Lord's Prayer. When she'd finished, they all said, "Amen," almost as if they meant it. Most of them were godless, but she'd found that even those without faith still wished their loved ones a safe journey through whatever might come after life.

"Feliks was a man of few words, so I won't disturb the quiet with a lot o' my own," Trinity said. She glanced at Oleg and then at Kirill, whose expression had never been more like stone. There would be no tears from this lot. "He had courage and dignity, and he defended his brothers with his life. God keep him."

For several seconds they all stood there, staring at the freshly turned soil. The wind blew, and somewhere a loose shutter creaked in the dark like the squeal of a frightened rat. They had dug the grave in the scrubland behind the motel, fifty yards back from the cracked, empty swimming pool.

Kirill realized she wasn't going to say anything more and cleared his throat of whatever thickness of emotion had lodged there.

"The traitors have taken another life," he said, speaking English purely for her benefit.

He'd mourned in his native tongue, but now he clearly wanted to include her, and it touched her deeply. For a long time she had been nothing but Oleg's woman to them, but now that they were at war, she had become family, for better or worse.

"Krupin and the others might not have been at Temple's ranch, but it was for them Temple acted. For Lagoshin. Feliks's blood is on his hands. Another of us dead because Lagoshin wants the Bratva business in this part of the world for himself. We have . . . What would they say here? Rules. These men have betrayed us all. They have murdered those who should be their brothers. We have been forced to strike from the shadows, to hide our heads because they have numbers and weapons we could not match. But now that has changed."

Kirill nodded at Oleg, Gavril, and Trinity in turn.

"We have as many weapons as we have hands and enough ammunition to kill our enemies and their entire families."

He surveyed those gathered around him. A chill went through Trinity, and she wiped tears and smudged dirt from her cheeks.

"Feliks died for these guns," Kirill said. "And we will use every last bullet."

Oleg nodded slowly, lips pressed into a tight line. "Amen," he said, as if Kirill's declaration had been another prayer.

"Amen," the rest of them echoed.

Trinity felt sick. Feliks's death, the digging of his grave, and this pauper's funeral had disturbed her enough, but this . . .

She whispered her own private little prayer and turned away, walking back across the rough ground and past the empty pool.

Oleg caught up to her just as she was entering their room, took her wrist and followed her inside, closing the door behind them. Her heart pounded, and she felt her face flush as tears spilled down her cheeks. She hated herself for crying, hated the vulnerability it made her feel, even though she believed that empathy showed strength, not weakness. Angrily, she wiped her eyes again.

"What is it?" Oleg asked.

Trinity turned away from him. "You mean besides Feliks being dead? Isn't that enough?"

Oleg grunted. He did that a lot. It was practically a third language for him.

"There is more. You turned your back on us, came rushing back here. Something upset you, and it wasn't just Feliks dying."

He touched her shoulder and she pulled away, then spun to face him.

"It wasn't a prayer," she whispered, barely controlling her fury.

Oleg frowned, grunted again.

"What Kirill said? I understand it. You don't grow up like I did and not understand violence . . . vengeance. I'm not gonna try to persuade you to turn the other cheek, 'cause in my life turnin' the other cheek just means givin' the bullet a clear path to your brain. But bloodlust is not prayer."

"Of course it's not!" Oleg snapped, throwing up his hands. "You think we don't know that?"

Trinity scoffed. "You said, 'Amen.' You all did."

"And what does it mean, 'Amen'?" Oleg said quietly, reaching out to touch her face, to lift her chin so that she would look him in the eye and see the love he had for her. "It means 'I believe,' Trinity. When I said it, that's all I meant. The others just repeated it."

She closed her eyes tightly and let out a shuddering breath. His touch had broken a dam of emotion within her, but somehow this wave of grief and anger stopped the flow of her tears.

"Don't say it like that again, okay? It means somethin' real to me."

Oleg kissed her forehead. "I promise," he said.

He kissed her gently on the lips, and then more firmly, and she pressed her body against his and let all of her emotions crash into him, shared it with him in a way she never had with anyone. She trusted him with all she felt, love and fear and rage.

To the end.

The eastern sky had begun to lighten by the time Jax, Chibs, and Opie rolled into North Las Vegas. It had been a long time since either Jax or

Chibs had paid the North Vegas charter a visit, but Opie had never been there before. Bone-tired, his jaw tight and his hands aching from gripping so long, Jax guided them into the parking lot of the Tombstone Bar, so named because the building had once housed a business that sold gravestones and other funerary monuments. The growl of the Harleys' engines echoed off the bar and the building across the lot, loud in the darkness just before dawn.

The Tombstone was a grade-A shithole, a dive with a faded, tilted sign above the door and dying neon beer logos in the windows that burned 24-7. It had just about the least curb appeal of any bar Jax had ever seen, which made it perfect for SAMNOV to use as the legitimate front for whatever illegal business they might do. Truth was, the North Vegas charter didn't invest a lot of time or energy into criminal enterprise. Their president, Rollie Thurman, didn't have much ambition beyond the fraternity of the club. He liked the bar, enjoyed its reputation as a dive and the sort of clientele that dragged itself through the door on a nightly basis. The way Jax remembered it, when Rollie wasn't busy, he liked to tend bar himself, listen to tales of woe from drunks and hookers, junkies and gamblers, and the occasional cop. SAMNOV pulled their weight when it came to fulfilling their obligations, protecting gun shipments, doing whatever distribution was required—and they'd gone to war to protect their territory more than once—but Rollie liked things simple and quiet.

Jax was counting on that.

He killed his engine, slipped off his helmet, and ran a hand through his hair. He hadn't gotten used to the shorter length, but it helped on a ride like this. Opie and Chibs shut off their bikes and dismounted. Chibs opened and closed his hands a few times even as Jax was massaging his own knuckles. They'd stopped plenty of times to piss and take a breather, but his hands still felt tight. He tried to imagine how much pain Clay was in every time they rode, given how bad his arthritis had gotten, and hoped he'd never have to endure that curse.

Opie gestured across the parking lot. "What's the story on that?"

Jax turned and smiled at the sight of the sign on the building next door. Once upon a time—he figured in the '70s and '80s—it had been a two-screen movie theater, one of those storefront jobs that had existed before the megaplexes had come along. Last time he'd been there, it had been a furniture showroom or something, but now it was a theater again.

The Tombstone Theatre. The marquee offered up a Hitchcock double bill and a midnight show of something called *Bubba Ho-Tep*.

"Looks like Thor got his wish," Jax said. "Guy's been talking about the charter buying that place and getting it running again for eight, nine years."

Chibs strode up between them. "You'd think the local law might get a bit suspicious when you've got two legit businesses guaranteed to lose money but somehow you manage to keep 'em going."

Jax shrugged. "As long as they pay their taxes, I guess."

They had pulled their bikes around the side of the bar. Behind it was a small paved yard enclosed with a chain-link fence, and Jax spotted a restored Ford Mustang, an old white box truck with the bar's name on the side, and four motorcycles. The eastern sky had continued to brighten, hinting at the approach of dawn and turning much of the sky a rich indigo. They walked toward the heavy old wooden door that, despite its appearance, was used by the charter as a side entrance to their clubhouse, which was in the rear of the building that housed the Tombstone Bar.

A loud clank echoed across the lot and the door dragged inward. A thin, hawk-nosed face peered out.

"Morning, Baghead," Jax said.

Bag rubbed his eyes as he opened the door further, his suspicion giving way to irritation.

"'Morning'? You see any goddamn sunshine out here?"

Jax kept back from the door, Opie and Chibs following his lead. They were all brothers here, but the charters had their own cultures, their own rules, and their own maniacs. Baghead had earned his name because he was a sociopath with no filter and no shame who'd pick up the homeliest woman in a bar, then make her wear a bag on her head while he fucked her.

"You sleeping light, or you supposed to be on guard?" Jax asked.

Bag stepped outside, putting away the gun he'd been hiding behind the door in case of trouble, and stretched tiredly. "Guard what? We're just sleepin' off what we finished drinking a couple of hours ago. I'm still fucking drunk."

"When aren't you?" Chibs muttered under his breath, so only Jax and Opie could hear.

For the first time, the real strangeness of their arrival seemed to hit Baghead, and he blinked, waking up a little.

"What's this about, Jax? You don't show up at asshole o'clock in the morning unless you got pressing business."

Jax started toward the door, his patience wearing thin. He needed a piss and a place to put his head down for a few hours.

"Look, brother, we rode all night because we wanted to get here before the sun came up. I don't want anyone knowing we're here, not yet. I'm gonna need to have a talk with Rollie. He wants you and the other guys in that conversation, I'm okay with that, but I need to talk to him."

"He ain't here," Bag said, as if they might go away.

Opie grumbled. "You're not gonna turn your brothers away, are you, Bag? That what Rollie would want?"

The invocation of Rollie seemed to fully wake Baghead at last. "Nah, of course not, man, it's just . . . it's early."

Rubbing at the corner of his eye with a knuckle, he stepped back to let them enter. Before Jax even crossed the threshold, he felt the weight of exhaustion descend on him, like he'd been holding it off until that moment. Opie and Chibs slung their packs off their shoulders and ambled inside, and Bag shut the door behind them.

"Bathroom's up toward the bar if you need a piss," Bag said, pointing past a huge metal door that must have been the beer cooler. Then he gestured the other direction, where another corridor branched off along the back of the building. "Jax, you know where the crash pad is. There're two empty beds back there but plenty of pillows and shit, and there's a sofa in the poolroom."

"You're not going back to sleep?" Opie asked him. "You said you haven't even been down a couple of hours."

Something was wrong with Baghead, but nothing that hadn't been wrong with him for years. He twitched, glancing shyly away as if he was uneasy with anyone expressing concern about him. *Sensitive guy for a sociopath,* Jax thought.

"Nah, man," Bag said. "I'm awake now. Sun'll rise soon, and once I see the sun, I can't even take a nap. I'll clean up the bar. No worries, though. I'll keep the clatter to a dull roar."

He turned and walked past the cooler and the bathroom, headed for the bar, leaving them to their own devices. Now that they were inside and he'd assured himself they posed no threat, Bag apparently felt no inclination toward hospitality.

Jax headed along the back corridor toward the crash pad. They passed the poolroom, a small space with a sofa, a pool table, and a little bamboo tiki bar that looked like it had been stolen from the courtyard of some Vegas hotel. "I'll take it," Chibs said, tilting his head toward the poolroom. "Opie's too tall, and we can't have our VP on the couch."

Jax gave him a nod of thanks and kept moving. The crash pad was actually two separate bedrooms with a third—a sort of TV room, from the look of it—between them. North Vegas was a tough crew. They'd thrown down with some savage clubs and come out on top, but there was something almost quaint about the setup, as if Rollie and his boys came from an earlier, more innocent era.

The bedroom on the left stank of stale beer and month-old vomit. He spotted a red-bearded monster in one bed, massive leg thrown over the side, sleeping like he'd been hurled onto the mattress by an angry god. *Thor,* Jax remembered, still doubtful that it was the big son of a bitch's real name. There were two other beds in there, one of which was occupied by a little olive-skinned guy called Antonio. The empty one was messed up enough that he figured it had been where Bag had been sleeping before the sound of their snorting Harley engines had woken him.

The other room had only two beds, one empty and one occupied by a man named Joyce, who had a bull's-eye of ugly burn scars where a member of the Iron Heart MC had held his face to a stovetop coil. Jax hadn't intended to involve the charter—that would defeat the whole purpose of their coming down here incognito—but a sense of dread took up residence in his skull like a ghost in an old dark house. He forced himself to shake it off. "Get some rest," he told Opie.

He went and dropped his bag beside the empty bed. Then he laid down and closed his eyes. Around the edges of the heavy blackout window shade, he could see the glint of predawn light.

Despite the long night's ride, it was quite some time before Jax managed to sleep.

7

The next time Jax opened his eyes, the sun was burning around the edges of the blackout window shade and the temperature in the room had gone up twenty degrees. He felt grimy, as if he'd been sweating through the night and it had dried on him, stiffening his clothes. Stretching, he glanced over to see the other bed empty, and he wondered what Joyce had thought when he'd woken to see SAMCRO's VP sleeping nearby.

He swung his legs over the edge of the bed and dragged his sneakers on. His wallet chain clinked quietly as he stood and swiped a hand across his tired eyes. With a groan, he shook himself, wet-dog style, and glanced around for a clock but didn't find one.

The rest of the crib was abandoned, with no sign of Chibs, Opie, or any of the SAMNOV guys, so Jax returned the way he'd come in the early morning hours. The poolroom sofa was vacant as well, but Joyce stood by the table with a cue stick in one hand, studying the arrangement of the balls. After a moment, he realized that Jax was watching and glanced up.

"You snore," Joyce said.

"We all have our faults," Jax replied.

Joyce chuckled, his smile causing his burn scar to stretch grotesquely.

"What time is it?" Jax asked.

"Too early to be up and too late to go back to sleep."

"Any chance you could be more specific?"

"Going on 10 a.m. Antonio called Rollie about an hour ago. I haven't seen him yet, but I'd guess he's out front already."

Jax nodded. "That bacon I smell?"

"We got a grill in the little kitchen by the bar. Thor likes to cook breakfast."

"He any good at it?"

Joyce gave a small shrug. "Couldn't make a decent pancake to save his life, but his eggs are fantastic. You'll see."

Jax made his way to the front of the building, stopping only to empty his bladder on the way. The main bar area took up about half of the building itself, mostly oak beams and thick floorboards soaked with decades of spilled beer and smelling every year of it. There were no shining brass railings in this place and no mirrors on the walls—the clientele the Tombstone Bar drew in weren't too fond of staring at their own reflections. There were booths and tables with mismatched chairs, simple and to the point. Behind the long bar were racks of alcohol built up like bookends on either side of a huge marble grave marker with Rollie's full name on it. The damn tombstone was the only thing in the bar that looked like anyone ever bothered to clean it.

"Morning, Jackson," Rollie said, rising from a stool near the plate-glass windows at the front of the room. His hair had more salt than pepper these days, and his gut had belled out a bit since Jax had last seen him, but he still exuded the same combination of warmth, intelligence, and mischief as ever.

"Rollie," Jax said. "Thanks for the hospitality."

Chibs and Opie were seated at the bar with Antonio, Thor, and Baghead, all of them digging into plates of breakfast. Opie raised an eyebrow and gave a nod, silently letting Jax know the food had his seal of approval. Chibs didn't even look up, and Jax had to smile. It had been a long ride, and his own stomach growled at the fantastic smells coming from the little kitchen.

Rollie shook Jax's hand and clapped him on the shoulder.

"If you'd let me know you were coming, I would've at least had the boys change the sheets back there," Rollie said, frowning in disapproval.

Anyone else, Jax would've doubted it, but he took Rollie at his word.

"I know you would have, brother. Couldn't do it, though."

"Bag said something seemed off," Rollie noted. "You guys are up at four in the morning, I got to figure there's trouble. Maybe you ought to lay it out for me."

Jax glanced over at Bag and the others. "You want to do that here or in your office?"

Rollie understood his meaning. "No prospects here this morning. You can consider whatever you say here just as sacrosanct as anything you'd say in chapel."

Jax nodded slowly. He wasn't sure how well Baghead could keep a secret, and he didn't know Antonio very well, but he trusted Rollie.

The service door swung open, and Hopper stepped through with a wide plate heaped high with food.

"Jax, come sit down," he said. "Thor wants his food eaten hot. He's been keeping it warm back there, but don't test his patience."

Jax shook his head. Hopper had his hair tied back with a rubber band and his goatee cinched together with a little iron ring.

"Damn, Hopper. I hope Thor makes a better chef than you do a waitress."

"Sit down, asshole," Hopper growled, sliding his plate none-too-gently onto the bar.

"Can you talk and eat at the same time?" Rollie asked. If it was a joke, he didn't let on.

"I'll manage," Jax said, ravenous now.

He walked to the bar and slid onto a stool, trading nods and greetings with the other men in the room. "You guys eat like this all the time?" he asked, digging his fork into the eggs.

"Couple times a week, when Thor feels like cooking," Antonio said.

"I might never go home," Chibs said, pushing away his empty plate.

Jax let business slide for a couple of minutes while he tucked into the plate of food, heaping eggs on top of toast.

After he'd finished half the plate, Rollie dragged a stool over beside him, a mug of coffee in his hand.

"All right, man from Charming. Your belly ain't growlin' quite so loud now. You want to explain your under-cover-of-night arrival and, more importantly, why you're not wearing your cuts? If I showed up at your place without mine, I don't think I'd have received such a warm welcome."

Jax wiped crumbs from his mustache, nodding. "It's appreciated, Rollie." He turned on the stool, facing Rollie and making sure as many of the other SAMNOV guys could see him as possible. "Short version . . ."

And he told them.

When he'd finished the story, Baghead choked up a mouthful of phlegm. "Goddamn Russkies," Bag said, and spat the wad into his empty juice glass.

Rollie laid a hand on his own prodigious gut, brows knitted in contemplation.

"We try to fly under the radar down here, man," he said. "You know that. We've been in our share of scrapes, but we try to keep business running smoothly, focus on the finer things. But family is family. Until you know your sister's safe, you've got whatever you need from us. Blood, sweat, and tears."

Jax leaned in toward Rollie. "Thank you, brother. I know you try to keep things looking legit. We'll do everything we can to avoid bringing trouble to your door."

"Aye," Chibs agreed.

Opie had turned to watch the conversation unfold, and he raised a coffee mug to signal his own agreement.

"What can we do?" Rollie asked.

Jax inhaled the stale-beer aroma of the bar, the warmth of it, and the camaraderie of the men of the North Vegas charter. These guys had a good thing going, and he didn't want to blow it for them, especially when things had been so tense in Charming. The last thing he wanted was to drag his shit over someone else's threshold.

"Right now, just a place to lay our heads and some information." He glanced around at Hopper, Antonio, Thor, and Bag. "Anything in the air about rival Bratva factions?"

A lot of shaking heads.

Rollie looked thoughtful and then shrugged. "We've got connections with the local PD. Cooperative relationships, ya know? And there are guys we could talk to who have deep ties to the old mob powers that still run most of the dark money in Vegas. I don't know how much help they're gonna be, but we can give it a shot."

Someone coughed at the back of the bar, and they all turned to see that

Joyce had entered the room. How long he'd been listening, Jax couldn't be sure.

"Bag, you gonna tell them about the Birdman's place?" Joyce asked, the bull's-eye scar on his cheek gleaming angrily in the daylight filtering in front of the bar.

Baghead frowned, hands fluttering toward his face as if he felt some insect harrying him and wanted to swat it away. He twitched, sniffed, and then nodded swiftly.

"Right, right, Harry," Bag said, one side of his mouth lifting in a smile. "Stupid of me, yeah? Should've thought of that without you making me think of it."

Harry Joyce. Jax had forgotten the guy's first name.

"Who's the Birdman?" Opie asked.

Bag flinched toward him as if he'd forgotten Opie had a voice. "Guy likes old jazz, plus he keeps a bunch of parakeets in the club. Strip club, called Birdland. People think the name comes from the girls, 'birds,' like they'd call 'em in London or whatever, but it's the jazz connection. Famous club in New York has the same name, but not the naked titties and definitely not the parakeets."

Chibs leaned back against the bar and crossed his arms. "I'm lost. How is this relevant?"

Jax glanced at Joyce, hoping for a rescue, and he wasn't disappointed.

"Birdland's always got a few Russian Mafia guys hanging around," Joyce said. "You wanna find out what the Bratva are up to in Vegas right now, that's the place to start."

"Got a contact at the club?" Jax asked, turning to Rollie. "Someone who can point us the right way?"

Rollie clapped him on the shoulder. "We can do better than a contact. Wait till tonight, and Joyce'll go with you. He'll know the faces and the names."

"I'm in," Joyce agreed. His smile didn't reach his eyes.

Jax nodded his thanks. He turned toward Opie, saw relief in his expression and a dark purpose in his eyes, and knew they reflected his own. They'd come to visit the Tombstone Bar expecting not much more than a place to crash. People so rarely exceeded his expectations that Jax found himself very happy when they did.

He looked at Joyce. "Thanks, man."

Bag snorted something back into his nose, then scoffed. "That's Harry Joyce. Never could resist a damsel in distress."

Chibs laughed softly. "Ah, well, it's clear you've never met Jax's lovely sister." He turned on the stool and looked around the bar. "Trust me, fellas . . . Trinity Ashby's not some swooning girl. She's nobody's bloody damsel in distress."

Trinity had never been the sort of girl who cried. To hear her mother tell it, she'd wailed like a banshee as an infant, screeching to wake the dead. Her mother's friend Kiera had once said baby Trinity's crying could have driven Christ off the cross, and Trinity had been perversely proud of that. But once she'd been able to crawl—to move without her mother lugging her around—her tears had ended. Oh, she'd wept at a funeral or two, but that was the sum of it. Romantic movies made her roll her eyes, and even in her teen years there had never been a boy who'd made her cry . . . though she'd bloodied a few of their noses.

This morning she was furious with herself for the tears she had shed last night. Feliks had died, and they'd buried him—grief was only natural—but she knew that she needed to be harder than that. She needed to be able to turn off the pain inside, to go numb, or she might not survive all of this.

For it's sure Feliks won't be the last to die.

Steeling herself for the blast of cold, she stepped into the shower. The desert morning was cool and the water much chillier than that. Gavril and Kirill had managed to get the well pump that served the motel—and the oil-stinking generator—running easily enough, but the furnace was broken, so there'd be no hot water. Still, the water sluiced the night's sweat and the previous day's dust off her body, and that part felt wonderful.

Trinity shivered as she ran the soap over her body, hurrying as best she could. Gooseflesh prickled her skin.

Feliks had been a good man, but in her experience the death of good men had always been one of life's few guarantees.

Not Oleg, she thought. She would not lose him. Oleg was a good man. Trinity feared that he might need to become a bad man to survive, but if that was what it took for her to be able to keep him, then so be it.

"Well, well," he said, stepping into the bathroom as if summoned by her thoughts.

Trinity glanced out through the dirty glass door. "What do you think you're doin'?" she asked, teeth chattering.

"I thought I might join you."

"You add one more second to how long this takes, and I'll have your guts for garters."

Oleg laughed and leaned against the wall. Trinity hung her head and let the cold water soak her hair, shuddering as she reached for the shampoo. Stepping back from the stream, she worked her hair into a lather, but all the while Oleg stayed there, hands jammed into his pockets, back against the wall.

"Enjoyin' the show?" she asked.

"Such beauty deserves an audience," he said, his accent thicker than usual.

Teeth chattering, she smiled nevertheless. She hadn't met every Bratva thug in the world, but she doubted many were eloquent, particularly in a language not their own.

"But somethin' else is on your mind," she said, before she braced herself and plunged her head into the frigid shower's cascade.

"We have weapons now," Oleg said. "With luck, soon we will learn where Lagoshin has been staying. Once that happens, we will have to attack, to kill Lagoshin and his lieutenants, or it will only be a matter of time before they find and kill us."

Trinity stepped back, squeezing excess water from her hair.

"None of this is news to me, love. It's why we're hidin' in a hotel near a haunted kiddie park . . . why we killed Temple and his bodyguards. You think I don't—"

Oleg cleared his throat. "I want you to leave, *kotyonok*. You being here . . . it makes me afraid, and I can't do what I need to do if I am afraid for you."

Trinity shut off the water, freezing water sluicing from her body, dripping from her breasts. She gritted her jaw, but not from the cold.

Sliding the door open, she stepped out onto the mat, her whole body crying out from the cold. A towel hung on a plastic bar within arm's length, but she did not reach for it, only stood and stared at Oleg as tiny rivulets of water ran down her naked flesh.

"*Kotyonok*—" he began, moving toward her, reaching for her hands.

"I'm not your fuckin' *kitten*," she snarled. "In bed, you can call me whatever you like. But this is somethin' else, so don't you dare be tender to me now. You listen. I love you, ya bastard. I'm not goin' anywhere. So don't tell me about your fears or how I'm your weakness. I should be your goddamn *strength*. I should be the iron in your blood. That's what love is! I don't know what kind of woman you thought you were gettin' when you asked me to leave my home and come with you, but I'll tell you this much . . . we survive together, or we might as well already be dead. You understand me?"

Trinity fumed, inhaling and exhaling loudly, face so flushed with her temper that she no longer felt cold. She saw the emotions raging on Oleg's face, anger and embarrassment and love and doubt.

Then he grinned.

"What in God's name are you smilin' about?" she snapped.

Oleg roguishly arched an eyebrow. "You get angry like this, and you breathe very hard. Watching your tits move up and down . . . it is like I'm being hypnotized. Or put under a magic spell."

She gaped incredulously at him, and he laughed.

Trinity punched him again, this time in the arm and not so hard.

"Don't bring up the idea of me leavin' again," she said.

He took her and kissed her, the water on her damp skin soaking through his clothes.

"I promise, *kotyonok*," he whispered.

Kitten. Again. The bastard.

This time, though, she didn't hit him. Instead, she reached for his belt buckle.

On the phone's first ring, Maureen Ashby only glanced up from the left-over stew she'd been heating up on the stove. The phone had fallen silent again, and for half a second she wondered if the ring had been her hopeful imagination. A cat yowled out in the alley behind her place, and she heard one of the neighborhood kids laughing loudly, a cruel sound followed by the shattering of glass and a much more frightened, irritated screech from the cat.

The phone kept ringing.

Poor thing, she thought, on the surface of her mind. She ought to open a window and give those kids hell for tormenting the animal. That Kenny Donovan was a vicious little shit.

Underneath that, though, a voice was screaming at her to answer the phone. When it rang again, Maureen felt as if an electric shock had jolted her. She dropped the wooden spoon from her hand and launched herself toward the phone. Almost nobody called her on this line—her friends used her mobile—so unless it was a sales call . . . but no, there it was, the international code.

America. Please be Trinity.

"Hello?"

"It's Jax. You alone?"

Good news, she wondered, *or the unthinkable?*

"Tell me you found her, Jax. My thoughts are strayin' into very dark corners these days."

Crackling on the phone. At least there was only a little delay. Only a little.

"—Nevada," Jax was saying.

"Wait, what? Sorry, start again."

"We're in Nevada," he repeated. "No sign of Trinity yet, but I wanted to touch base because I don't know how long it'll be before I can call again."

Her heart sank, but she forced herself to buck up. No news might not be good news, but it was better than the nightmare of the phone call that she dreaded so desperately.

"If we have a chance of finding her, it's gonna be through her Russian boyfriend. Oleg and his buddies are gonna be way more memorable to people than Trinity, so we're gonna start with that. But, listen, Maureen . . . is there anyone out here she'd know? Anyone she might go to if she got into trouble?"

She could hear the dark accusation in his voice, that of course if Trinity had been in trouble she ought to have called her brother. Maureen agreed, but given the issues SAMCRO had with both the RIRA and the Russians, she also understood why her daughter might have hesitated to introduce her half-brother to the new man in her life.

"Let me think on it," Maureen said.

Jax read her off a number. "You've got the cell number I gave you last time. I've still got that burner on me. But if you can't reach me, you can call here. It's a bar, but if you ask for me, they'll take a message."

Maureen exhaled. Somehow, despite her fears, Jax had managed to soothe her. Perhaps it was the gruff confidence in his voice, that rumble that reminded her so much of his father.

There was still that other conversation they needed to have—about the letters she'd put in his duffel just before he left Belfast, hoping he'd read them when he got home. He deserved to know that part of his father's life. Of course he'd have read them by now, but Jax hadn't brought it up when they'd talked before—maybe because Gemma had interrupted the call—and that was just fine with Maureen. If Jax felt like talking about those letters there'd be time for it later. Right now, Trinity was her only concern.

"Jax," she said, her voice firm. "Your sister—"

"I'll find her."

"More than find her. You'll send her home."

"I can't promise that, Maureen. Trinity's not some kid. I can't make her—"

"She's fallen in love with a Russian gangster. I knew there'd be danger when she went off with him, but she didn't give me a choice. Now it's happened already, just a handful of months later, and I can't allow her any more choice than she gave me. You didn't grow up as brother and sister, Jackson, but she's your flesh and blood, and you care for her. I know you do. Just like I know you understand the danger loving this bastard is puttin' her in. So, yes, I expect you to promise me, to swear on your father's soul, that you will send her home to me."

The line crackled with static.

"Jax?" she said, worried that she'd lost the connection.

"I'm still here," he said, his rough voice a distant ghost.

"Promise me."

"I promise. I'll send her home even if I have to bring her there myself."

Jax hung up without saying good-bye. Maureen kept the phone to her ear for a few seconds, listening to the static and the ghost of a past she'd cherished and a future she'd never had.

8

The Sons rode into Birdland's parking lot two by two, Joyce and Chibs in front, Jax and Opie in back. Harley engines roared the news of their arrival, and a handful of people in the lot glanced up and watched as they rolled by. Jax ignored them, just as he'd ignored their surroundings on the ride over. The day had seemed like an eternity, but now night had fallen and it was time for answers.

They parked their bikes in the corner of the lot, far from the exit but near a stretch of dirt that led out to the curb. If they needed to make a quick departure, they wouldn't worry about pavement. One by one, they killed the engines and removed their helmets.

They started toward the entrance to Birdland, admiring the neon sign depicting a woman with wings. She had them covering her breasts one moment, and the next they were unfurled, revealing small hearts over her nipples. Classy joint, Jax thought, but he appreciated the oddness of it. Jazz music played from speakers outside the door as they approached.

Opie sidled up beside Jax. "You sure you don't want me to ask the questions?"

Jax glanced at his dour expression, the concern in his eyes. "I've got it."

"I've seen that look on you before, Jax," Opie said quietly. "I'm just thinking you may not get answers if everyone you ask thinks you're a heartbeat away from caving in their skulls."

Jax shot him a look that silenced him. "Cover my back, Op."

Opie nodded. He didn't seem satisfied, but he wouldn't push it any further.

Joyce led the way, opening the door and moving into a darkness broken by flashing colored lights. Jax and the others followed, taking in every detail, watching for exits and for trouble. The foyer had a bathroom door, an old pay phone, and a curtained-off section that could've been anything—a party room, a coat check, stairs leading to an attic. A single doorman sat on a stool beside a podium, a black bodybuilder with a shaved head and a thin goatee. A strong guy, but not a fighter. Jax could see it in the way he held himself, even the way he stood and fronted them as they approached. He was a man used to intimidating with his size. Maybe he'd been in his share of scuffles in this place, a fistfight now and again, but he wasn't a boxer, a soldier, or a street fighter, and so Jax wasn't worried about him until he saw the bulge of the gun sticking from his belt, underneath his shirt, and he reassessed. The gun was a threat, even if the doorman might not be.

"This is a nice place," the doorman said. "Boss doesn't like trouble."

Chibs held out his hands, palms open. "No trouble here, brother."

The doorman sized them up. "Twenty-dollar cover, right?" Joyce asked, handing over a pair of folded tens.

The doorman hesitated, studying Joyce in apparent disapproval, then took the bills. As the others passed him, he took their money without another word, but as they moved through an arched doorway flanked by two huge bouncers, Jax knew they'd been marked. The doorman would tell the bouncers to keep an eye on them. One of the bouncers, a vampire-pale white guy, looked like he worked out at the same gym as the doorman, but the other bouncer had cold eyes and stood with his back to the wall in a stance that said he was ready to hurt someone. *Jarhead*, Jax thought.

The music outside had been jazz, but inside it was whatever the girls onstage felt like dancing to. Right now, two girls were twirling topless around the same pole to AC/DC's "You Shook Me All Night Long," while a third marched up and down a smaller stage in the back. They all had glitter sparkling on their breasts, like they'd grown up doing little art projects at the kitchen table and this was all that remained of their girlhood imagination. The room was an L shape, and off to the left, on the leg of the L, was an area with four pool tables. There'd be rooms in the back for private dances. Waitresses in next to nothing wandered the floor selling alcohol Jell-O shots, and bartenders worked at inhuman speed behind the counters, slinging eight-dollar beers and twelve-buck whiskeys.

Then there were the birds.

Behind the bars, above the stages, even in the corners of the pool area, there were huge cages either hanging from the ceiling or standing on poles like those the strippers used. Inside the cages were parakeets, parrots, macaws . . . even a goddamn toucan, and in the lulls in music, Jax could hear the birds calling to each other.

Planning an escape, he thought, amused and horrified at the same time.

"Guy who owns this place must be a loon," he said, moving up beside Joyce.

Joyce shrugged as if to say, of course he is. "On Sundays, he'll only play jazz in here. The girls who want to keep him happy . . . they've learned how to dance to that stuff. You'd be surprised how many people show up for it, too. They do brunch."

"It's shit, though, right?" Opie said, raising his voice to be heard over the grind of AC/DC. "I've never eaten anything in a strip club that didn't taste like ass."

"Might be best we don't talk about what you've eaten in strip clubs," Chibs said aloud.

Opie gave a sheepish grin, and Jax laughed. Joyce seemed curious, but it was a story for another day. Jax glanced back toward the bouncers, saw their eyes tracking him and the others, and clapped Chibs on the back.

"End of the bar. Shit goes down, the jarhead's yours."

Chibs knew better than to look at the bouncers. He nodded and moved off immediately toward a waitress picking up drinks from the end of the bar. She had dark skin and bright red hair and was wearing a half-shirt and a skirt so short it displayed her pink panties in all their glory. Chibs said something to her, and she grinned. Jax had seen the soulless smile that hookers and strippers put on for the men who were paying their bills, and this wasn't that. Something about Chibs just charmed them. Part of it was the accent, but Jax thought the scars did something to them as well— suggested the beginnings of a story that they finished in their own heads. Lost girls liked broken men. Jax had a taste for women like that, but today he kept his mind on the job at hand.

The bartender came over to make sure Chibs wasn't troubling the waitress, glancing at the bouncers, but the girl touched Chibs on the arm and must have passed along his drink order, because when he turned toward the bar to set up camp there, nobody tried to move him along.

Jax didn't know how many people Birdland drew on its busiest nights, but tonight's crowd was substantial. Clusters of young guys in business suits were side by side with truckers and contractors and housepainters, not to mention the occasional freak. The freaks were the easiest to spot because they sat alone, usually at the rounded corners of the stage, and they doled out single dollar bills and nursed watered-down beers for hours. Jax had seen a particular brand of strip-club freak more than once, guys who would lean in when the girls came near, inhaling deeply, trying to catch a whiff of pussy that would carry them through their daydreams for months.

Joyce led them past the pool-table area and into the thick of the crowd around the stage. A waitress in a see-through plastic top brushed close against Jax, her smile like a mannequin's, but he only scanned the faces ahead. Opie stuck close behind him, but Jax wasn't expecting trouble unless they started it themselves.

The music switched over to "Crazy Train," and the two girls on the main stage used side snaps to remove their panties. They did it in synch, facing each other and then air grinding so that their hips nearly touched. It was almost enough to coax a smile out of Jax. Not all the girls looked like they were having fun, but those two did.

Joyce changed direction slightly—moving like he owned the place— and Jax stayed with him. The rear stage was less populated than the one at the front of the club. A group of middle-class suburban types were along one side, probably a bachelor party, but on the other side, not far from the beaded curtain that led into the back room—and presumably to the back exit—there sat a trio of darkly clad men with rugged, stony Slavic faces. The stripper there, a Latina with enormous fake tits, crawled toward them on her hands and knees to retrieve the trio of twenty-dollar bills the three men had laid upon the stage. Two of the men wore wolfish grins, but the third had an expression Jax could almost have called a sneer. He watched the girl closely enough, but almost as if she disgusted him.

"Opie," he said, nodding toward the beaded curtain at the back.

With a wary glance, Opie moved toward the curtain. He stopped ten feet away, near a high round table laden with abandoned glasses. A waitress would approach him quickly enough, and he would order a drink, but it was a strategic location from which he could observe the rear section of the bar. His attention would not be on his beer.

The Russians saw them coming. One of the wolves tapped the sneering man, who looked up to watch as Jax and Joyce approached. The second wolf stood and moved to block them, but Joyce didn't slow. He sidled a bit, moving like a snake rising from a street charmer's basket.

"Down, boy," Joyce said, one hand raised as he spoke loud enough for the Russians to hear over the pounding music. "It's Yurik, right?"

The grizzled Russian nodded. "I know you?"

"Naw, man, but we have friends in common. Lizzie Broski, you know her? She pointed you out at a party one night. That's how I recognized you."

Yurik looked confused. When his mouth opened, Jax saw yellow teeth and a bit of sweat on his lips. The guy's pupils were pinpricks in his glassy eyes. He was high on something, and suddenly this seemed like it might have been a terrible idea.

"What you want?" Yurik asked.

Which was when the sneering man rose up behind Yurik, put a hand on his shoulder, and physically moved him aside. He stared a moment at Jax, then turned to Joyce. His sneer had deepened.

"Go away, you idiots. Don't you know you don't interrupt a man when there are naked girls around?"

Jax smiled.

The sneer died on the man's face. "Did I say something funny?"

Jax stepped in close to the sneering man, almost but not quite crowding him. He opened both hands to show he held no weapons and stared right into the Russian's eyes, knowing he could match the bastard cold stare for cold stare.

"I'm real sorry we interrupted your pussy gazing. It's pretty clear you're a serious man, and I'm not going to waste your time. I'm looking for a guy named Oleg Voloshin, and I heard you guys might be able to tell me where to find him."

The sneering man blinked in surprise, studying Jax more closely.

Yurik said something in Russian, guttural and full of arrogant condescension. The name Voloshin appeared in the midst of a host of other words that sounded like made up spy language to Jax. But he'd heard that one.

Thanks, Yurik, Jax thought. Now he knew which side these pricks were on.

"What you want with Oleg?" the sneering man asked.

Jax glanced at Joyce as if trying to decide whether or not to confide in these Bratva goons, but he didn't need Joyce's reassurance.

"Nothing he'll enjoy," he said.

The three Russians stood together a moment, looking like nothing so much as a trio of black crows on a telephone wire, the uniformity of their black coats and shirts and pants almost laughable, if not for the guns they surely carried and a history of murder.

"I am Iov," the sneering man said, moving closer, so that he and Jax were intimately, uncomfortably near. "What if I told you Oleg is my brother?"

The music throbbed and the lights flashed. Glasses clinked and men whistled and howled for the new batch of strippers as they began to remove their tops, revealing first one breast and then the other, playing coy. They were the worst actresses in the world.

"Iov, my name's Jack Ashby," Jax lied. "If Oleg's your brother, then you and me—we've got a problem. The prick has my sister."

The Russian cocked his head dubiously. "Oleg kidnapped your sister?"

Jax shook his head. "Nah. She took off with him. Left home. But from everything Oleg said before they left, I know there's some serious shit going on with you and your people and I want to get my sister back before she ends up in a ditch with a bullet in the back of her head. I want to get her out of this, and I'll do whatever I have to do to make sure she gets home safely."

Iov scratched at a spot under his left eye, thinking.

"You want us to help you find your sister? To tell you where to find Oleg?"

"He's not your brother, is he?" Joyce asked, looking a little squirrely. A sheen of sweat had formed on his forehead.

"I can pay," Jax said.

Iov's eyes sparkled. "I work for a man who would also like to find Oleg. Right now, we don't know where he is, but maybe my employer will want to meet you. Maybe you can help him, and he can help you."

He sent Yurik to make a call, and the thug headed toward the men's room, where the thumping music wouldn't prevent him from hearing voices on the other end of the line. Los Lonely Boys' "Crazy Dream" came on the sound system, and the girl on the rear stage dropped down and began pumping her lace-covered crotch at the bachelor-party guys. All the while, she stared longingly at Iov—the Russians tipped way better than suburban dads. She caught Jax watching her and scowled at him, pissed that he'd drawn her best customers away.

A waitress floated their way, a lithe brunette who looked closer to fifteen than twenty, which had to be an illusion given the law. Her purple eye shadow had sparkles in it that changed color with the shifting lights in the club. She wore a little tartan skirt that must have sparked a thousand Catholic-schoolgirl fantasies, and she made a beeline toward Joyce. Her eyes lit up like she knew him.

"Hey, Harry. Give a girl a taste?" the waitress asked. "You've always got the good stuff."

Joyce gave her a dark look. "Now ain't the time."

Jax bristled. He didn't much care if Joyce was using drugs to buy favors from strippers, but if he was selling in clubs, that was the kind of small-time shit that could get the whole charter jammed up. It was something for Rollie to take care of—and Jax would bring it to his attention—but right now the girl was just a distraction.

Jax saw Opie signal him and looked toward the front of the bar to see what had gotten Opie's attention. One of the bouncers—the bodybuilder, not the jarhead—stood beside the main stage watching Jax and Joyce talk to the Russians.

"Maybe next time, honey," the waitress said, before she turned to the rest of them. "What'll you have, boys?"

"Go away, girl," Iov rumbled.

She glanced at Jax. "You look like a whiskey man."

Iov grew angry. "Are you blind or stupid? We want a drink, we find you. Now fuck off."

She looked him up and down with the belittling disdain only a beautiful young woman could muster.

"I can't decide if you've had too much to drink or not enough," she said, and then she turned to Joyce, moving close enough to give him a whiff of the perfume that had already filled Jax's nostrils. "I'm dancing in about half an hour, honey. I hope you'll stick around for my show. Trust me, you won't be—"

Iov shoved her. The girl's arms pinwheeled, flinging away the trayful of Jell-O shots. For a heartbeat, the music stopped—just between songs—and Jax could hear the little cry of surprise as she staggered backward and fell on her ass, tartan skirt flipping up to reveal the tiny patch of pink lace between her legs.

Joyce tried to wade in. "Hang on, man, there's no need for that."

"Stay out of it," Jax told him, shoving him backward.

Iov barely glanced at them, but he wasn't stupid. The Russian had to have noticed Joyce's obedience, recognized that Jax was the one in charge. His eyes narrowed, but Jax wasn't sure if it was with appreciation or suspicion.

Yurik came out of the bathroom but stopped with his phone in his hand and a stupid look on his face. The girl had risen to one knee and was glancing around at the splotches of Jell-O and little paper cups strewn around her, cursing like a lunatic in the drunk tank. Opie started to leave his position in the back corner, but Jax gestured for him to stay put, thinking he could salvage the whole thing . . .

The bouncer who'd been watching marched toward them, looking confident in his strength and his purpose. Anger rushed like fire through Jax's veins—any other day, this bodybuilder wouldn't have been an issue, but he needed to finish his conversation, and time had just run out. One of the bartenders emerged from behind the bar, and a couple of customers— good old boys with noble intentions—had started shuffling as though they might also step in.

The girl came surging to her feet and spit in Iov's face.

He backhanded her, the slap so loud that the stripper on the little rear stage stopped dancing to stare, and so did the bachelor-party guys. Jax swore under his breath and went to intervene, but the bouncer beat him to it. The muscle head slid between Jax and Joyce, brushed by the waitress, ducked a punch from Iov, and grabbed the Russian's arm, twisting it behind his back in one smooth move.

The third Russian, who'd been lingering the whole time, kidney punched the bouncer, and the poor bastard roared in pain and went down on one knee, releasing his grip on Iov. Jax almost felt bad for the guy— the way he'd subdued Iov, he'd been better at his job than Jax had expected—but when shit turned ugly, you had to know how to read the situation if you wanted to keep your head from getting caved in.

Slapping the girl had done it.

The bartender punched Joyce just for standing there. The noble civilians waded in, but by then all hesitation had passed. Jax stepped inside the reach of the first guy and leaned into his swing, punching the man in the gut so hard he heard the burble of vomit about to spew from the hero's mouth. He stepped out of the way, saw the guy fighting the urge to puke, and nailed him in the temple with enough force that he dropped straight down.

When Jax looked up, Opie had the bartender from behind, crushing his larynx, and Joyce had started to pound on the second Good Samaritan. People were shouting, and the stripper on the stage had stood up and was screaming, covering herself like Eve after her first bite of the apple.

Jax grabbed Joyce's shoulder, blocked the guy's instinctive retaliation, and then spun around. "Opie! We're going!"

Opie gave the bartender a shove and started moving. Jax glanced over at the Russians, who'd started kicking the fallen bouncer and took over after Opie abandoned the bartender. He knew they should stay, knew that no matter the consequences these assholes were his best chance to find Trinity, but jail would mean going back to Stockton. As it was, he wasn't supposed to be out of the state of California. Jail would also likely mean they'd figure out who he was, and he couldn't have that.

In a place like this, the management wasn't likely to bother calling the cops for a bar fight—not with the backroom blow jobs and front-room drug deals likely happening on the premises—but he couldn't chance it.

Ablaze with fury, he shoved his way through the bar with Opie and Joyce in tow. Several times guys tried to get in the way before seeing the rage on Jax's features and changing their minds. Chibs had stayed by the bar, where Jax had left him. He saw them coming and drained the last of his beer, dropped some money on the bar, and smiled at the same waitress he'd charmed when they'd come in. She tucked a piece of paper into his hand that might have been her number, and he stroked his goatee like he was one of the Three Musketeers.

"Glad you're enjoying yourself," Jax snapped.

Chibs didn't have time to reply. The doorman had taken over for the jarhead bouncer, who moved to block their path.

Jax threw his hands up. "The trouble's back there, brother, and we don't want any of it. Step aside, and you won't see us again."

The jarhead flared his nostrils and for a second, Jax thought he would put up a fight. Then he moved to let them pass.

"Don't come back," he said. "The Russian pricks have connections. I throw them out twice a month, no choice in the matter. But you guys ain't Russian."

Joyce started to say something, but Jax shoved him forward, into the foyer, and then all four of them were pushing out through the front door and into the parking lot. They were awash with piss-yellow light from the lampposts, and Jax kept moving until they were in the darkness beyond that sickly illumination, not far from where they'd parked their bikes.

"What happened back there?" Chibs asked.

"One of the girls was a little too eager," Joyce said. "Got on the Russians' nerves."

"You didn't help," Opie said. "You could've gotten rid of her before it blew up like that."

An eighteen-wheeler blew by on the main road, kicking up wind and grit. Joyce turned to glare at Opie like he'd just insulted his mother.

"I just did you a favor, asshole." The coiled burn marks on his face had a pearlescent hue, catching the light from the parking lot. When he grimaced, one side of his mouth did not move as freely, thanks to those burns.

"You let it fall apart," Opie said.

"All right!" Jax barked. "We'll figure out another angle. Let's just—"

Chibs tapped him on the back. "Jackie."

Jax turned and saw Yurik emerging from Birdland. The Russian glanced around, looking jaundiced in that yellow glow. Jazz still played on the outdoor speakers, a jubilant tune that seemed almost absurd as theme music to this hardcore Bratva leg breaker. Yurik spotted them and started over.

"Careful," Joyce said.

"He's alone," Jax muttered. "If this was trouble, you think he'd put himself out here like this? You guys keep back."

Jax strode back across the lot—back through that piss-yellow light, awash in too-happy jazz—and met the Russian halfway. Yurik had a split lip and a bloody nose and his left eye had started to swell, and Jax wondered if it had been the bartender who'd managed it or if one of the noble bystanders had gotten in a lucky punch.

"There's a Russian Orthodox church on E Street, right across from the park. Ninety minutes, you be on the steps of the church."

"You can help me find my sister?"

Yurik dragged a hand across his nose, leaving a bloody streak on his arm. "Ninety minutes. Maybe you help us find Oleg. Maybe we let you take your sister away before she gets hurt."

9

Behind the hotel was a rusted old swing set that sat on a concrete block with grass growing up through cracks. Trinity could see it from the window of the room she shared with Oleg and had felt the lure of it for days. She'd resisted, mainly because she had earned a level of respect from Kirill and the other men in Oleg's Bratva and she thought sitting on the faded, dirty yellow swing and kicking her feet back and forth would undo the image she'd cultivated with them.

Tonight, she didn't care. Oleg and Gavril had gone into Las Vegas, searching for any sign of Lagoshin and his men. Boredom and anxiety had crept inside her, made nests under her skin, and now the little twitchy spiders of dread were being born and crawling all through her body. Some of those spiders were doubt—doubt about her choices, doubt about her love, doubt about her chances of surviving the next twenty-four hours, never mind the next twenty-four days.

So she sat on the swing. After a little while, alone behind the hotel in the middle of nowhere with the red hills behind her, she began to gently kick her feet, swinging a few inches forward and backward. Little flakes of rust dusted onto her hands where she held the chains of the swing, and the whole apparatus creaked, but she didn't mind. It was a lovely, familiar sound, almost like an old friend from childhood whom she hadn't seen in far too long.

She thought about Sacha and Vlad and the other guys who were still inside the hotel, and she wondered what must be on their minds. Kirill and Logoshin both answered to Bratva higher-ups back in Moscow, men who had once been allies, part of the criminal hierarchy that ran the Russian Mafia. When their operation in America had fallen apart, ripples had traveled all the way back to Moscow, leading to the violent deposing of the man at the top, Anton Maksimov.

The Bratva boss had fled Russia, or so it was said, and the Bratva had splintered in two. A quiet civil war had erupted, with each man attempting to persuade the rest of the Bratva captains that he was the right choice to lead. It was mostly a chess match, a power struggle in which each man attempted to assert his control over pieces of the Bratva's business, and if Trinity understood it correctly, the largest remaining piece was the money that came from their operations on the west coast of the United States. Whoever won this fight would win it all, and that meant violence and bloodshed. The squeak of the rusty swing turned into something else, and Trinity paused, dragged her feet to stop herself. To silence the swing. She sat and listened. Had she really heard a howl in the distance? The romantic in her wondered if it had been a coyote or a wolf. Were there wolves in Red Rock Canyon?

The wind picked up, and she shivered despite her thick, wine-red sweater. With a glance up at the stars she began to swing again, throwing her head back to study the constellations.

Off to her left, there came a cough. She glanced over but did not stop her slow swinging. In the darkness, someone struck a match. In the flare of orange light, she saw Kirill light his cigarette and then shake the match out. A dark silhouette from that one ember burning in the night, he approached her slowly and sat down on the swing beside her without a word. He drew deeply on the cigarette and exhaled a cloud of smoke, and then he began to swing.

"It's nice here," Kirill said, taking another drag on his cigarette. "Quiet."

Trinity glanced at him, making her swing twist sideways. The barbed-wire tattoo that circled his neck seemed blacker than black in the moonlight, and it made the sight of this killer on a swing set even more absurd. She couldn't help but smile.

Kirill understood without asking, and he smiled in return. It faded instantly.

"Feliks was a good man," Trinity said. "A good friend."

"A good brother," Kirill said, swinging his legs, making the rusty swing shriek as he rode higher.

They were lost in memory for a moment, and Trinity allowed herself to swing a bit higher as well, forgetting her fears of looking foolish. With Kirill beside her, the other Bratva men could hardly think less of her.

When Kirill stopped pumping his legs, Trinity did the same, and slowly their pendular motion ceased.

"It is frustrating, yes? Being stuck inside the hotel?"

Trinity nodded. "I'm gettin' claustrophobic. Not just with the hotel—"

"I feel it as well," Kirill interrupted. "We are trapped by our desire to stay alive. We must keep out of sight because we know they are hunting us, but remember: we are also hunting them."

"They don't seem intimidated by it," Trinity said. "There are more of them. More guns, more shooters, more money."

Kirill glanced up at the stars, perhaps wondering if Feliks's kindness had earned the key to heaven, in spite of his sins.

"This is why we hide," he said. "They believe they are smarter and stronger, that they will destroy us. But their confidence can be used against them."

"You sound sure."

He smiled, but this was a different sort of smile—thin and cruel. "There is nothing for you to fear, Trinity. Soon we will not be hiding. We will kill them or they will kill us. Either way, it will be over."

"That's not as comfortin' as you seem to think it ought to be," she said.

But Kirill wasn't listening.

They heard footfalls coming around the side of the hotel. Trinity stiffened a moment, but when she saw that Kirill wasn't troubled and heard the calm, easy pace of the crunching steps, she relaxed. The silhouette that appeared from the corner was tall and whip-thin, and she knew it had to be Timur. He'd been a thief and pickpocket as a child and into his teen years before he'd been caught and sent to prison, where the Bratva had taken him under their protection. Oleg didn't trust him, which meant Trinity didn't like him, but the skinny thief slunk toward Kirill with the proper air of deference, and so Kirill approved of him.

Timur said something in Russian.

Kirill took another drag on his cigarette. "Be polite, Timur. Speak English."

The thief sniffed the air, as if he'd smelled something he didn't like. He glanced at Trinity, but only for a second.

"Gavril called in," he said. "There was a fight at Birdland—"

"The strip club?"

Timur nodded. "There was a fight earlier. Some of Lagoshin's men were involved. The doorman heard them talking about a meet at the Russian church on E Street. You know the one?"

Kirill flicked the ashes from the end of his cigarette. "Stupid question. I assume Oleg paid the doorman?"

"He paid."

"Too easy. How sure is Gavril that this isn't a setup?"

Trinity frowned. "They couldn't have known you'd have people there tonight, askin' questions."

Kirill smoked and knitted his brows. "Maybe not. But if they know we're looking, they could be setting out bait for us all over. No way to confirm if they've laid a trap or not."

"How many of our men are with Oleg and Gavril?" Kirill asked.

"Two others."

Kirill nodded slowly. "All right. Tell them to be careful. And to kill as many as they can."

Timur grinned a weasel-like grin, then turned and slunk back toward the motel.

Trinity felt as if she'd turned to ice. She stared at Kirill. "You're just gonna stay here? The rest of us need to go, right now, and back them up. We have enough guns now. They need—"

"Stop." Kirill took a long drag, then flicked his cigarette onto the cracked concrete. "They are all the way on the other side of the city. By the time we reach the church, whatever is going to happen will have happened. If it is not a trap, four men will be enough to cause problems for Lagoshin. If it *is* a trap and we all go, then they will kill all of us, instead of only four."

He pushed off, rusty chains creaking, and began to swing again.

Trinity stared, feeling hollow inside. *Only four,* he'd said. But one of those four was Oleg.

"Breathe, Trinity," Kirill said. "Whatever comes, it is out of our hands right now. In this moment, at least—when we can do nothing and we do not yet know the consequences—we are free."

The swing set squeaked and squealed. She felt as if she ought to speak, to protest. Once again she thought she heard something howl in the distance.

She exhaled. In some perverse way, Kirill was right. What happened next was not within her control. Slowly, she pushed backward and then raised her feet, letting herself swing forward.

Breathing, for now.

They parked the Harleys a block from the church, away from the nearest streetlight. The sky to the west was lit up with the neon brilliance of the Vegas Strip, but here on what the locals called the alphabet streets, there were no jackpot winners. Some houses had been kept up well or recently restored, an attempt to drag the neighborhood into the light, but others had cracked or boarded windows, cars on blocks in the driveway, and badly peeling paint. Tourists wouldn't come here, and in Jax's experience with neighborhoods like this, the police wouldn't bother to swing by very often either.

"Stick with the bikes," Jax told Chibs. "If there's trouble, you make the call. Joyce, you're with Chibs."

Joyce made a little noise about the order, but Jax ignored him. He and Opie headed for the church without looking back. If things went to shit, Chibs would either wade in, bullets flying, or he'd withdraw and make sure word got back to Rollie—and to SAMCRO—that the situation had changed. Jax wanted to keep the Russians in the dark about who they were dealing with, but if things went so badly wrong that he and Opie ended up dead on the curb, the Sons of Anarchy would go to war. Every member of the Bratva in Nevada—both factions—would meet Mr. Mayhem.

"Joyce ain't happy," Opie said as they approached the church steps.

"He can leave anytime he wants," Jax replied.

The Russian Orthodox church had been beautiful once. The domes still gleamed gold, and the crosses on top of those were stark white, but the building looked faded and tired, as though it had surrendered to its own abandonment. Long planks had been hammered across the front doors and cardboard NO TRESPASSING signs hung there, torn and dusty. Jax couldn't decide if the houses that were kept up indicated a neighborhood on the road to recovery or a last handful of homeowners fighting a losing battle, but it seemed the patriarch of this particular church had given up a long time ago.

"His lead was good," Opie said. "Birdland got us here."

"The lead was good, yeah, but he nearly pissed it away, not handling that waitress better back at Birdland. Didn't inspire much faith."

Opie glanced around, watching the street. Jax studied the front of the church, just in case there were men hiding in its shadows. He felt the comforting weight of the gun tight against the small of his back.

"We need all the backup we can get," Opie reminded him.

Jax shook his head. "Joyce is a wild card. Too easy to tip your hand with a guy like that around."

Headlights appeared at an intersection two blocks up—a black sedan. It turned the corner and slid toward them, and the headlights went off as it drew up to the curb a hundred feet from the church. A hulking SUV followed the same path and pattern, dousing its lights before it pulled up behind the sedan.

"Here we go," Opie said.

The drivers did not turn off their engines. Three men climbed from the sedan, five from the SUV. Jax glanced across the street at the trees in the park, then around at the roofs of neighboring houses, and he wondered if there were other eyes watching them. As far as these Bratva men were concerned, he and Opie were just civilians with a mutual interest. For the Russian Mafia, there were no repercussions to killing a couple of civilians who stuck their noses into Bratva business. They'd destroy the bodies or just make them disappear, and they'd do the same thing to any witnesses foolish enough to agree to testify against them.

Jax flexed the fingers of his right hand. He would have felt a lot better with his gun in hand instead of tucked against the small of his back.

"Hey," Opie said quietly. "You okay?"

Jax nodded. Opie had reason to be concerned. There had been times when Jax's temper had gotten the best of him, and now would be a bad time for him to let it off its leash. But Opie also should have known better. When Jax came face-to-face with men like this—cold-blooded bastards who thought they had all the leverage in any conversation—an almost reptilian calm descended on him. His anger never went away, but it hid in the shadows, biding its time.

The Russians mounted the wide, cracked stone steps of the church. They fanned out, surrounding Jax and Opie in a half circle. The man in the center stood about five-five and had his head shaved down to stubble that matched his chin. He didn't seem like a natural leader, but the proud, upward tilt of his chin said otherwise. To the left of him and one step back was a much taller man, late forties but in murderous physical condition, with pockmarks on the right side of his face that had been left behind by shotgun pellets instead of acne. His bodyguard, Jax figured.

"Name," the little stubblehead said.

"Jack Ashby," Jax replied. "And this is—"

Stubblehead grinned, never taking his eyes off Jax. "His name doesn't matter. Is you who are looking for this woman, yes?"

Jax felt the cold serpent of that reptilian calm slither into him. "What about you? Does your name matter?"

Stubblehead nodded as if in appreciation of his brass balls. Then he turned to the guy with the shotgun scars. "Hurt him a little."

Opie tried to get in front of Jax and all the Russians moved at once. Jax put up a hand to push Opie backward, then stood facing Stubblehead and Scarface with his own chin raised defiantly.

"You heard the man," he said, staring at Scarface's black shark eyes. "Hurt me."

The big man—six foot three and built to inflict pain—took a step up and plowed a fist into Jax's skull as casually as if he'd waved hello. Stars exploded behind Jax's eyes, and he staggered to the side and up another step. Scarface went to follow him, but Stubblehead put up a hand.

"My name is Viktor Krupin," Stubblehead said.

Head ringing, Jax smiled thinly. The son of a bitch hadn't cared about giving up his name, only about Jax's having the balls to demand it. Opie's jaw was set, chest rising and falling, ready for a brawl, and Jax mentally noted how funny it was that Op had been concerned about *his* temper. Back where they'd left the bikes, Jax could see that Chibs had a hand on Joyce's shoulder, keeping him in place. That was good. Chibs would do as he'd been asked, trusting that Jax knew what he was doing. Maybe until it was almost too late.

"I thought we were gonna meet someone named Lagoshin."

Krupin sniffed. "Mr. Lagoshin doesn't waste his time with street trash."

Jax glanced around, made a show of noticing how many Bratva men had come to this little meeting on the church steps. He wanted Krupin to see that he recognized bullshit when it was spoken to him. Lagoshin might not have come to the meeting, but he'd taken it seriously, or he wouldn't have sent all of these goons.

"Look, this is supposed to be simple. My sister's with this Oleg guy, thinks she's in love with him. The family doesn't want her to end up catching a bullet, so I'm here to bring her home. If he works for you, all I'm asking is—"

Krupin shook his head. "Oleg does not work for me. And we don't know where he is, or if your sister is with him."

Jax cocked his head. "Then why the hell are we talking?" He glanced at Scarface, head still aching from that one punch.

"It's very simple, Mr. Ashby," Krupin said. "We wanted to tell you that if you find your sister with Oleg, you're going to let us know where Oleg can be found. And we want to make sure you are who you say you are."

A ripple went through Jax. They had no idea where Trinity was—this meet had been a waste of his time. His temper began to slip.

"You're telling me you don't have a single lead?"

"We have a few, but nothing very helpful," Krupin replied.

"Anything you feel like sharing?"

"You keep asking the wrong questions."

Jax nodded slowly. "All right. I'll bite. How are you gonna make sure I am who I say I am?"

Krupin grinned. "I thought you must be smarter than you looked."

He gestured with his right hand, almost a flourish, and the Bratva men drew their guns—all except for Scarface and Krupin himself.

"Only a complete fool would have come here without a gun," Krupin said. "Carefully take out your weapons and walk them up to the top step, leave them there, and then return."

Jax complied immediately, drawing his gun with his fingers, letting the Russians see the whole process. He turned, holding the gun out to one side, and started climbing the eight remaining steps to the boarded-over doors of the church.

"This is a bad idea," Opie muttered as he passed by, even as he drew out his own gun.

"If you've got an alternative, I'm listening," Jax replied quietly as they climbed the last few steps together.

They both knew shoot-and-run was not an option—not with so many guns, and not even with Chibs and Joyce as backup.

With the guns on the top step, they descended back toward the Russians. Six steps. Seven. Scarface didn't wait for Jax to reach the eighth step. Jax tried to deflect the punch, but the big bastard's fist glanced off his jaw hard enough to nearly unhinge it. The metallic taste of blood flooded his mouth. He shuffled sideways, turned and lunged inside Scarface's reach, hit him with three fast gut punches and one to the kidneys, but the big man dropped an elbow down on his shoulder, and Jax went to his knees. Wheezing, trying to catch his breath, he fought the blackness at the edges of his vision as pain washed over him.

He heard a chorus of guns cocking, glanced up, and saw that half of them were aimed at Opie and half at him.

"No, Mr. Ashby," Krupin said. "There is no defending yourself."

Jax exhaled through gritted, bloodstained teeth. Then he opened his fists and climbed to his feet. Pain radiated through him but he breathed, letting it spread and diminish. Once again, he turned toward Scarface and let the man hit him.

Opie swore and took a step, and one of the Russians jammed a gun against his throat.

Punches rained down on Jax. He felt his lip split and tasted a fresh gush of own blood. A fist to the gut and a knee to the balls were followed by another crashing blow to his skull, and those black waves swept in again at the edges of his vision. He blinked, on his knees again, trying not to go down. Even then, in the midst of pain and with blood running freely from his nose and mouth, he understood that Scarface was going easy on him. He could have broken hands, arms, ribs . . . anything. He could have shattered Jax's nose or crushed his kidneys. They wanted him bloody and in pain but not broken.

He let it go on. At one point, he heard shouting and caught a glimpse of Chibs and Joyce over by the bikes, at the edge of the park. Joyce had started toward the church, and Chibs had restrained him because Chibs understood—maybe had understood before even Jax himself. If Krupin wanted to kill him, they wouldn't have met somewhere so out in the open.

Maureen, he thought, *you owe me.*

But he wasn't doing this for Maureen Ashby. And, as much as he liked Trinity, he wasn't really doing it for her, either. He let the punches land, let his blood flow, for his father's sake. JT had not been perfect, but Jax could not let his old man's daughter die.

Scarface stood over him. "Your name?"

He speaks, Jax thought. "Already told you. And fuck yourself."

The fist came down again. Jax barely felt it. He blinked and realized that his cheek was pressed against granite—he was sprawled on the church steps and had lost a few seconds of time. Voices cursed in Russian.

Jax spat a wad of bloody spittle and pushed himself up to a sitting position. Ears ringing, head and ribs throbbing, he looked up at Krupin. The little man seemed to nod with approval, though whether he was expressing appreciation for Scarface's efforts or Jax's ability to sit up seemed unclear.

"If my friend thinks you are lying, he will continue to hurt you," Krupin said. "So tell me, Mr. Ashby, are you what you seem to be? Just a piece of biker trash worried about his family?"

Jax nodded slowly, his eyes never leaving Krupin's face. "Yeah. That's me. Biker trash."

The words translated differently inside his head, where they were a promise that he would make sure Krupin took a hell of a beating before he and the boys left Nevada. But Trinity came first.

Krupin produced a business card and slipped it into the pocket of Jax's leather vest. "On this card is a number where you can reach me," Krupin went on. "If you discover any information that will lead you to your sister, you will call me immediately."

Opie swore quietly, and the men guarding him took a step away. He stayed where he was. Jax spat another bloody wad.

"If you're searching for Oleg and his friends, you must have something you can tell me," he said. "Anything. Point me in a direction to get me started, one of the things you're pursuing."

Krupin glanced at Scarface, and Jax thought the big man would hit him again—he tensed, not sure he could keep himself from fighting back this time—but, instead, it was Scarface who nodded. *What the hell is this?* Jax wondered.

"A gun dealer named Oscar Temple and his bodyguards were murdered last night," Scarface said. "We know that Oleg and his friends were hoping to acquire guns. If you can learn anything about those murders, it might help you in your search."

Oscar Temple. The name sounded familiar, but if the guy dealt illegal guns, that was not a surprise.

But as the Russians all turned and began to make their way back to their vehicles, guns vanishing back into holsters, it wasn't Oscar Temple who was foremost in his mind. He stared at the retreating men.

"Lagoshin," he said.

Krupin and the big man turned—the big bastard with his shotgunned face and his bloodied fists.

"A pleasure to meet you, Mr. Ashby," Lagoshin said, his voice smooth as silk, almost elegant, despite his brutish appearance. "When you are icing your injuries later, remember that they were inflicted merely to make a point. If you have lied to me, or if you discover your sister's location and hesitate to share it . . . well, I'm certain you don't need me to explain. Mr. Krupin believes you are smarter than you look. I hope he is not mistaken."

As Lagoshin and his men climbed back into their vehicles, a squeal of tires ripped through the night air. An engine roared. Jax and Opie whipped around to see a gray Camaro tearing up the street toward the church. The Russians scrambled, bumping into each other as some tried to get into the car and others tried to get out.

"Down!" Opie said, and he slammed Jax to the steps.

Jax blinked, head still ringing, and from that angle—with his cheek against the granite again—he saw Krupin and three other Bratva men draw their guns and start to take cover behind the cars and the open doors. They were too slow.

The Camaro's engine sounded like thunder. A gun barrel poked out the open window, glinting in the moonlight, and the Camaro's passenger pulled the trigger. The staccato bark of the assault rifle echoed off the steps and the face of the church.

One Bratva man slammed back against the SUV, his head snapping to one side as blood and brain and bone erupted from his skull. A bullet took Krupin in the shoulder, spinning him around in a fan of bloody mist. Two or three shots stitched the chest of a third man, who hit the ground with a wet, meaty slap.

Then the Camaro had gone past. Chibs and Joyce shot at the car as it whipped by them, but it skidded into a left turn at the next corner and vanished as instantly as it had appeared. The engine screamed as it raced off through the neighborhood.

Lagoshin's men were shouting in confusion, trying to help the wounded even as Lagoshin himself shoved his way out of the SUV and started barking orders. The sedan tore away from the curb in a hopeless pursuit. Even groggy, Jax knew they had no chance of catching the shooters.

Fury etched on his face, Lagoshin stormed up the church steps toward them. Jax realized Opie was no longer pressing him to the steps, and he sat up wearily, sneering. He knew the look on Lagoshin's face, and now he wished he and Opie hadn't left their guns up in front of the church door—hell, he wished he hadn't let the guy beat the shit out of him.

"What in hell was that?" Lagoshin roared, one of his men scrambling up behind him, alternately watching the street for further attack and covering Jax and Opie with his gun.

Jax spit again. Not so much blood this time. He took a deep breath to clear his head and staggered to his feet. Gun barrels swung his way.

"Are you shitting me? You think we had something to do with that? Those bullets were flying our direction, too, asshole."

Lagoshin's huge fists opened and closed. "Two of my men are dead—"

"It's your business that almost just got us killed!" Jax snapped.

"But you two are unharmed!" Lagoshin shouted, pointing toward the park. "And your men there . . . they're still standing!"

"My friends were shooting at the damn Camaro!"

"Hey . . . ," Opie muttered.

Jax didn't like the tone of his voice. Troubled, he turned to see Opie pressing a hand to his left side, dark stains soaking into his T-shirt and spreading.

"Shit, Op . . ."

Opie hissed in through his teeth and took his hand away, showing the center of the blood spot blossoming on his shirt. "Grazed my ribs, I think. Nothing some stitches and a shit-ton of whiskey won't cure."

Pressing his hand against the wound again, Opie turned to Lagoshin. "You still think we're in with whoever those guys were?"

Doubt flickered across Lagoshin's scarred features, and he exhaled loudly, deflating. He waved his man away, and the guy hesitated only a second before starting back toward the SUV. The driver had gotten out and was putting the dead man into the trunk . . . the other corpse had been in the sedan that rushed away.

Police sirens warbled in the distance.

"Oleg works for a man named Kirill Sokolov," Lagoshin said. "The men in that car were Sokolov's—"

"You saw their faces?" Jax asked.

Lagoshin bared his teeth like a snarling dog. "I don't need to see their faces." He gestured toward Opie. "Do not think a little blood is very persuasive. We all bleed."

The police sirens grew louder as Lagoshin turned and hurried down the steps to the waiting SUV, which tore away from the curb the moment he'd climbed inside.

"We gotta go," Opie said, wincing as he started toward the street.

Wounded, he'd forgotten the guns. Bruised and bloody, head still ringing, Jax hurried to the church doors and retrieved them, then hustled back down. Chibs and Joyce were already on their bikes and kicked the engines into life. Jax and Opie straddled their bikes. Joyce started asking questions, but Chibs snapped at him to shut up and turned his bike around, glancing back at them, ready to fly.

"How we gonna play this?" Opie asked, ignoring Joyce. He grunted in pain as he kick-started his bike.

Jax started up his Harley. "Follow the lead we've got. Oscar Temple."

Opie glanced at him. "You really gonna call Lagoshin if we figure out where Trinity and Oleg are holed up?"

With a grunt of pain, Jax wiped blood from his mouth and stared along the street where the Russians' vehicles had gone.

"Damn right I am," Jax said. "I can't wait to see that prick again."

They tore away from the church, two by two, maybe fifteen seconds ahead of the cops' arrival. Jax held on tight as he rode, blackness swimming at the edges of his vision. His head and ribs throbbed with pain, but he held an image of Lagoshin in his mind, and that helped him focus.

He wasn't leaving Nevada without Trinity.

But he also had no intention of leaving without seeing Lagoshin again.

10

Trinity heard the rumble of the Camaro's engine and put aside the copy of *The Great Gatsby* she'd found under the counter in the motel's lobby. Reading more classic literature had been on her to-do list for years, but she'd never been able to stick to it. Oleg had suggested *Anna Karenina* because he wanted her to read something Russian, but Trinity had always despised the very idea of classic novels about melodramatic rich girls struggling with love. Maybe she shouldn't judge, but sappy shit like *Pride and Prejudice* made her want to puke.

Tugging her shoes on, she shut off the light and left the room. They'd cleaned up some, but walking around the abandoned hotel barefoot would have been stupid. There had been enough teenagers partying around the place that shards of broken beer bottles were more plentiful than spiders, and there were plenty of those.

She crossed the cracked parking lot. A door opened behind her, and she glanced back to see Pyotr emerge from his room. The young Russian had blue eyes so pale they were almost white. Oleg liked him, and Trinity was trying, but Pyotr barely spoke to her. Even now he only nodded and kept his stride steady, making no attempt to catch up and walk with her. She did the same, reaching the rear door of the lobby ahead of him. The main entrance and the lobby were dark except for the moonlight, but she only had to pass through and head down a side corridor to reach the motel's conference room.

When she walked in, most of Oleg's Bratva were already there. Cigarette smoke swirled and eddied in the room. Heavy blackout curtains covered the windows, and so they congregated there, out of sight of the road. Trinity could have waited out back for Oleg and Gavril—even now they would be parking the Camaro back there—but she wanted the others to see her as herself, and not just the ginger who followed Oleg around. Some of them already had accepted her, and others, she knew, never would.

"Trinity," Ilia called as she stepped inside. "Have a drink with me!"

He raised a bottle of rum—his beloved—and shook the remnants of it around so it sloshed against the glass.

"I'm grateful, but no, thank you." She smiled at him, and he seemed happy enough with that. She wondered how drunk he had to be before it pissed off the rest of them.

Kirill was in the small office adjoining the conference room. He had made the place his own and had maps of Las Vegas and the surrounding areas all over the floor, lines and circles drawn in red marker indicating areas they'd identified as likely haunts for Lagoshin and his men.

Voices came along the corridor, and then Gavril walked in, followed by Oleg. He smiled at her, and Trinity nodded to him, but he had more pressing matters on his mind than his girlfriend. Oleg knocked on the office door, and Kirill called that he'd be right out. A few moments later, they were all clustered even more tightly around the conference table.

"You found them," Kirill said as he came out of the office. "I see it on your faces."

Oleg nodded grimly. "We hit three or four of them. There were two I don't think will be getting up again. One was Vasily. I didn't see the face of the other."

"Krupin?" Timur asked.

"He was hit in the shoulder. Probably not a killing wound," Gavril replied.

Kirill frowned, studying them. Trinity noticed that they all seemed to be holding their breath.

"There is something you're not saying," Kirill observed.

Oleg and Gavril exchanged a glance, and then Oleg nodded slowly.

"Lagoshin was there," he said. "I'm sorry, Kirill. We could have ended it tonight if we'd gotten him."

Silence descended among them. The whole hotel seemed to tick and shift, as if she could hear it breathe.

Kirill said something in Russian. Trinity had listened to them talking enough that she understood a little, knew it translated roughly to "good job" or "you did well."

"Lagoshin is down by two men, maybe more if the others who were shot are badly wounded," Kirill went on, scanning the room. "I call it good fortune. Our friends are looking out for us."

Ilia scoffed. "Friends."

Kirill glared. "Don't let the bottle speak for you, Ilia."

"We have no friends or we would already know where to find Lagoshin and Krupin and the rest," Ilia said, all of his drunken amiability turned to slurring scorn.

"You can't blame them for being wary," Oleg said, and from his tone, Trinity realized how much Ilia's remarks unsettled him. "Our contacts are afraid. They want to help us, but if they do so openly and Lagoshin is the victor here—"

"Cowards!" Ilia snapped. He stood drunkenly and moved to the heavy drapes, peering out between them at the darkness. "They are cowards, and so are we, hiding here and striking from shadows. I say we talk to our 'friends' again, let them know they can't stand by and wait to see who is still standing at the end. They must choose, and if they do not choose us, then we make them regret the choice."

The room seemed to hold its breath. Trinity glanced at Pyotr, Sacha, and the others and realized that they agreed. This was why Oleg seemed so wary of Ilia's words, because he knew the others felt the same.

"Throwin' away through haste what might be gained through strategy is a fool's gambit," she said.

They all stared at her, and she felt more than ever like an intruder. Even Gavril curled his upper lip in disapproval of her interference. Only Oleg looked kindly upon her.

Kirill walked slowly to Ilia. Even drunk, he had the good sense to take a step back as his captain approached.

"It is my brother lying out there in a grave with no name," Kirill said. "I want Lagoshin dead more than any of you, but I want to do it without burying anyone else in this desert. I agree that we must put more pressure on some of our friends to choose sides, but it must be done carefully and wisely . . . and soberly. In the morning, Ilia, we will speak of this again."

Ilia looked terrified, but he raised his chin in a show of defiance and, in his own language, agreed.

Kirill turned from him. "Oleg, Gavril, come into the office."

Oleg and Gavril followed him into the little side room with its maps and markers while the others began to disperse, realizing that nothing more would be happening until morning.

Ilia, who had been so welcoming to her before, paused to glare drunkenly at her. "If they find us before we find them, they will kill us all."

Trinity nodded slowly. "They might. But if we rush into their gun sights without a plan, we die even faster."

The drunken man flinched, sniffed at her logic, and marched out of the conference room. The trouble was that she agreed with him. He was drunk and foolish, yes, and she didn't think they ought to do anything without preparing for the consequences, but the time had come to force the truth out of the Bratva's local contacts, even if it meant pain. Even if it meant blood.

No more hiding in shadows.

The crowd at the Tombstone Bar was significantly more subdued than the usual suspects back at Birdland. Chibs stood by the bar and waited on Baghead, who'd slipped behind the oak counter and grabbed a bottle of whiskey. Hopper had been tending bar, pulling pints of local ale off the tap and setting them in front of patrons with the foam still spilling over the rims. Now he turned to glare at Baghead and mutter something sharp. Bag replied, and Chibs saw Hopper look up, search the bar, and settle on him, then nod. Bag may not have explained exactly what was going on in the back room, but he knew it wasn't good.

Chibs and Joyce had let Jax and Opie ride in the lead, just in case one of them took a spill. Despite the blows to Jax's head and Opie's blood loss, they'd made it back to the Tombstone without any real difficulty and guided their bikes into the lot at the rear of the bar. Patrons leaving the last showing at Rollie's little next-door movie theater stared at the snorting Harleys as they vanished behind the gate. Chibs hoped the darkness had hid the crimson soaking Opie's shirt and the blood on Jax's face.

"Got it," Baghead said proudly as he emerged from behind the bar. He did a little two-step as if to celebrate his achievement, and Chibs wondered just how crazy the guy might be. With Tig and Happy, they had their own madmen back in Charming, but Bag seemed to walk a fine line between good-natured idiot and raving lunatic.

"Brilliant," Chibs said as they fell into step together.

Bag handed him the bottle as they strode toward the back hallway, and Chibs nearly choked. Talisker single malt, twenty-five-year-old scotch. A rare beast, and surely one of the most expensive bottles of liquor behind the bar.

"This isn't the sort of thing you give a man to take the edge off," Chibs said.

Bag shrugged. "Honored guests, man. Jax is VP of the mother charter. You guys get the best. Rollie said so."

Chibs thought Rollie might shit his pants when he saw how literally Bag had taken this instruction, but he stopped arguing about it. He was looking forward to a little taste of the fine stuff himself.

They went through the back of the building to the crash pad. In the poolroom, Joyce and Thor were playing a round of eight ball while Rollie used peroxide to clean the wound on Opie's right side. Jax had already washed most of the blood off his face and lay on the sofa with a plastic bag full of ice against his head.

Chibs raised the bottle of Talisker. "If you need a painkiller, Jackie, this one's a beauty."

Opie extended a hand for the bottle. "Whatever it is, pass it over."

Rollie glanced up from his handiwork and sighed. "Shit, man, that's a three-hundred-dollar scotch."

"Honored guests, that's what you said," Bag reminded him.

Chibs took a sip and handed the bottle to Opie, who slugged back several long gulps.

"Get it done," he said.

"Let's give it a bit for the scotch to work its magic," Chibs said.

Opie took another swig, this one not as deep. "Just do it. We can't waste time."

"You're going out again tonight?" Joyce asked, clearly surprised.

Baghead sniffed."You deaf or stupid? Opie already took a bullet. If the Russians are getting close to an all-out street war, Jax's sister is gonna be right in the middle of it. We've gotta get her out before that happens."

"Not 'we,' Bag," Rollie said. "I don't want you near any part of it."

"Yeah, yeah. I can't keep my cool. I'll only make it worse," Bag replied, waving his prez's words away as if they were irritating houseflies.

Chibs wondered how long Clay would have put up with the guy. A wild card could be useful, but a loose cannon was always a danger to the club. He hadn't yet decided which one Baghead might be.

"Stitch him up, Chibs," Jax said from the sofa.

Rollie stepped out of the way to let Chibs work. It wasn't the first time a member had been stitched up in this room, and Chibs figured it wouldn't be the last. Fortunately, that meant Rollie had everything he needed to sew up Opie's wound. "Turn," he said.

Opie shifted sideways to present the wound, and it pouted open a little. Chibs has treated his share of wounds as a medic in the British Army, and taken care of more than a few for his brothers in SAMCRO, but the scotch could only do so much. When he started stitching up the wound, Opie grimaced.

"So," Opie said, taking another pull from the Talisker bottle. "How we gonna take these pricks down?"

Jax sat up slowly, and took the ice pack from his head, steadying himself. Chibs had thought he'd cleaned up more, but now he saw the blood in Jax's beard and the swelling on his face and jaw. At the church, he hadn't been close enough to see how bad Lagoshin had beaten Jax. Now his hands twitched with the desire to throttle the big Russian.

"I'm not worried about taking them all down," Jax said. "They're already trying to kill each other, so all we need to do is get out of the way. We get Trinity, make sure Lagoshin goes down, and we're done here."

Opie grunted, teeth grinding as Chibs sewed.

"From what Lagoshin told you, the only lead we've got is the murder of this Oscar Temple," Chibs said.

Jax nodded painfully. "Which is why we talk to a cop."

Rollie glanced over at him. "How hard did that Russian hit you?"

Jax stared at him. "I know you have someone on the local PD who'd be willing to give up information at the right price."

Thor sank the seven ball in a corner pocket and glanced up. "There's Izzo."

Joyce snickered. "Izzo, man, you can't trust that guy. He'd sell his mother for a line of blow."

"We don't want his mother," Jax said. "But he does sound like a man we can do business with."

They met up with the cop in the parking lot of a defunct home-improvement store just south of Nellis Air Force Base. Jax put his bike up on its stand as the echoes of its engine died on the wind. He sat astride it for a few seconds as the throbbing pain in his chest and head subsided.

After a moment, he dismounted and forced himself to stand up straight.

"You all right?" Opie asked, coming toward him.

Jax cocked an eyebrow at him. Opie's features were pale and drawn from the blood he'd lost, but he seemed remarkably well for a guy who'd been kissed by a bullet a few hours earlier.

Chibs killed his Harley's engine and climbed off just as Thor circled round to them. He had led them here and then taken a quick ride around the building to be sure they would be alone. Jax had always liked Thor Westergaard. With his imposing size, he seemed an unlikely candidate for chef, but he conducted himself with a calm, methodical style that belied the motorcycle-club lifestyle. Now Jax could see that Thor brought the same Zen aura out into the real world. They'd never been under fire together, but Jax had a feeling that Zen calm would carry over.

"Where's your cop friend?" Opie asked.

"Izzo's not a friend," Thor said. "But he has his uses."

They heard tires on pavement and the low murmur of an engine. Headlights illuminated the corner of the abandoned home-improvement warehouse . . . and then went out. The car came around the building slowly, almost crawling, and Jax and the others stood away from their bikes a little, making sure that the moonlight would be enough to allow Izzo to see them.

The car's headlights flickered, letting them know the driver had seen them. It neither slowed nor sped up, only rolled toward them until, at last, it puttered to a halt. In the darkness behind the windshield, Jax could see the burning tip of a cigarette. The orange glow flared a moment as the smoker inhaled.

The driver's door opened. The dome light inside the car did not go on— the man was used to meetings in dark places where he didn't want to draw attention. He left the car running as he climbed out, studied them as he took another drag on his cigarette, then reached back inside to shut it off, apparently deciding that if they were going to ambush him they would've done so already. Jax made a mental mark against his intelligence level, but they didn't need a genius, just an informant.

"If it ain't the mighty Thor," the cop drawled, cigarette hand dangling at his side. "And friends. Which one of you is Iron Man?"

"You missed your calling, Detective," Thor replied. "I'm sure there's a spot for you on stage at Caesars."

Izzo offered a pained smile, waiting. Thin and jittery, he needed a haircut and a shave. Thor and Rollie had explained that he was a detective with the Las Vegas vice squad and that he dipped into the product of his arrests more often than not—hookers, drugs. He wasn't the sort of cop who wanted to be a kingpin, just a guy who couldn't control his taste for the forbidden.

"Mike Izzo, meet some friends of mine," Thor said at last.

"No colors on you boys," Izzo said, gesturing with his cigarette toward their clothes. "No gang affiliation?"

"Sons of Anarchy isn't a gang, Detective," Thor said.

"I know, I know, it's a 'motorcycle club,' but these guys ride motorcycles, too."

Jax gave a shrug—small, but enough to make his body remind him of Lagoshin's fists.

"We're not the joining type," he said.

"They're friends of mine," Thor said, as if that explained it all. "My friend here is searching for a missing family member and thinks some of her associates might be connected to the murder of Oscar Temple."

Izzo cocked his head, eyes narrowing. He smoked and exhaled through his nose.

"You've got interesting friends," he drawled, but he nodded. "Trouble is, I don't know shit. Homicide's not my beat."

Jax stiffened. Had they wasted their time with this cokehead?

"You sing this song every time, Mike," Thor said. "We both know you've always got your ears open, hoping to hear something you can sell or trade."

Izzo flicked ash off his cigarette. From the way his nostrils flared, he hadn't liked Thor's observation much.

"Maybe that's true," he said, "but this is fresh. Happened yesterday."

Jax glanced at the others. Chibs looked pissed, turned and spat onto the cracked pavement. Opie seemed to have been drifting, barely listening, maybe because of the blood loss, but suddenly he perked up.

"Who found the bodies?" he asked in his familiar low rumble.

Izzo stared at him. "You boys don't look too good," he said, turning to study Jax. "And you look like you got your ass handed to you. What are you really after?"

"We told you the truth, man," Jax said, hands up. "We're not bringing trouble. We're trying to get my sister out of it."

Izzo nodded knowingly. Vice detective in Las Vegas, he'd seen more than his share of sisters in trouble.

"Wish I could help," he said. "Not least because I could use the scratch Thor and his boys would pay for information. But the investigation is just ramping up. I can give Rollie a call at the Tombstone if they turn up anything. What I can tell you is that Oscar Temple's in the gun business—sponsors the big gun show out there in Summerlin—and homicide figures it was a side deal gone wrong."

Chibs glanced at Jax. "Illegal guns?"

Izzo scratched at his stubbled chin and took a drag on his cigarette. "I know, right? People breaking the law. Can you imagine?"

Jax cocked his head to one side, trying to figure the cop out. "You never answered my friend's question."

"Sorry, right," Izzo replied, waving toward Opie with his cigarette. "One of the dealers from the gun show, an old friend of Temple's, went up to the house to have coffee or something after he'd packed up. Found the bodies."

"This gun dealer, does he have a name?" Thor asked.

"He's an old dude. Older, anyway," Izzo said. "Irish guy, I think. Last name is Carney."

Thor stiffened. "John Carney?"

Izzo dropped his cigarette, crushing it under his shoe. "You know the guy?"

"Heard of him," Thor admitted.

Jax watched Izzo's eyes and realized the detective was thinking precisely what he'd been thinking—that if Thor knew the old man's name, maybe John Carney hadn't gone up to Oscar Temple's house for coffee at all.

"I'll keep you posted if I hear anything," Izzo said, digging out his keys as he returned to his car. He paused just inside the open door. "You make sure you do the same. I could use a little career boost."

"I'll keep that in mind," Thor told him.

None of them believed it, not even Izzo.

11

John Carney had slept poorly ever since the death of his wife. Over time he'd developed the habit of falling asleep in the recliner in the living room, bathed in the flickering blue light of the television. Living in Arizona required air-conditioning, but his backyard opened up to nothing but scrub and distant hills, and it could get awfully cold at night. He kept the windows of his little adobe house open and covered himself with a thick blanket, never taking his slippers off. Past the age of fifty, his feet had begun to feel cold pretty much all the time. And he'd left fifty in the rearview mirror quite a while back.

Tonight he moaned and shifted in the chair, rising up from the shadows of dreamtime, cobweb memories of a nightmare clinging to him. He frowned and rubbed his eyes, sleepily contemplating the possibility of leaving the chair and actually sleeping in his bed for once. Instead, he pulled the blanket up to his neck and nestled deeper into the chair. The ghost of his dead wife occupied that bed, and he figured it always would. Whenever he tried to sleep in there, he felt her presence. *No, that ain't it,* he corrected himself. He felt her *absence.*

Drifting in that gray fog between sleeping and wakefulness, Carney thought he heard voices. He groaned softly and slitted his eyes open. One of his animal shows played on the TV. A baby gorilla clung to its mother, and the sight made him smile, still more than half-asleep. His animal shows could be grotesque at times, and even then they were fascinating, but there was something soothing about the programs concerning bears and monkeys and apes.

Knock knock.

Thump thump.

Carney jerked in the chair, adrenaline burning him awake. He threw the blanket aside and stood, barely noticing the arthritis pain in his knees. Turning slowly, he tried to locate the source of the noise, and it came again. *Thump thump.* He spun, staring at the short little corridor that led into the rest of the house.

A rapping came from the back of the house, a fist on glass, urgent but not angry. Not on the verge of shattering.

Carney twisted the little iron key, opened the body of the grandfather clock, and stopped the pendulum's swing with his left hand. With his right he reached past it and grabbed the shotgun that always sat waiting there, just behind the tick of the clock.

The knock came again as he made his way down the little corridor, giving him a chance to zero in. The sound hadn't come from his bedroom or the bathroom or the smaller second bedroom he used as an office. There wasn't much house out here in the desert, but how much house did an aging widower need?

He ducked into the kitchen, stared at the blinds that hung over the sliding glass door that led onto his patio. A low adobe wall ringed the patio. On any ordinary night there'd have been nothing but snakes and coyotes beyond that wall, but snakes and coyotes didn't knock on the wall or rap on the glass. The blinds were closed. The patio light was off.

"Who's there?" he shouted at the closed blinds, leveling the shotgun at the slider. If they wanted to kill him, his voice gave them a location. They could start shooting right now. But did murderers knock?

"Friends, Mr. Carney," came a reply, a raspy voice—not an old man's rasp.

Carney slid to the side, toward the stove, and sidestepped past the kitchen island so he came at the blinds from an angle.

"In my experience," he called back, "friends don't bang on your back door after midnight."

"Sorry if we woke you," that voice rasped again. "The lateness couldn't be helped. It's pretty urgent I talk to you."

I guess it must be, Carney thought.

"You armed?" he called.

"Yes, sir. But none of us have weapons drawn. If we wanted to do more than talk, there are open windows." Carney reached out and opened the blinds. Through the slats he could make out five men silhouetted by moonlight. Shotgun leveled at them, he flicked on the patio light, and the men blinked at the sudden brightness. The one in front squinted but didn't raise his hands to shield his eyes, too smart to want to spook Carney into pulling the trigger.

"Hands up, slowly," Carney said.

The men complied. The guy in front, blond and bearded, was the first to do so, and the others followed suit. In the back of the group, a massive red-haired man was the last, and his reluctance was obvious.

Carney studied the faces. "I don't know any of you."

"I know how this must look," said the blond, the owner of the raspy voice. "My name's Jax. I think you may've met my sister, Trinity—"

A memory flashed through Carney's mind. Gunshot and blood spatter in Oscar Temple's kitchen. The woman's face floated across his thoughts, and he saw the resemblance. Carney's heart had been thundering in his chest, and now it skipped a beat as the copper stink of blood returned to him.

"Irish girl?" he asked, voice raised to be heard through the sliding glass door.

"That's her." Muffled. Quieter.

"You don't have an accent."

"Different moms." The blond man put the palm of one rough hand against the glass and gazed calmly at him. "She's not safe, Mr. Carney. I just want to get her the hell out of here and home to her mother."

A fine sentiment. Carney had taken a shine to the girl from the moment she'd approached him at the gun show, and not just because her accent reminded him of home. She had a raw energy that he'd admired. But that wasn't why he lowered the shotgun.

The rough men on his patio seemed surprised when he raised the blinds all the way and unlocked the slider. He stepped back and covered the door with his shotgun, but he kept his finger outside the trigger guard. John Carney had gotten old, and his hands trembled sometimes. If he shot somebody, it would damn well be on purpose.

"Just you," he told Jax. "Your friends can make themselves comfortable on the patio."

A goateed man with startling scars on his face looked disappointed. "Any chance of a cup of coffee?"

Carney heard the mix of burr and brogue in his voice and smiled. "You're not a guest. You're a stranger who woke me in the middle of the night."

The man beside him, pale and bearded with his hair tied back in a small knot, nodded. "He does have a point."

Jax slid the glass door open and entered the kitchen as the other four made themselves comfortable on the patio furniture, sprawling as if they hadn't a care in the world. They weren't worried about him killing them with his shotgun, which told him they had no intention of trying to kill *him*. But he hadn't gone to Oscar Temple's house thinking anyone was going to die, either.

"Lock it behind you," he told Jax, who complied without complaint.

"Can I sit down?" the man asked.

"You're not getting coffee, either," Carney told him.

Jax smiled, but it turned to a wince. Carney flicked on the light above the kitchen table, and now he saw the bruises and swelling on his visitor's face.

"Rough night?"

"I'm alive," Jax replied. "I'd like to stay that way, and keep Trinity alive, too."

"She told me her name was Caitlin Dunphy. I heard one of 'em call her Trinity, but I didn't put it together that it was her name till you said so. I would've known who you meant regardless, though. You resemble her a little. Plus, she's the only woman I've run into in a long time that I figure might cause armed men to show up on my patio. How did you all get here, anyway? You got a van out front?"

"Bikes," Jax said.

Carney almost laughed at the image of these five leg breakers riding bicycles out here with the lizards and dust devils. Then he realized the guy meant motorcycles, and his humor dissipated. Had he slept through the roar of five approaching engines? A disturbing thought. If they'd meant to do him harm, he really *would* have been dead by now.

He lowered the shotgun and leaned against the counter.

You're crazy. Letting this man into your house.

Motorcycles might mean they were part of a biker gang. That made a certain sense. He'd caught a glimpse of what looked like some kind of logo on the vest that the big red-bearded bastard had been wearing out on the patio. Oscar Temple dealt illegal guns—a *shitload* of illegal guns—and Jax's sister had been trying to make a deal with him on behalf of some Russians.

"You involved in the gun business, too?" Carney asked.

Jax cocked his head. "I'm told you used to be pretty involved yourself."

"I'm not casting aspersions, lad. Just trying to figure out all the connections here."

"The only connection that's relevant is that I'm a concerned brother. I don't want to involve you in anything that's going to cause you trouble—"

"Your sister involved me already," Carney said.

Jax nodded, said nothing more.

Carney sighed deeply and then shrugged. "She did save my life, I suppose. Though it wouldn't have needed saving if I'd never met her."

Jax opened his hands, palms up as if in surrender. "Question is, What are you gonna do right now? Tonight?"

Carney turned the question over in his head. He glanced out at the men on the patio. Would there be consequences for the wrong answer? Jax seemed intense, but not intimidating. Was it an act?

"I spoke to the police already," he said, hesitating.

"I can hear a 'but' coming."

Carney raised the shotgun slightly, barely noticing that he'd done it. Maybe his subconscious mind wasn't as sure of Jax's motivations as his conscious mind was.

"I liked her the moment I met her," Carney went on.

"She has that effect," Jax said.

"I didn't want the police to find her, but I wasn't just protecting her."

"You were protecting yourself. Makes sense. I figure you told the police being up there at the ranch was a coincidence, but whatever deal Trinity and her boys were trying to strike with Temple, you were a broker. Maybe coming out of retirement?"

"One night only, like all the great Vegas comebacks," Carney said. "Anyway, I wasn't in a hurry to help the cops track them down."

Jax leaned across the table, blue eyes alight. "So you do know where they went?"

Carney's hands felt sweaty on the metal of the shotgun. "No. But someone else might. One of the men your sister was with mentioned a name, after the killing was done. Something about how they had to make sure they couldn't be tracked back, or Drinkwater would have to find them a new place."

"That name mean something to you?"

"Louis Drinkwater is a local real estate guy. Never met him, but I've seen him in the papers. He's had his share of legal trouble."

Jax stood abruptly, the chair scraping linoleum. Carney flinched, raised the shotgun, but Jax had almost forgotten he was there. The biker unlocked the slider and snapped at his men.

"Let's go," he said. "The night is young."

"Drinkwater has a lot more money that I do," Carney said. "Probably has better security, too. Maybe you oughta wait till morning."

Jax stepped onto the patio, then turned to look back through the door. "If I get my sister home safe, we're both gonna owe you one. Thanks for your help. And sorry again for waking you."

I did it for her, not for you, he wanted to say. But the men were leaving and taking their guns with them, so he thought it best not to antagonize them.

Jax liked to ride late at night, when the world was quiet and dark. Even if he wasn't riding alone, it still felt like solitude. Even more so with the dry wind blowing down from Desert Hills and Red Rock Canyon. They'd gone south to visit Carney, but now it was past one o'clock in the morning and they were roaring along the beltway with Jax in front and the other guys riding two by two. Joyce had put in a few hours at the Tombstone and then met up with them before the visit to Carney.

Headlights strafed Jax from a truck headed the other direction. He let himself drift back to Belfast, back to his first meeting with Trinity. They had recognized something in each other that had been difficult to identify. She had a core decency that he admired, but also blunt, rough edges. She wasn't a part of the RIRA, but her family was inextricably linked to it, and maybe being raised in that family wasn't so different from Jax's life with SAMCRO. He'd practically been born on the back of a Harley, heir apparent to the gavel.

He'd felt a kinship with Trinity even before he'd learned they were actually kin . . . and they'd learned that bit of truth just in time. The connection between them had been powerful. They'd been halfway undressed and well on their way to enthusiastic, if unintentional, incest. If their mothers hadn't interrupted, and immediately revealed the truth to avoid any chance of a second try . . . The memory made his stomach turn into an awkward knot, but not nearly as awkward as if the revelation had come a day later.

Jax didn't like to think about it, and he was sure Trinity shared that reluctance. With the violence and chaos that had erupted around SAMCRO's visit to Belfast, they hadn't really had a chance to figure out what it meant to be brother and sister before Jax had to return to the States. He wondered if their awkwardness would prevent them from figuring that out now. Hoped it wouldn't.

A low roar came from his left, and he looked over to see Opie riding up alongside him. Opie tilted his head, indicating something behind them. Jax cast a look back and spotted a silver BMW gliding along. He and Opie exchanged another silent communication. Was someone tailing them?

Jax slowed, letting Chibs, Joyce, and Thor pass him, and he took another glance backward to be certain of what he thought he'd seen. Sure enough, two men on bikes were following the BMW.

He saw an exit sign for Cheyenne Avenue, twisted the throttle, and blew past the others, signaling them to follow as he left the beltway. At the bottom of the exit ramp, he turned west, away from civilization instead of toward it. Opie and the rest followed him, but so had the BMW and the two assholes on motorcycles. He raced beneath the overpass and then skidded to a halt, propping the bike on its stand before taking cover. Then he drew his gun.

Opie, Thor, and Joyce did the same on the opposite side of the street. Thor moved up against the concrete foundation of the overpass, using the corner to shield himself.

Chibs skidded up beside Jax and jumped off his bike.

The BMW slowed as it rolled beneath the overpass, and the two men riding behind it throttled down. The car's driver had seen them pull over—he couldn't have missed it—and given their body language, the way they were taking cover, the way they all held their gun hands down at their sides, just out of sight, even an ordinary citizen would have known they were ready for a fight.

The BMW did not turn around, only rolled slowly until it stopped in the middle of the street, dead center in what would be the cross fire if bullets flew. The two guys on motorcycles—sleek red Kawasakis—halted fifty yards back, far enough that they could bolt if things turned ugly, report back to the boss.

The passenger window of the BMW slid down. In the darkness of the underpass, without even starlight to illuminate the face of the man inside, Jax could not make him out. A dome light inside the BMW clicked, and he flinched, surprised that the men inside would expose themselves like that.

The guy in the passenger seat was Viktor Krupin. He looked pale but fairly hearty considering he'd been shot in the shoulder a few hours earlier.

"Mr. Ashby," Krupin said, his voice echoing against the concrete sides and roof of the underpass. The BMW purred, and the two Kawasakis growled quietly. "I would have thought the beating my boss gave you earlier would have discouraged you from breaking your agreement with us."

Jax stared at him, thinking fast. Either Lagoshin had a way to track them or one of the Russians had been tailing them since the Orthodox church. Both options seemed unlikely.

"I haven't broken any agreement," he said, stepping out from behind his bike as he slid his gun back into his rear waistband. "And I figure if you're up and riding around with that hole in your shoulder, it'd reflect badly on me if a couple of punches in the head kept me from doing the same."

Krupin frowned. "You were to call me as soon as you had a lead on your sister's location."

Jax put up his hands. "That *was* the deal, but I don't have shit. Just a string of names, people who might help narrow it all down for me. I didn't see the point in boring you with that kinda thing. Figured once I had a location—"

"What *do* you have?" Krupin asked. He rested his elbow on the frame of the open window, deceivingly casual.

Jax's whole body ached as he remembered the beating he'd received.

"I'm not going to have you and Lagoshin going around beating the crap out of anyone who might have seen my sister. I want to find her, not scare her off . . . and I sure as hell don't want you and Sokolov's guys getting into a shooting match with her around."

"We can guarantee her safety," Krupin said reasonably.

"No one can guarantee her safety," Jax replied. "Not even me." He pointed up the road toward the men on the Kawasakis. "I'm gonna figure out where she is. Then I'm gonna get her out before the shooting starts. You want to send those two guys with us as insurance, that's fine. I figure they're gonna follow us anyway. Something happens that you won't like, your guys can take care of business for you."

Krupin narrowed his eyes. Jax could practically feel him searching for duplicity. The son of a bitch *knew* things weren't what they seemed, but it was clear Krupin also felt very confident in Lagoshin's ability to terrorize people. And Jax had no doubt that sending the two bikers to babysit him had been the plan from the outset, or Krupin wouldn't have brought thugs on motorcycles.

Someone in the car began to speak to him in Russian. Krupin snapped angrily at the man, then opened his door and stepped out. Jax saw the driver of the BMW drawing a gun. Across the street, Opie, Joyce, and Thor still had their weapons out, ready for things to turn bloody.

Krupin beckoned to the Kawasaki riders, and the two men spurred their bikes forward, riding up to stop directly behind the BMW. They wore helmets, but when they raised their visors, Jax could see that one had gray eyes and one a cold blue. Krupin introduced them as Ustin and Luka.

"You go with him," Krupin told them. "When you know the sister's location, report back to me." He turned to Jax. "Once I hear from them, you will have one hour to get your sister to safety. One hour. If you are still there when we arrive, or if you warn Sokolov and his men, you will all die together."

Jax nodded slowly. Krupin stared at him a moment. Then he climbed into the BMW and it pulled away, power window gliding up. Despite all the talk of murder, Krupin had treated the whole thing like a business meeting, and Jax thought maybe that was all any of it was to him. Business. Nothing personal.

The thought made Jax want more than ever to shoot him.

As the others remounted their bikes, glaring at Ustin and Luka, Jax walked over to Thor, who sat on his idling Harley, putting on his helmet.

"Head back to the Tombstone," he said quietly. "Tell Rollie what's going on. Tell him I may need backup and that I need your club on standby. Stay with him till you hear from me."

The big man scratched at his red beard. "You don't want me to just *call* him?"

"No. I don't."

"I guess you don't want to tell me why."

Jax hardened his gaze. After a second, Thor just nodded, buckled his helmet, and took off without speaking to any of the others. Jax watched him go and then turned to his Russian babysitters.

"Try to keep up," he said, and then he started for his bike.

12

Trinity and Oleg had made love quietly, well aware of the proximity of his comrades. His brothers. After several nights of broken sleep and days of emotional exhaustion, she had curled into the comforting crook of his arm and fallen asleep listening to his heartbeat and trying to decipher the meaning of the tattoos on his chest.

In the small hours of the morning—she guessed it must be 2 a.m. or so—her eyes opened and she was suddenly, irritatingly awake. Some nights she woke with a jarring disorientation, a terrible sense of dislocation, but tonight she knew precisely where she was and why.

Really, the why was the only thing that mattered, and the answer was: *Oleg.*

The hotel room's window stood halfway open, letting in the cool night air. During the day the room baked, and even after dark it could remain muggy and stifling. Now, though, it was pleasant—almost chilly. If she let herself drift, just studied the stubble on Oleg's jaw or the taut skin of his abdomen, she could almost forget the murder of Oscar Temple and the imminence of more bloodshed.

She caressed his chest, ran her fingers along the prominent lines of his rib cage. He shuddered in his sleep, edged slightly closer to her, and a small grunt came from deep inside him. Whatever Oleg had done, in slumber he looked innocent, his brow free from the troubled lines carved by life. It hurt her heart to think how much she loved him.

Why had she fallen for him, and so quickly?

She knew the answer, or at least part of it. She'd grown up thinking her father was a soldier named Duffy, who'd died in the service. Her real father was a man named John Teller, who'd died on the side of a California roadway. Trinity was still angry with her mother for keeping that secret. No matter what sort of man John Teller had been, she wished she had known him.

Men were a puzzle she'd spent her whole life trying to solve. Most of the men she'd admired as a girl had disappointed her in one way or another. Some had been RIRA, which had seemed noble to her when she was too young to know any better, and others had been unreliable. Drunks or gamblers. Men who liked to keep their thoughts primitive and their emotions buried.

The boys she'd grown up with spent their time in pubs, making a joke of everything. If they treated a girl sweetly, it was only to rope her in. Once they had her pregnant and dependent, it was back to the pub with the same jokes and the same lads, a game of darts and a few pints of ale. Trinity had seen it happen far too many times.

In Oleg, she had found a man with a sense of adventure and a listless dissatisfaction with daily life that reflected her own. He wanted to *go*, and *do*, and *act*, and he wanted her at his side as a companion, not a conquest. Oleg had a brutal honesty that struck at the core of her. His life could be violent and bloody, and certainly dangerous, but he had never tried to hide that from her. From what Trinity could see, it had never even occurred to him that he should. This was a man she could respect . . . a man she could love.

Love had complicated the hell out of her life.

She slid her hand beneath the sheet, began to stroke the inside of his thigh. Using her fingernails, she scratched him gently, her pulse quickening.

"Mmm," Oleg said, and he took a deep breath as he opened his eyes. "What are you doing, *kotyonok*?"

"I can't sleep," she whispered, heart full of him. Hand full of him.

"So because you cannot sleep, I cannot sleep either?"

Trinity grinned. "Are you complainin'?"

Oleg drew her toward him . . . drew her on top of him.

"Does this seem like complaint to you?"

Louis Drinkwater woke with a gun to his head. Jax stood beside his bed, mostly in shadows, and pressed the cool metal of the gun barrel to the man's temple. He gave a nudge, then another, speaking in a low, clear voice.

"Wake up, asshole."

Drinkwater blinked awake, scowling and wiping at the spittle on the corner of his mouth, like his maid or somebody had disturbed his sleep. It wasn't until Jax repeated the words that the guy seemed to get it. The real estate agent froze, eyes wide and staring. His breath quickened into short, choppy gasps, almost as if he might break down sobbing. He glanced at Opie, who'd been wearing a pained grimace all through the evening's

ride, thanks to the stitches in his side. Opie bared his teeth like he might
rip out the real estate agent's throat.

"Oh, God, what do you want?" the man whined. "Take . . . take anything. Just . . . just . . ."

Jax took a step back, gun still aimed at Drinkwater's skull. The sheets
were soft—high thread count—and whoever had decorated the place had
expensive tastes and a sterile soul. The house was a stucco minicastle complete with turret room, the home of a moderately wealthy man in a neighborhood of moderately wealthy people, not rich enough to have high fences
or any significant security. Drinkwater had an alarm company sign in the
front yard, but they'd been able to see the keypad through the back door;
he was one of the fools who paid for the alarm system but only used it
when he was away from the home, confident no one would dare enter while
he was in residence.

Opie poked around the room, opening closet doors and drawers. The
third drawer he opened, he chuckled softly to himself and reached inside
to pull out a large purple vibrator. With a look of disgust, he dropped it on
the floor.

"Who the fuck are you people?" Drinkwater moaned, either unnerved
by Jax's silence or gaining new confidence now that he was more awake.

"Quiet," Jax said. He stepped forward and bumped the gun barrel
against Drinkwater's forehead, just to remind him of its weight. "One question."

The man blinked. He was thin and olive-skinned with an accent Jax
couldn't identify and a thin little mustache that made him look like he'd
just stepped off the set of a 1970s porn flick. In his mind, Jax found himself comparing Drinkwater to John Carney. He'd had a good feeling about
Carney.

Not so, Louis Drinkwater. The decor alone told Jax what kind of prick
he was dealing with. He had no good feelings for this guy.

Opie laughed softly, and Jax glanced over to see that he'd produced a massive black latex dildo from the drawer.

"What?" Drinkwater asked. "What do you want to know?"

"You're helping some Russians stay out of sight," Jax said. "Tell me where."

Drinkwater flinched, wet his lips with his tongue, and gave a nervous laugh. "Russian? You think you're living in some spy movie?"

Opie stepped forward, swung hard, and cracked the skinny guy across the face with the dildo, hard enough to split his lip and make blood spurt from his nose. The thing was huge and heavy and Opie was strong. Drinkwater groaned and reached for his nightstand, missed a handhold and slipped out of bed, falling to the gleaming hardwood in a tangle of sheets. Opie hit him again and the dildo came back streaked with blood. When Drinkwater spit a gob of scarlet onto the floor, a broken bit of tooth came with it.

Jax crouched beside him. "I'm not a patient man. You tell me where you've got the Russians stashed, and we'll make it look like your place was broken into. My friend here is gonna duct-tape you to a chair. If the Bratva—or anyone else—figures out you told us where they are, you'll be able to say you were beaten and your life was threatened. I'd say your chances of them not killing you are fifty-fifty. But if you don't tell me right now, you got zero chance of surviving the night."

Drinkwater tried to rise, put his hand on the bed to lever himself up. Opie brought the massive dildo down on his forearm nearly hard enough to break bone. The guy crumpled to the ground again, tears springing to his eyes.

"You're a businessman, Louis," Jax said. "You can do the math here even better than we can." He shook the gun in his hand to draw the Realtor's attention to it. "I could count to ten if you need some drama or whatever."

Clutching his bruised forearm, blood trickling from his nose, the man stared at Jax and Opie with an expression of such horror that it stripped all the pretense away from him. Even the world's biggest asshole had been a kid once, and Jax figured he was seeing the stripped-down face of young Louis.

Opie let the heavy latex cock dangle in his hand. "Ugly way to die, Louis," Opie said. "Skull caved in with your own damn dildo."

Drinkwater looked at Opie. "When you duct-tape me . . . I have a deviated septum. If you cover my mouth completely, I won't be able to get enough air. You'll suffocate me."

Opie shrugged. "I'll use an old-school gag. A rag or something. You can breathe around it, but it should keep you quiet for a while."

The little man nodded enthusiastically. "Okay, okay." He rose slowly and sat on the edge of the bed. "They're at the Wonderland Hotel. Place is abandoned, up for sale. I'll give you the address, but you've gotta promise to let me use the toilet before you duct-tape me. Could be my daughter who finds me—she comes by for lunch sometimes. I don't want to piss my pants."

Jax hesitated, thinking the guy might make a break for it or try to get to his phone. But Opie would be keeping an eye on him.

"Address," he said.

Drinkwater gave it up. Opie dropped the dildo, wiping his right hand on his jeans, then gestured for the Realtor to walk ahead of him to the bathroom.

Jax went into the kitchen, pulled out a chair, then waited until Drinkwater emerged and told him where to find the duct tape. Every house had a roll, even moderately wealthy shitheads. Opie taped the guy to the chair, wrists and ankles bound tightly enough that he could not possibly escape, and then went back into the bedroom for a minute.

"What was that about?" Jax asked when he came out.

Opie shrugged. "Guy's daughter might come by. I put his dick collection back in the drawer."

Jax shook his head, stifling a laugh. Opie gagged Drinkwater, and they left, the Realtor sighing sadly before slumping in the chair as much as the duct tape would allow.

They left the stucco castle by the back door. Joyce and Chibs waited there with their two Russian babysitters. The two Bratva pricks had wanted to come inside, but Jax had refused to allow it. Drinkwater would be more reluctant to give up the location if he knew for sure that he was sentencing his Russian buddies to death. At least that was what Jax had told them, and with the tension between the Kawasaki Russians and Jax's guys, they wisely declined to argue.

"Well?" blue-eyed Ustin demanded when Jax and Opie came out the back door.

Jax bumped shoulders with the Russian as he walked by, heading for the bikes. Chibs and Joyce were already there, waiting with Lagoshin's other thug, Luka. Ustin caught up to Jax and Opie as they were climbing onto their bikes.

"Where are they?" Ustin demanded, lowering his voice an octave and attempting to intimidate them.

Jax strapped on his helmet. "I told Lagoshin the plan. I'm going in after my sister. When we get there, you won't need to ask the address. He promised me an hour, and that hour starts ticking the second you call him. Just follow me. You can call him when you see the place."

Luka sniffed imperiously, as if he'd smelled something revolting. "You don't trust Lagoshin?"

Jax winced at the bruises on his face and the way every breath hurt, thanks to the kicks he'd taken to the chest.

"You're joking, right?"

He kick-started his Harley and twisted the throttle, tearing out of the parking lot. Chibs, Opie, and Joyce had been ready and followed him out. It took the Kawasaki Russians a few seconds to get themselves together, but they caught up fast enough. Jax had no intention of trying to lose them—not when they could prove valuable to him.

Dawn was still many hours away, but Jax could practically feel it creeping up. Too many pieces were in motion, not just Lagoshin's and Sokolov's crews, but SAMNOV and the cop, Izzo, not to mention Carney and Drinkwater, whose daughter would find him in the next ten to twelve hours, if not sooner. The night air grew heavy around him. Normally, riding was freedom, but in the small hours of that night it felt claustrophobic to him. Caution could only take him so far.

Two miles from Drinkwater's house, on an access road that led along the property line of a dried-up ranch and back toward the beltway, Jax pulled off onto the shoulder. Dust swirled up around his Harley. He pulled off his helmet and dismounted. One by one, the others followed suit, ending with Ustin and Luka. The Kawasaki Russians looked pissed when they ripped off their helmets, although the difference between joy and fury would be hard to discern on those unforgiving faces.

"What you doing, man?" Ustin demanded, marching up to Jax, hand drifting behind his back, trying to decide if he should pull his gun. "You try an' cut Lagoshin out, you know what's gonna happen."

His accent was Russia by way of LA gang-speak, like he'd learned English from watching bad cop shows.

Jax held his hands out at his sides. "Don't be stupid. My sister's in the middle of all this. You really think I'm gonna risk her life if I can help it?"

Opie and Chibs stood in the road, watching for approaching cars, but this time of night, nobody would be out driving this dusty ranch road unless they were up to no good. Joyce had stayed next to his motorcycle, an anxious look on his face. Jax was being unpredictable, and it was very clear that unpredictable scared the shit out of Joyce tonight.

Ustin pointed at Jax. "Why we stopping, then?"

"I changed my mind. Lagoshin sending his men in after these other Russian pricks might work in my favor. Provide a distraction. Go ahead and call him."

A thin smile touched Ustin's lips, snide enough to be sinister. He nodded.

"Smart man," the Russian said, and he dug out his cell phone.

Jax drew and shot him twice in the chest. The gunshots boomed across the dried-up ranch, so loud it almost seemed to be the noise that blew Ustin backward in a fanning spray of his own blood. His cell phone spun in the air and hit the ground almost at the same instant he did. The smell of blood and gunpowder swirled around them.

"Son of a bitch!" Joyce cried. "What are you—"

Luka roared and lunged toward Jax. Opie and Chibs reached for him, knocked his gun away before the barrel could clear his waistband, and drove the gray-eyed Russian to the dirt shoulder. Opie slammed him twice against the ground and then stood back, picked up Luka's gun and pointed it at him.

Opie glanced over at the guy Jax had killed. "Ustin . . ."

"Don't say it," Chibs said.

Opie grinned. "We have a problem."

Luka stayed on the ground but let loose with a torrent of what could only be Russian profanity.

"Jax, what are you doing?" Joyce asked, shaking his head and staring, slack-jawed, at the dead Russian. "We had a plan—a good plan that would have protected Trinity. Now Lagoshin's going to kill you both!"

Jax stood over Ustin, watching blood run out of him and pool in the dirt. Crimson turned black in the moonlight.

"Either Lagoshin sent hitters to Charming to try to take out SAMCRO, or Kirill Sokolov did," he said. "Do you know which one?"

Joyce scowled. "Of course not."

"Me either," Jax replied, with a glance at Opie and Chibs. "I show up where Sokolov's people are and they figure out who I am—maybe Trinity's told them she's my sister, I don't know—they're gonna kill me. That is, if they're the Russians who want to destroy SAMCRO."

He wandered over to Luka, bent, and did a quick search, taking away the Russian's cell phone and a small knife strapped to his leg. Dirt rose up from the hard-packed shoulder, the grit getting into Jax's mouth.

"I bring them our friend Luka," he went on, "and maybe they listen long enough for me to get Trinity out of there. Bringing Luka to Sokolov shows goodwill, and maybe if they poke him a bit, they can make him tell them where Lagoshin's holed up. Everybody wins."

Joyce just shook his head, backing up. He glanced at Opie and Chibs as if expecting their support. "This is crazy. Stupid."

Ice spread through Jax. His upper lip twitched as he let the mask he'd adopted fall away, and he sneered at Joyce.

"Figured you'd feel that way, considering."

Joyce went silent and still. Stared at Jax. "What are you talking about?"

He glanced around, saw Opie and Chibs watching him with expressions as cold as the one Jax wore, and started shaking his head. "I don't know what you think—"

"Now's not the time to lie," Chibs said. "We've no patience with it."

Joyce went pale. All emotion leeched from his face, and he turned again to Jax. "I'm just looking out for you and your sister, man."

Anyone who saw Jax in that moment and didn't know him well might have been forgiven for thinking he smiled just then. A flicker. The expression, however, was one of disbelief.

"Don't make it worse by being a pussy, Joyce. You had the balls to turn on your brothers, take money from the Russians . . . at least have the balls to face the music now that it's here."

"I didn't, though . . . I would never . . ."

Opie held Luka's gun. He raised it, aimed at Joyce's head. "Someone told them we were headed to Drinkwater's house."

"That could've been any of the guys! Thor, Hopper, even Rollie. Shit, man, Baghead is a basket case!"

Jax shook his head. "Only it wasn't any of them. I should've known it back at Birdland. You were so clued in about the Russians, where and when they'd be there. Started trouble with 'em because you figured you could. You'd dealt with them before. Guy wearing a cut has to be stupid or damn sure he's not gonna eat a bullet if he's gonna start trouble like that. Something seemed off then, but when Krupin rolled up on us after the visit with Drinkwater, I knew it had to be someone from SAMNOV, and you're the only one who makes sense."

Jax cast a quick glance at Luka, saw the way the Russian was watching them, and he had his answer.

Desperation had Joyce sweating. His chest rose and fell in quick breaths. He shook his head again.

"I promise you, this wasn't me," he said. "You don't believe me, fine, take it to the table. You're not in Charming. Talk to Rollie, man, if it'll make you feel better—"

"Exactly what I'm gonna do," Jax said.

Which was when Joyce went for his gun.

Opie shouted in alarm, but he had nothing to worry about. Joyce never had a chance. Jax shot him through the skull, and Joyce flopped backward onto the dirt.

"Idiot," Chibs snarled, staring down at the dead man. "Who goes for his gun when he's got one pointed at his head?"

Jax exhaled, staring at the spatter of Joyce's blood in the dirt. "He knew it was over for him. If we took it to the table, it would've ended the same way. Maybe he just figured this was quicker."

Opie wiped his prints from Luka's gun, then pressed it into the grip of

Ustin's dead fingers. Luka muttered a curse in Russian, seeming to have abandoned English entirely since the tables had turned on him.

"What are we gonna do with this guy?" He pointed at Luka, and all three of them stood there for a moment contemplating their next move. They had nothing but motorcycles. No way to get Luka where they needed him without the risk of the guy taking off.

"Shit," Opie muttered.

Chibs laughed humorlessly. "Don't be too hard on yourself, Jackie. Situation's changing fast. We're making this up as we go along."

Jax scuffed his shoe against the dirt. "We can't call Rollie unless we feel like taking the time to convince him Joyce betrayed the club."

"Never mind that he went for his gun," Chibs added.

"He'll lose his shit that we didn't take it to him before getting into this situation," Opie finished for him. "We could just say Ustin killed him, but this other piece of Bratva shit isn't going to cover for us."

They all stared at Luka for a few seconds, Jax trying to decide how much they needed Luka. Enough to go to all the trouble it would require to get him where they needed him? He swore quietly. They might not need Luka to convince Kirill Sokolov, but if they did . . .

"Drag the bodies away from the road," he told Chibs and Opie. "Dump the bikes on the other side. I'll get to cover, keep him guarded, while you two go find us a truck."

Luka had a smile on his face, enjoying their frustration.

Jax cracked him across the face with his gun, then turned to Opie and Chibs.

"Make it fast, or this whole thing is going to fall apart around us."

13

As Oleg shook her, Trinity fought to stay asleep. She sighed, grumbled, and batted his arm away. In that bleary state between sleep and wakefulness, she became aware of the thin line of drool on her cheek and the dryness of her throat.

"Come on," she heard Oleg growl. His hand clutched more tightly at her arm, and he shook her so that her head lolled back and forth like an old rag doll's. "Trinity!"

Her eyes snapped open. They burned, craving sleep, but she batted his hand away more forcefully and propped herself up, glaring.

"What time is it?" she demanded, the question accusation enough.

"Get up, love," Oleg said, more gently this time, although his gaze carried a grim urgency.

Trinity threw back the single sheet, untangling her legs. Oleg handed her jeans over, and she slid into them. She wore no bra under her tank top, but he seemed too impatient to wait for her to put one on, so she grabbed a thin sweater from the bedpost and slipped it over her head even as he ushered her into the corridor.

"What the hell—" she said, voice muffled by the sweater.

As she drew it downward, trying to keep her footing, she heard voices coming from other rooms, saw Timur and Gavril rushing up behind them with guns in hand, and fear burned the last cobwebs of sleep from her mind.

"Lagoshin," she said. "Is it—"

"No," Oleg said, taking her by the hand as they hustled toward the lobby. "In answer to your question, it's nearly four in the morning. You didn't hear the truck pull up?"

"I was dead asleep."

Oleg pushed through the door to the lobby, drawing his gun. In the darkness, the moonlight that came through the lobby windows turned the gun a ghostly blue. It seemed strangely alive, as if it were more at home with deeds done in dark.

"I've got her," Oleg said.

Trinity glanced past him. Kirill stood over by the lobby doors, up against the frame with his gun pointed at the ceiling, keeping himself shielded from bullets that might fly through the doors. Vlad and Pyotr were positioned on either side of the uncurtained section of glass at the front. She saw nothing but darkness outside, had no idea what might have spooked them so completely.

Kirill pushed the door open just a bit, careful to expose as little of his body as possible. "Put those headlights back on!" he shouted.

Twin spots blazed to life, so bright that she had to shield her eyes. She blinked, getting used to the glare.

"If it's not Lagoshin, then—"

"Step into the light!" Kirill called to the front parking lot.

A single figure stepped from the darkness into the brilliance of the truck's headlights. A halo of white light silhouetted him, but then he walked a dozen steps nearer to the lobby doors, and the angle of the light changed. She saw the beard and the cut of his features. Trinity knew that face, and that walk.

"Son of a bitch," she whispered.

"You know this man?" Oleg asked curtly.

Trinity stepped away from him, crossing the lobby. He called her name, reached out, and grabbed her arm, fearing that someone might start shooting.

She turned and looked at him, feeling almost as if she were in a dream. "That's my brother."

Oleg's eyes darkened. "You never told me you had a brother."

A chill went through her. There'd been a dangerous edge to his tone just then, and it scared her a little.

"Half-brother. It's a long story."

"You'd better tell it."

She nodded. "I will."

Then she turned from him, walked toward the door with Kirill and the others staring at her. Kirill held up a hand to stop her.

"Look, I brought you a present! Something you need!" Jax shouted from the lot. "What I need is to see my sister."

Kirill glared at Trinity with deep mistrust. It hurt her, that look, but desperate men were always paranoid, and she couldn't blame them for being uneasy about surprises. It shocked her that there had not been any gunfire yet. She could picture it in her mind, though . . . Jax rolling up in this old pickup, getting out, calling out to whoever had been on guard. Knowing the Bratva were here in the hotel—*And how had he known that? How had he even known she was in Nevada at all?*—he'd just put himself out there as a target. Bloody fool could've been gurgling up blood from his lungs by now. If Trinity had been on watch and someone had come strolling up, knowing they were there, she'd have made sure he had at least one bullet in him by now.

Had they hesitated for her, because he said he was her brother?

That alone could have its own complications, if they thought she had told anyone where to find them.

"Kirill," she said, "I swear I don't know how he found us. But he's a good man. You can trust him. If he's got somethin' for you, it's gonna be somethin' you want."

Oleg came up behind her. Despite feeling that she'd sinned by omission with him, he seemed to support her. After a few seconds, Kirill nodded.

"Come ahead slowly!" Kirill called.

Trinity glanced at the truck's headlights and wondered how many other men were out there. Jax made his way toward the lobby doors, lights playing strangely over him, so that at times he seemed barely there, but then he reached the door, and Kirill unlocked it. Jax came through with his hands up. Kirill backed into the lobby again, covering him.

"What the hell are you doing here?" Trinity said, crossing her arms.

Grim and troubled was Jax's resting face, and tonight he certainly had reason to be wary. For a moment, though, he smiled, and it reminded her how much his grin made him look like a little boy.

Jax stepped toward her.

"Not yet," Oleg rasped, pointing his gun at Jax's chest.

Kirill aimed at Jax's back. The others stayed where they were, ready for any attack from the parking lot.

"What's this gift you have for us?" Kirill asked.

Jax's eyes went cold, his features hard. "Outside in the truck. I've got two of my guys with me. I rode the motorcycle—they came in the truck with the present."

Kirill pressed the gun against Jax's back.

"That's enough," Trinity said, knowing her own eyes had gone cold, her features hard. They had not grown up together, but there were many things she and Jax had in common—chief among them, an unforgiving nature.

Jax gave a single shake of his head, letting her know not to make a fuss.

"You must be Oleg," Jax said, glancing from Trinity to her lover. "I'm gonna guess the guy making demands behind me is Kirill Sokolov. You'll be happy to know, Kirill, that your buddy Lagoshin's down two more men. One of them, Ustin, is dead on an old ranch road about fifteen minutes' drive from here. The other one, Luka, is alive. He's out in the truck. I'd have wrapped him up in shiny paper and put a blue ribbon on his cock, but the stores are closed this late at night."

Trinity wanted to laugh, but she was too confused.

"What are you doing here, Jax?" she asked again.

"Needed to see you."

Understanding dawned on her. "My mother called you. Told you I was in the States."

Jax nodded toward Oleg. "Told me about your new guy. Congratulations, by the way. You two make a cute couple."

She thought Oleg might say something, but when she glanced at him, she saw only suspicion and anger in his eyes.

"Jax," Kirill ventured. He gave Jax a little shove with the nose of his pistol. "Take off your shirt so I can see you wear no wire."

Jax hesitated. Trinity could see the request worried him, and she didn't know why. *No. Don't tell me you could be that stupid.*

"Do you not want Luka?" Jax asked. "I figure he can tell you where to find Lagoshin and you guys can end this little standoff."

"How do we know you didn't bring them here? That Lagoshin and his men are not out there right now?" Kirill demanded.

Jax shook his head, scoffed a little. "If Lagoshin was here, you'd all be playing out the Alamo together, and I'd be on the inside. You think he'd have waited while you fetched my little sister before he started shooting?"

Kirill slapped the back of his head. Jax bared his teeth, started to lower his hands.

"Shirt off!" Kirill snapped.

With a sigh, Jax slid out of his vest. "Trouble is, when I take my shirt off, we're gonna have a lot more to talk about. Maybe we ought to talk about it now?"

Kirill slapped him again. Jax froze, muscles bunching, fighting the urge to slap him back. The many guns in the room apparently persuaded him this would have been unwise, because after a few seconds he exhaled and stripped off his shirt.

Trinity saw the way Kirill stared at her brother's back, and it baffled her, and then she had an epiphany. She'd never told Oleg about her brother or her father, never said who they were. Now she wished she'd warned them.

"You're Jax *Teller*," Kirill said.

"SAMCRO," Jax confirmed. He locked his gaze on Oleg's now, ignoring Kirill and Trinity alike. "My club's had a long history with the Bratva, some good, some bad. A few days ago, one side of this conflict you're in tried to kill me, and the other side saved my ass. I figure you'll understand when I ask which one of those sides you're on."

Trinity felt a sick tightening in her gut. She'd tried to avoid the politics, the ugliness, and now it had crept up on her in the dark and wrapped its hands around her throat. She and her brother both waited for an answer.

Kirill narrowed his eyes. He stared at Jax for what seemed like an eternity. Then he gestured with his gun.

"Put your shirt back on, Mr. Teller. Let's see what your little Christmas present out there can tell us," Kirill said. "Then we'll all get to decide whose side we're on."

Oh, shit, Trinity thought, glancing at Oleg, who refused to meet her eyes.

That was not an answer.

꧁ ꧂

Opie stood beside the truck, trying to calm the thunder in his heart. The pickup's passenger door hung open, but they'd smashed the dome light inside, an excess of caution. The weight of his gun dragged at his hand, whispering to him that it would be much lighter if he fired some of its bullets. Just nerves, he knew. Nerves and exhaustion and blood loss.

He managed a calm front, and most of the time that reflected an inner resolution and acceptance of whatever might come. Tonight, though, they had stuck their hands in a hornet's nest. Jax's plan of action had been the most direct, but it sure as hell wasn't the wisest or most cautious approach. If Kirill Sokolov and his men were the Bratva faction that had tried to murder Jax and Opie on the way back from the cabin, things were headed down a dark road. Opie exhaled, stretched the fingers that clutched his gun, and waited.

"What do ya see in there, brother?" Chibs called from the cab of the pickup.

"Same thing as you," Opie said. "Jax just put his shirt back on."

"Sounds like we're gettin' somewhere," Chibs said.

Maybe, Opie thought. Times like this, dealing with professional liars and killers, there was no way to know. *Professional liars and killers. What does that make us?*

Up in the truck, Luka tried to cuss them out from behind the gag in his mouth. Chibs took a fistful of his hair and slammed his face into the dashboard, not for the first time. When Luka glanced dazedly around, fresh blood dripping from his nostrils, his eyes had the desperation of a coyote with its leg caught in a trap. Opie figured if Luka could have gotten away by gnawing his leg off the way a coyote sometimes would, he'd have done it—and he'd have been smart to make the attempt. The rest of his life could be measured in the number of breaths it would take for him to tell Kirill Sokolov what he wanted to know about Lagoshin. Luka had to know that.

"Here he comes," Chibs said.

Spotlighted in the truck's headlights, Jax strode from the hotel and crossed the parking lot toward them. As always, he moved as if he carried a dreadful weight on his shoulders. One of the Russians came behind him, a thin, bony man with sunken eyes and sharp cheekbones.

"Bring him out," Jax called.

Opie gestured toward the open passenger door. Chibs gave Luka a shove, and the bleeding captive slid to the edge of the seat. He slid out. The moment his feet hit the ground he lunged at Opie, hands tied behind his back as he tried to turn himself into a battering ram. Opie tightened his grip on the gun, but he didn't shoot the fool, just sidestepped and gave Luka a push. Luka lost his footing and went down on the pavement, twisting so that he landed on his shoulder, scraping flesh from his arm and smacking his head on the ground with a satisfying crack.

Luka rolled on his back and sat up, staring at the Russian who'd come out of the hotel, someone he probably knew. Not long ago, the two warring Bratva factions had been one. They might as well have been SAMCRO going to war with SAMTAC or SAMNOV. Brothers weren't supposed to try killing each other, but whenever there was a power vacuum, the potential for bloodshed was like the electric crackle in the air right before a thunderstorm hit.

The skinny Russian stood over Luka. "Stand up."

Luka glared at him, not wanting to do anything to hurry himself toward his fate. After a moment, though, the stalemate ended, and Luka managed to get his knees under him and rise.

"We good?" Jax asked the skinny Russian.

"Good enough," the Russian replied with a slow nod. He grabbed Luka and twisted him toward the hotel, directing him at the lobby doors.

Trinity emerged from the hotel before Luka reached it, another Russian behind her. Opie thought she looked rough, not unhealthy but uncared-for, as if she'd just come off a long ride—and maybe that wasn't a bad comparison. Her hair was a mess. She wore jeans and a thin sweater that clung lovingly to her, but her feet were bare. The Russian behind her took her hand as they passed Luka and the skinny man, who were headed the other way.

Chibs climbed down from the pickup, moved out to one side, his hand hovering near his gun. Opie didn't figure Trinity's appearance for trouble, but they couldn't be too careful.

Trinity and Oleg walked until they'd reached Jax. Oleg glanced at Chibs and then at Opie's gun but didn't attempt to reach for his own. The lobby windows were dark, but inside there would still be men aiming guns at the truck—Oleg knew his visitors wouldn't try anything stupid.

"Hello, Trinity," Opie said, nodding warily.

She smiled. "Opie." Then she introduced him and Chibs to Oleg as if they were at a damn cotillion instead of the parking lot of an abandoned hotel full of Russian gangsters.

The gun felt suddenly light in Opie's hand, as if it wanted to float upward all on its own. "What's the story, Jax?"

With Oleg and Trinity looking on, Jax went to Chibs and held out a hand. Chibs handed over his Glock, and Jax slipped it into his rear waistband. He held out his hands like a magician proving he had nothing up his sleeves and turned to Oleg.

"This going to be a problem?"

Oleg shook his head, expressionless. Noncommittal.

Jax seemed to take that as a positive sign, but Opie wasn't so sure.

"Chibs, you and Op take the truck back to where we stashed your bikes," Jax said.

Opie froze. "Not a chance."

Jax stared at him. "You want to leave the bikes out there?"

"I'll go," Opie said. "Chibs can stay."

Chibs shook his head, obviously not liking this plan any better. "How are you gonna get the bikes into the back of that pick up on your own?"

"I'll dig around, find something to use for a ramp. I'll figure it out."

Jax hesitated, but he didn't argue, and Opie knew why. This might not have been a very good plan, but it was the only one they had.

"Half an hour," Opie said, making sure Oleg and Trinity heard him. He went around to the driver's side of the truck, convinced they were making a mistake. If what the Bratva wanted was Jax Teller dead, he had just served himself up on a platter. That was a damn big *if*.

As he drove away, Opie kept glancing at the figures in the rearview mirror until they vanished in the retreating darkness.

"This is stupid," he muttered, thinking they should've just knocked Oleg out, grabbed Trinity, and thrown her in the truck. Granted, she didn't look like she wanted to leave, never mind that they probably wouldn't have made it to the truck without being shot. He told himself it would be all right, that they weren't even sure which side Sokolov's men were on, but he was sure that he *did* know.

He pressed harder on the accelerator, flying through the night as a pre-dawn glow lit the eastern sky.

Trinity forced herself to breathe. Scant minutes ago she'd been dreaming, and now she found herself all too awake. She rubbed at her sleepy, itchy eyes and studied the tense uncertainty that filled the space between Jax and Oleg. The sky had turned the perfect indigo of predawn, black fading to the deepest blue, and the stars had begun to vanish as if the coming day snuffed them one by one.

"We need to talk," Jax said. He had a laconic nature, the kind of man who thought people ought to be able to intuit his designs and desires.

"Jax—"

"It wasn't easy, tracking you down," he went on, with a quick glance at Oleg and Chibs. "This situation . . . it's got a fuse burning at either end. I've got some things to say, and you should hear 'em now, before whatever's gonna happen happens."

"I didn't need you here, Jackson Teller," she said, her Irish brogue thickening with her frustration. "I'm perfectly capable of takin' care of myself."

Jax pressed his lips into a thin line and cocked his head. She imagined that he'd envisioned himself as some kind of white knight riding to rescue the damsel in distress. Whatever danger his arrival might have put them both in, she did feel safer having him nearby. But she wasn't going to admit that to him.

"You're tough, Trinity," he said. "But you're not bulletproof. I came a long way. All I'm asking is a few minutes to talk."

Trinity nodded slowly. "Give me a second."

She took Oleg by the hand and led him away, off toward the southern end of the parking lot, away from Jax and Chibs. Away from anywhere the members of Oleg's Bratva might overhear. His eyes were still hard and sharp as flint, and he gazed at her as if she were someone he only vaguely knew and did not like very much.

"Trinity," Oleg said.

She punched him in the chest. Did it a second time.

Oleg reached for her wrist, but she dropped her arm away.

He blinked. "You knew we had business with SAMCRO—"

"And I didn't want it to be *our* business. I'm a Belfast girl. I've never been to California. Jax and me, we share a father. Wasn't too long ago we'd never laid eyes on each other. I didn't want you and me to be about SAMCRO any more than I wanted it to be about the Real IRA or the Bratva or any of the other brotherhoods whose loyalties might interfere with our loyalty to each other. Now I see your eyes turn to stone when you look at me, and I want to slap your stupid face."

With a sigh, he ran his palms over his skull, dipping his head toward her. Oleg groaned.

"We could've killed your brother," Oleg said softly, and when he looked up again, his eyes were full of sorrow. "You don't want this to be about other people, but what if we'd killed him? Would the history between SAMCRO and my people still not matter?"

Trinity stared at him. She had her back to Jax and Chibs, but she could feel them watching her with Oleg. This should all have been simple. She shouldn't have to choose between family and love. Truth was, she didn't know Jax very well, and her feelings about her father and his legacy with the Sons of Anarchy were complicated at best. But her mother had raised her to put family first, above all.

"It *was* your people who went after him?" she said quietly.

Oleg shifted, glanced toward the hotel.

"What now?" Trinity asked.

"Now we see if Kirill thinks killing Lagoshin is more important than finding out what really happened to Viktor Putlova, the man who used to run Russian interests in this part of the world."

Trinity shivered. The eastern horizon bled yellow and gold, colors heralding the imminent arrival of the sun. She put her hand on Oleg's chest, right where she had punched him, and spread out her fingers.

"He's my *brother*," she said.

Oleg nodded, but then he turned away so that she could not read his eyes.

"Don't be long," he said, more to Jax than to Trinity, as he walked toward the lobby doors. "If you want to hear what Luka's got to say, you should come inside while he's still alive."

14

Jax stuck his hands into his pockets and waited for her. Trinity watched Oleg until he'd returned to the gray darkness of the hotel and then turned to Chibs, who gave her a nod and went to stand by the lobby entrance, lighting up a cigarette. In the sepia hue of imminent dawn, she looked rough and beautiful in equal measure, and Jax could see the hesitation in her—the love she had for this man she'd chosen.

I'm the least of her concerns, Jax thought. Trinity had put herself in the middle of a quiet little desert war zone. Maybe she hadn't known what she was getting herself into, but Oleg had known, and if he loved Trinity, he could have kept her out of it. *Should* have.

Jax kept his hands in his pockets as Trinity approached him.

"You didn't tell Oleg and his buddies who you were."

"I told them who I was," Trinity explained. " I just didn't tell them who you were, or who my father was. It didn't seem relevant. Sort of like us talking about Belfast—it seemed like it could only do more harm than good."

Jax smiled. "It's good to see you, Trinity."

She shook her head with a sigh and put her arms around him, forcing Jax to pull his hands from his pockets and return the embrace. Trinity trembled slightly, and he pulled her tighter.

He had a sister. The idea had taken some getting used to, but here and now, with her solid and alive, he felt a bond he'd never imagined.

"I wish you'd known Tommy," he said quietly.

Trinity backed away, one hand still on his arm. "So do I."

Jax nodded. "We live through this, we're gonna have to get to know each other a little more."

She smiled, but thinly, as if she had zero faith in both of them surviving their time with the Bratva.

"So you found me," she said. "What now?"

"Maureen wants you home."

The sun breached the horizon, warm light spilling across the land. Her face glowed with the bright gold of morning.

"I'm not goin' anywhere. I—"

"You love him," Jax interrupted. "Figured you'd say that."

"And?"

Jax touched the bruised flesh on the left side of his face, wincing. "I've got my own issues with Lagoshin now. Not to mention, I want to make sure I'm leaving you safer than I found you. Can't very well tell Maureen I left her baby in the middle of a gang war. I figure we'll throw in with your pal Sokolov, settle debts, make some new peace. As long as they don't try to kill me."

Trinity exhaled. This time it was she who put her hands in her pockets.

"They've got to know if they kill you, they'll have to kill me, too."

"You think they won't?" Jax asked.

"I'm not an idiot," she said. "I know they'll put their brotherhood before anything else. Maybe even Oleg, if it came to it. He loves me, but I can't be sure, ya know?"

"That's not an answer."

Trinity shrugged. "I think most of 'em would hesitate before tryin' to kill me."

"Somehow I don't feel reassured."

Jax glanced along the road, wondering how long before Opie returned. Then he gestured for Trinity to lead the way to the hotel.

"Let's go," he said. "I don't want them taking Luka out without me there. I want to make sure they remember who brought him to the dance."

With the sunrise creeping across the parking lot, they joined up with Chibs and went through the doors into the hotel lobby. Two of the Bratva men were still there, but there was no sign of Kirill, Oleg, or Luka.

"Where are they?" Trinity asked.

The Russians eyed Jax and Chibs with distrust. "Swimming pool."

Again, Trinity led the way. Jax felt the weight of his gun against his lower back, but he ignored the alarm bells in his head. These guys weren't going to shoot him in the back while he walked away, not without the boss's orders, and he didn't think they'd been given that green light just yet.

The hotel corridors had a dry, dusty smell, with just a hint of mold. They passed one numbered door after another, a dead ice machine and a soda machine whose face had been pried open, a handful of soda cans left inside.

A heavy metal door at the back of the building led out into a fenced area on the east side of the hotel. The main road was visible from the walkway between the back door and the gate, but inside that fence and the overgrown shrubbery around it, they would be shielded from sight.

As Trinity grabbed the gate and dragged it open with a scrape of rusty hinges, they heard Luka cry out in pain. Jax quickened his pace and Chibs followed.

The pool was empty, caked with a thin layer of grime. The patio around it was cracked and shot through with weeds. Down inside the pool were Kirill, Oleg, and three other Russians. One of the faded deck chairs had been placed in the center of the empty pool, and Luka sat there bleeding.

"Scream in pain if it makes you feel better," Kirill said. "But don't scream for help. No one out here is going to help you."

Jax cleared his throat to get their attention. All six men whipped around to stare at him, then noticed Chibs and Trinity. The hope on Luka's features was pitiful.

"I can see you're in the middle of something," Jax said. "But if you can spare two minutes, I'd like to talk about where we stand."

Kirill stared at Jax as if he might spit on him.

"Think of it this way," Jax said. "The longer you keep him waiting, the more he's gonna torture himself thinking about how long he'll be able to keep from telling you what you want to know. It'll be agony."

Trinity stood at his side, shoulder to shoulder. Kirill glanced at her, saw the solidarity there, and then looked at Oleg. The nod was almost imperceptible—not enough to make the other Russians question who was in charge—but it was clear that Oleg was Kirill's second, and the boss valued his input.

"Timur," Kirill said to one of his men, "break both his thumbs."

Luka did not beg. He glared at Timur and bared his teeth, refusing to show fear.

As Kirill walked up the steps from the empty pool, Timur started his work. Luka screamed. Instead of a triumphant smile, Kirill wore an expression of deep sadness.

"He'll talk," Jax said.

"Of course he will," Kirill said. "But I wish he wouldn't make us hurt him. We were friends once."

"You and Lagoshin are at war. Unless one of you waves the white flag, a lot of your friends are gonna die."

Kirill gave him a sidelong glance, his face a grim mask, but he said nothing. They went out through the gate, and Kirill set off around the back of the hotel. Chibs followed, but stopped outside the gate, where he could keep an eye on them without Kirill thinking he was trying to eavesdrop. Jax and Kirill strode together to a broad swath of scrubland that looked out on the foothills as the sunlight seared the tops of the mountains, the hot line of its glare moving downward, touching more of the land.

Kirill stopped, staring at the golden aura of early-morning light on the mountains.

"Just so we have no misunderstandings," Jax said, "you should know I'm armed."

"I expected you would be."

"That doesn't concern you?"

Kirill turned to face him. "You'd have to be suicidal to kill me right here."

"I have no interest in killing you."

Kirill smiled thinly, as if to remind Jax that the feeling was not at all mutual. "You wanted to speak with me privately," he said. "Here we are."

Jax scraped his fingers through his beard, choosing his words carefully. "I've had a lot of new beginnings in my life lately. Not anything you'd give a shit about. Personal stuff. The past relationship between the Bratva and my club is complicated. There's a lot of bad blood there. You think we killed Putlova. Clearly I'm not gonna convince you otherwise, just like you're not going to confirm it was your men who tried to put me and Opie in the ground the other day."

Kirill studied him thoughtfully.

"Lagoshin may be down a few guys," Jax went on, "but I'm betting he's still got you outgunned. I can help with that."

"There are three of you," Kirill scoffed.

"Three of us, but we got you the thing you couldn't get for yourself . . . a direct line to Lagoshin's location," Jax countered. "And there are three now, but I've got a charter here in Vegas who will send in reinforcements."

"In exchange for?"

Jax threw his hands up. "Hey, I'm just a guy trying to keep his sister from getting killed. She loves your boy, Oleg, and it looks to me like he feels the same. That makes you and me practically in-laws. All I'm suggesting is that we throw in together until Lagoshin's in the ground and you're running the Bratva's operations in the western U.S. When it's over, we maintain the current status quo. SAMCRO and the Bratva stay in our separate corners . . . and your people stay away from the Irish."

Kirill's eyes lit up. "I see, now. This is business for you."

"This is *family*," Jax said darkly. "My club is my family as much as Trinity is. I don't want anybody else dying for no reason."

He held out his hand, kept it rock steady as he waited.

Several seconds passed, but Kirill grasped his hand and shook.

"Good," Jax said. "Now let's go see what Luka has to say."

As if on cue, they heard Luka scream. The anguished cry echoed off the walls of the empty pool and out into the desert sky. A massive red-tailed hawk circled overhead, watching the show.

Jax leaned against the wall of the empty pool as he and Chibs watched the Russians beat the shit out of Luka. Kirill mostly just observed, leaving the bloody-knuckle work to Oleg and a guy named Gavril. Oleg looked like he had no taste for the brutality. Regret hung on him like a sheen of sweat. When Gavril cut off the little finger on Luka's right hand, Oleg had turned away. But when Luka still wouldn't talk, it was Oleg who stormed in with a cry of rage and hit Luka so hard the chair tipped over, and the prisoner smacked his head on the concrete floor of the pool.

Luka had been beaten and cut, lost two fingers and four teeth. His face was split and swollen and bloody, and he slumped in the chair as if he'd been an inflated man and all the helium was slowly leaking out of him.

"He dead?" Jax asked, growing frustrated.

Kirill rounded on him. "You want to take a turn? You think you can do better?"

Jax pushed off the wall.

"Jackie," Chibs said quietly, worriedly.

Jax strode over and began to circle Luka. "You could cut off his balls, threaten to take his cock as well."

Kirill and Oleg both blanched. Gavril only looked defeated.

Luka spat bloody phlegm at Jax's feet.

"This guy used to be your brother," Jax said. "I get it. Nobody wants to torture a guy who used to get you a beer when he went to grab one for himself. But Luka's not your brother anymore. He betrayed you. Lagoshin ordered him to stick with me, follow me till I found you, and then call it in. They were gonna come here and kill all of you."

Oleg glared at Jax. "You think we are so weak?"

Jax frowned. "Nothing weak about brotherhood. You're men of honor. But we all know this ends with Luka dead." He crouched down, eye to eye with the prisoner. "Hell, *Luka* knows that. Thing is, he's a man of honor, too, right? So the only way he's gonna tell you what you want to know is if you make it so he'd rather hurry up and die than hold on to that honor."

Luka glared at him. Jax stood up and glanced around at the Bratva men, who seemed to like him almost as much as Luka did.

"It's not about honor," Trinity said, walking down the steps into the empty pool. She tossed her hair back and turned to Jax. "It's dread."

"What?" Jax asked.

"They're takin' their time, buildin' up to worse, lettin' him fill up with pain and fear," she said, glancing at Oleg and then Kirill. "This is barely torture. It's foreplay."

"We don't have time for foreplay," Jax said.

Trinity walked to Gavril and held out a hand. "Give me your knife, Gav."

Gavril knelt and slid up the leg of his pants, retrieving a small dagger from the sheath strapped around his calf. Trinity took it from him as she passed by, moving into the deep end of the empty pool. Jax watched her curiously. Luka sniffed in derision and spit again, disdainful of the very idea that a woman could intimidate him.

She edged past Oleg, her back to him, controlling the space between herself and Luka.

Trinity grabbed a fistful of his hair and yanked his head back. Jaw tight, muscles standing out on her forearms, she pressed the knife against the skin just beside his left eye. In the morning light, Jax saw the trickle of blood drip from the wound.

"Bitch," Luka sneered, eyes pinched closed.

Trinity dug the knife tip into his eyebrow, and Luka cried out as she sliced downward, splitting his eyelid. He tried to tear his head away, tried to use his body weight to move the chair back, but she held him tightly, and the position of the knife blade forced him not to fight too hard.

"She's your sister, all right," Chibs said quietly.

Jax stood away from the wall, staring at her. Trinity had grown up with the RIRA in the family, lived a life no stranger to violence and murder, but she had never been a part of that violence as far as he knew.

"Hey," he said quietly, "don't."

Trinity shot him a hard look. If she understood that this blood she'd spilled had changed her, that she'd just given up a sliver of her innocence, he didn't see it in her eyes. Jax knew she was no little girl, and he wasn't the guardian of her innocence or humanity, but the moment still felt like a loss.

"Open your eyes," Trinity told Luka.

The prisoner complied. Blood ran from the slit in his left eyelid, but he seemed to still have the eye. Luka stared at her, all his defiance and disdain obliterated by fear and pain.

"That's just to prove I'll do it," Trinity said. "Five seconds, and I slice out your eye like I'm shuckin' an oyster. The address where we can find Lagoshin."

She had barely started counting when Luka blurted out the answer.

Task accomplished, Trinity let go of his hair. She handed Gavril's bloodied dagger to Oleg and turned from the Russians, walking over to Jax. Where others might have worn a satisfied smile, Trinity had gone pale. She braced her hands against the inner wall of the empty pool and took a deep, shuddering breath.

Jax put a hand on her back. "You all right?"

Trinity took another deep breath. "If I can keep from pukin' my guts up, I'll be right as rain."

Trinity hurried along the corridor, headed back to her room. The real estate agent had not wanted the water to the hotel turned on, but he'd supplied the surveying map, and Pyotr had managed to do it himself. By the time the water department noticed, they would long since have departed.

Just now she could have kissed Pyotr. There were days when a shower— even a cold shower, which was all they had—could save your life. Her face felt flushed, and she couldn't seem to unclench her fists as she turned the corner. When she saw the door to her room, she managed to exhale, then shuddered in revulsion at the thought that the stale-smelling, dusty hotel room could offer her such reassurance. The building seemed to be closing in around her.

"Trinity!"

She spun, fists still clenched. Oleg had followed, and now he strode quickly after her. *Two doors away, almost made it.*

An argument had been brewing between them—she'd kept secrets, he'd thought he knew her—but she couldn't have that conversation right now.

"You knew it was important, your relationship with Jax—"

"He's my brother."

"You knew it would complicate things for us."

"I didn't know how much, but, yeah, I knew. Do you blame me for keeping my mouth shut when I was falling in love with you?" She ran her hands through her hair. "Honestly?"

Oleg reached out to touch her cheek, lifted her chin. "And if you have to choose?"

Trinity's breath quickened. She cocked her head, trying to mask her alarm. "Are you going to make me?"

"If you had to," Oleg said, "who would you choose?"

Trinity gave a small laugh and shook her head. Her life back home had sometimes been troubled, sometimes lonely, and sometimes dangerous, but to her it had always been a beautiful life. School, working in the bakery and later in Keegan's Pub, seeing her friends, and fighting with her mother. There were churches and cobblestones, and on a nice day there were musicians busking all through the city. Beautiful.

There was beauty here as well. The badlands and the mountains. At night, even the lights of Las Vegas had a brittle beauty. Trinity had believed that she and Oleg could make a beautiful life, but she felt apart from it now, as if the only loveliness she could see was through the barred windows of some prison cell.

"A man who loved me would never ask me that question," she said.

Oleg nearly growled. She saw him fighting within himself, the grim Russian demeanor in conflict with his feelings for her.

"A woman who loved me would be able to answer it," he replied.

"You bastard . . ."

He reached for her, but she shook his arm off. "All I'm asking is . . . if it came to that . . ."

Trinity pointed a finger at his face, bared her teeth. "He's my *brother*, which makes him the only thing my father ever gave me. He's family."

A brutal silence descended upon them.

They heard the shush of clothing and a heavy footfall, and they turned to see Jax coming around the corner at the end of the hall. He stopped, meeting Oleg's gaze in an open challenge, and Trinity wondered how much he had heard.

"You got a minute?" he asked.

Oleg scratched at his stubbled chin. "She's got all the time in the world." He turned to walk away, but Jax called him back. "I was talking to you."

Chin high, Oleg regarded him coolly. "Go on."

"Me being here complicates things for you," Jax said. "I recognize that. Kirill and I have an understanding. At the end of this thing, we may not all be friends, but we're not gonna be trying to kill each other. I get the impression you and I need an understanding of our own."

Oleg wetted his lips. "Putlova recruited Kirill. Kirill brought me into the Bratva, freed me from an ugly life. I had great respect for Viktor Putlova."

Trinity watched her brother's face. His features betrayed nothing, were as smooth a mask as Oleg's.

"I respected Putlova, too," Jax said. "But it's hard to keep respecting a guy when you've got a knife in your back. Or at your throat. Trinity loves you, so I'm gonna promise you something. All my cards are on the table. My only agenda is to make sure my sister is safe. I know you want that, too, Oleg, but I have to ask . . . are all of *your* cards on the table?"

Oleg hesitated, glanced at Trinity, and a veil of aggression seemed to fall away from his face. "Yes," he said, "all the cards."

For a second, Trinity thought they might shake, but Jax did not extend his hand, and Oleg only nodded and turned away, striding along the corridor until he reached the turn in the hall. She heard the sound of the metal release bar on the exit door, then listened as it thumped shut.

"That went well," Jax said, not bothering to hide his sarcasm.

"I think it did, actually," she said. "He may not want to respect you, but I think he's startin' to. Harder to hate a man if you know him."

Jax laughed softly. "Yeah, that's not really been my experience."

"Regardless, we're allied now, all of us. Once Lagoshin's out of the way, all of this fear will end."

For half a second, Jax stared at her as if she'd grown an extra head. His doubts aside, she believed that this alliance would be propitious. Awkwardness lingered between them, but it was quickly being replaced by a deep kinship. Jax had made it clear that he had her back, no matter what, and though she'd spent her life learning to deal with men who disappointed her, she had begun to believe in *this* man. Her brother.

Trinity told herself she would never have to choose between her new life and her old one. She could almost believe it.

15

Thor felt a hand shaking him. He felt the crick in his neck and the ache in his spine and tried to twist himself into a more comfortable position. The hand shook him again, like God had reached down into his dreams and rousted him. He pulled away, determined to cling to sleep, but as he moved he slid off the sofa cushions that he'd laid out on the floor of the poolroom in a makeshift bed, and just that two-inch drop to the ground was enough to make his eyes pop open.

"Up and at 'em, thunder god," Baghead said, worried sincerity in his eyes. His breath could have peeled a century's worth of paint off a barn.

"Bag . . . ," Thor managed to say, too tired for any imaginative profanities. He pulled away from that hideous breath. Glancing around, he found the hair band he'd taken off the night before and used it to pull his red mop into a topknot, keeping it out of his face.

In the midst of this, Bag kept putting his hand out. Thor blinked and realized his friend was trying to give him something.

"Phone's for you," Bag said.

Thor squinted, rubbed his eyes, and glanced at the door. Was it morning yet? Had the sun come up? Sure as hell didn't feel like it could be morning.

He took the phone. "It better be fucking good o'clock," he said. "Who the hell is this?"

"It's Izzo," a raspy voice said. Someone else who didn't like being awake at this hour. "Trust me, I'm not happy to be talking to you, either. Something I figured you and your MC would want to know."

Thor felt a tightening in his chest. He glanced up, saw Baghead watching him intently with those mad little rat eyes of his. "Get me coffee, Bag."

Thor watched Bag retreat from the room. He had to go around Antonio, who'd been sleeping on the floor but who now raised his head to gaze blearily around the room. Jax had sent Thor back to the Tombstone the night before with a request that Rollie keep them ready to move, which meant every member of SAMNOV in the area had bedded down in the rooms at the back of the bar. Baghead had been sleeping in the other crash room with Mikey the Prospect, who was a nineteen-year-old ex-football star, and a short brute with a shaved head and blond eyebrows that they all called Clean.

"You call just to breathe heavy?" Thor asked.

"I thought you were still talking to your buddy," Izzo said. "Guy sounds half-crazy, by the way."

"Maybe both. You're stalling, man. Tell it."

Thor could hear Izzo sigh over the phone, almost as if the cop was afraid to speak the words that would come next. The sound was chilling.

"Little more than half an hour ago, we got a call from a guy out doing his morning bike ride. Found two bodies on the side of a remote road in North Vegas, runs through an old family ranch that was foreclosed on a couple of years back."

A small wave of nausea undulated in Thor's belly.

"One of the dead guys is a Russian. Our gang task force ID'd him as one of Lagoshin's men. The other is your man Joyce."

Son of a bitch. Thor exhaled, the news a gut punch. He and Joyce had argued over the years, even brawled more than once over the sweet little Korean girl at the bakery with her tattoo fetish. But the MC made them brothers, and he knew Joyce would have taken a bullet for him, and vice versa.

"What's it looking like?" he asked.

"You know it doesn't work that fast," Izzo replied, some of his natural growl absent from his voice. "Crime-scene guys are still there. Forensics will take their time."

"Not what I asked you, man. You know Rollie's going to want to know, so tell me . . . what does it *look* like?"

The phone went silent, so flat it seemed like he'd lost the call. Then Izzo spoke again.

"Definitely other people involved. Fresh tracks from a truck and a bunch of bikes. Three bikes were there. One's a Harley—I'm guessing Joyce's—but the other two are Japanese rockets, and I know you MC guys wouldn't ride those bitches even if your mamas asked you nicely."

"Two bodies but three bikes?"

"What I said," Izzo muttered. "Detective on the scene thinks the Russian shot Joyce and then someone else tagged him for it. But the scene's still hot. Got nothing else for you right now."

Thor took a deep breath. He heard a grumbled voice in the corridor and the creak of floorboards under substantial burden, and he glanced up to see Rollie standing in the doorway with Baghead hiding behind him like a third-grade tattletale. Antonio had pushed himself up to lean against the wall.

Rollie had gone deathly pale.

"Call me when someone needs to ID the body, and let me know when we can pick him up," Thor said, the words sounding callous even as he spoke them.

He ended the call without a good-bye and sat a moment, gripping the phone so tightly it hurt his hand.

"Joyce?" Rollie asked, his body filling the door frame.

Thor nodded, then laid it out for him exactly as Izzo had explained it. When he'd finished—and it only took seconds, so little time to sum up the end of a life—Rollie slammed a hand against the door frame. A dark intelligence glittered in his eyes, reminding Thor how often people underestimated SAMNOV's president. Rollie acted like he was everybody's friend, a big amiable bear of a man more interested in obscure movies and even more obscure beers to put on tap at the Tombstone. But the man was president of the North Vegas charter of the Sons of Anarchy for a reason.

"No word from Jax or his guys?" Rollie asked, staring at the floor, his hands clenched into fists.

"Nothing," Thor said. "I left him three messages during the night."

The room seemed to shrink, the floor to tilt. The air felt strangely heavy.

"You know what I'm wondering?" Rollie asked.

"You're wondering why Jax sent me back here last night instead of just calling you," Thor replied. "I figured maybe it was personal."

Rollie huffed like a bear unhappy with its dinner. He turned to look into the hallway, where Bag twitched and scratched himself as he waited.

"Baghead . . . wake everyone right now," Rollie said. "I want them up and moving in ten minutes."

"Moving where?" Antonio asked, still rubbing at his eyes. "What are we doing?"

Rollie shot him a frigid glance. "I've got questions," he said. "You guys are going to find me answers."

"Where do we start?" Antonio asked.

"You start by finding Jax Teller."

Izzo sat in the faux-leather reclining chair in his family room with a tumbler of spiced rum and pineapple juice in his left hand. He'd dropped his cell phone on his lap, and now he stared at the gleaming colors of his wall-mounted flat screen and wondered how this business with the Russians and the MC was going to shake out. He still paid alimony to his first wife, and his second—a blackjack dealer named Sarajane—liked shopping even more than Izzo liked booze or pussy. He was starting to think that a second alimony might be less expensive than his second wife.

Something made him glance down, and he realized his cell phone had been buzzing for a while without his noticing.

"Izzo," he said, picking up.

"It's Thor."

"I just hung up with—"

"Last night I brought that guy to you," Thor said. "You gave up John Carney's name. Rollie wants you to head over to Carney's and ask him what he told the guy."

Izzo drank again. Sweet fire in his throat. He'd had a pleasant buzz going before he'd gotten the call about the dead bodies on the ranch road, and now this. Why the hell did he keep answering his phone?

"The sun just came up, and I haven't been to bed yet," Izzo rasped, swirling the ice in his drink. "Let me get a few hours' sleep and kiss my wife. Carney won't want visitors this early anyway."

He could hear Thor breathing, heard him curse quietly.

"Joyce is dead. You think we give two shits how much sleep you got or whether Carney is feeling friggin' hospitable? I'd go over there myself, but you're a cop. The old man's less likely to shoot you. If I show up at his door right now . . . Look, Rollie wants you to do this. Whatever Carney told him, we need to know. Right now."

Right now.

The trouble with having a second job that involved illegal dealings with violent criminals was that you could never call in sick.

Izzo downed the rest of his drink. Suddenly the pineapple juice had started to taste sour in his mouth. Couldn't be the rum.

"On my way," he said, setting his glass down. He thumbed the button that ended the call. "Asshole."

The drive to John Carney's place took a little over half an hour. Izzo passed joggers and bicyclists trying to get some exercise in before the day heated up any further. He saw a woman running with her dog, the beast too small to keep pace with her without struggling, and he fought the urge to roll down the window and shout at her.

At Carney's place, he pulled into the driveway and sat a moment, watching the house. It seemed very still, very quiet. You couldn't be a cop as long as Izzo had without developing some intuition. His told him the place was empty, but it made more sense to think that Carney was still sleeping.

He stepped out and gently closed the door, then walked to the garage. Carney's old Cadillac sat inside the gloomy space, dust motes spinning in the light streaming in from the small windows in the garage doors.

Izzo went to the front door and knocked, but the sound came back hollow. Nothing moved inside, no curtains were drawn back. The house itself seemed disinclined to creak. Most houses seemed to breathe, but not this one.

He drew his gun, pulse quickening. Moving around the side of the house, he looked in windows as he passed. In the back, he saw broken glass on the patio and then turned to see the shattered kitchen door.

"Shit," he whispered, quickening his pace.

He didn't have to go any farther than the door. The diffuse morning light reached through the window above the kitchen sink and the jagged shards of glass jutting from the door frame. That golden glow cast a sepia tone across the floor and the tipped-over chair, revealing the sprawled corpse of John Carney. Izzo spotted a single bullet hole in his temple and a pool of drying blood that made a deep scarlet halo on the floor around his head.

Whatever the old man had told his visitors, Izzo would never know.

Jax hesitated before calling home, but it had been too long since he'd spoken to Tara, and he wanted to hear her voice before the day's violence began. No way of knowing if he'd still be standing by nightfall.

She answered sleepily after the third ring. "Hey. You're up early."

The tightness drained from Jax's body, and he felt himself smile. "Sorry. Been a long night, and we've got a long day ahead."

"You find Trinity?"

"Yeah. I just left her and her boyfriend."

"What's he like, this Russian?"

Jax weighed the question. "Jury's still out. Seems like a stand-up guy, but being in his life could get her killed."

Silence on the phone. Jax felt like he could hear the world breathing, there on the line.

"You still there?" he asked.

"That's the same thing people say about me," Tara said. "And the life *you* lead."

Jax had been standing by the window in his temporary hotel room.

Morning sun shone through the glass, and the small boxy room had begun to heat up. Now he went to the bed and perched on the edge, staring thoughtfully into a no-space in the middle of the room.

"I've made you promises, Tara," he said quietly, glancing at the door, not sure why he didn't want to be overheard. "I'm gonna keep 'em. We're getting out of it—all of us. You, me, and the boys."

"Be safe."

Jax bit back the words that tried to make their way to his lips—fighting the truth. How could he tell her that as long as SAMCRO was part of his life, he would never be safe? The MC was his family, looming larger in his life than anything else, almost a third parent, but it was going to kill him one of these days. He did not intend for that day to be today.

"What's happening there? The boys okay?"

"Abel has a low fever. Nothing to worry about," she said. "Some kind of virus that's going around."

"Good thing his mom's a doctor," Jax said. "I'll see you all in a couple of days."

A few seconds ticked by in which Jax knew Tara was busily missing him as much as he missed her. Things had changed between them while he'd been in prison. Tara had been hardened by his absence, and he couldn't help thinking she was keeping something from him. Something that troubled her deeply. He kept waiting for her to tell him.

"Would I like her, this sister of yours?" Tara asked.

"I figure chances are fifty-fifty. Either she'd be the sister you never had, or you'd want to kill each other. Neither of you puts up with bullshit."

"Two alpha females in one room can get tricky."

Jax grinned. "That what you are? An alpha female?"

"Come home and I'll show you."

He laughed quietly. "Couple of days, babe. Then I'm all yours."

"Okay," Tara relented. "I hope I get to meet Trinity."

A knock came at his door. "Babe, I've gotta go."

"I love you. The boys love you," Tara said.

"Kiss them for me," Jax told her. "See you soon."

He ended the call as he went to the door, not bothering to draw his weapon. They were in the lion's den here, among people who had tried to kill him and Opie, totally exposed, but he had to count on them having mutual interests right now. They wouldn't do anything stupid—he hoped.

Jax drew the door open to find a wary looking Chibs standing in the hall, one hand on the butt of his gun.

"Opie's back with the bikes. We're all set," he said, and then gestured over his shoulder. "And you've got a visitor."

Oleg stood behind him with a gleaming black assault rifle in his hands. Jax's thoughts raced as he wondered how fast he could drop his phone and reach for his own gun. Then Oleg held the assault rifle out to him. "Call it a peace offering."

Jax blinked, tossed his cell phone onto the bed, and took the assault rifle. Incredibly lightweight and shiny black, it had a long, curved magazine.

"What is this?" Jax asked. "Never seen one."

"Nine-millimeter TsNIITochMash. Subsonic bullet speed. Silencer. It will punch through body armor at four hundred meters. Very new and very difficult to smuggle into this country, but Oscar Temple had several of them."

Jax felt the light weight of the gun in his hands, testing its balance. He preferred a handgun and knew from the glint in Chibs's eyes that he would have liked this monster for himself, but it would have been an insult for him to pass it on. Oleg was trying to break the ice between them.

"Thank you," Jax said, and meant it. "I'll put it to good use."

Oleg nodded, unsmiling. "I'm sure you will."

He began to turn away, but changed his mind and glanced up at Jax again. "Kirill will not say it—particularly because of the strife between our people and your club—but we are both glad you are here. The reinforcements will be helpful. Perhaps these mutual interests we have will make us friends."

"Or at least not enemies," Jax said. "Let's not get ahead of ourselves."

Oleg nodded grimly, completely missing Jax's attempt at humor. *Russians,* he thought.

"Listen, Oleg, about one of our 'mutual interests.' You know Trinity has to stay behind today. She won't like it, but—"

"It will make her furious," Oleg agreed, "but she must at least suspect it. You could leave one of your people here with her, but we will need every man when we go up against Lagoshin."

"She'll be all right here?" Jax asked.

Oleg smiled, turning his grim features boyishly charming for a moment. Jax could see, then, the ordinary guy beneath the Bratva strongman.

"We will be busy killing all those who could threaten her," Oleg said. "None of them will be alive to cause her trouble."

"All right, then," Jax said.

Clutching the assault rifle in his left hand, he reached out with his right. Oleg took his hand, and they shook, a pact not unlike the one Jax had made with Kirill, but more personal.

"Let's see what other toys you guys picked up from Temple," Jax said. "Then we'll go give Lagoshin his morning wake-up call."

Rollie was in his bar, wolfing down a plate of scrambled eggs and toast, when Thor came trudging out from the kitchen.

Rollie turned, figuring he was ready to leave, but he spotted the cell phone in Thor's hand and froze.

"Tell me this isn't more bad news, bud."

Thor shrugged. "Well, it ain't *good* news. The old guy Izzo put Jax onto—John Carney—is dead."

Rollie swore and smashed a fist down on the bar. The fork he'd been using bounced off the wood and spun to the floor at his feet.

A dark thought swept through him. "You were with them when they talked to Carney?"

Thor nodded. "You know I was. It all seemed fine. Not to mention that Carney had kept information back from the cops that might've put them onto Trinity. I know what you're thinking, but Jax had no reason to go back and hurt this old man."

"All right. Go track down an address for the real estate guy Carney gave up to Jax. What the hell was his—"

"Drinkwater."

"Him." Rollie nodded. "Meet me out back. We'll let the others search for Jax or some Russians. You and me are gonna take Bag, Mikey, and Bronson over to see this Realtor and see what he knows."

Rollie took one last bite of his toast and then rubbed a finger over his teeth. He shoved back the stool he'd been sitting in and headed for the back hall.

"What if Drinkwater's already dead?" Thor asked.

Rollie paused, glanced over his shoulder. "Oh, I'm expecting to find him dead. Seems to be the theme of the morning. But that doesn't mean we can't learn anything from him."

16

Jax sat in the passenger seat of a black Audi, the interior of which smelled like cigarette smoke and body odor. No new-car smell for Ilia, the Russian behind the wheel. In the backseat, Oleg kept a gun jammed up against Luka's rib cage and snapped questions at him in Russian that Jax figured amounted to "right or left?" Luka was their human GPS this morning.

The air conditioner buzzed, turned all the way up, but for Jax all it did was chill the smoky, dank interior of the car. The Audi should have fit all four of them comfortably, but he felt claustrophobic. He'd hated having to leave the Harley behind. Worse than that, he despised having to sit idly in the passenger seat while Ilia did the driving. He didn't know the

Russian, had no idea how Ilia would respond if things went to hell. Oleg wouldn't have put him behind the wheel if he hadn't been a capable driver, but Jax kept opening and closing his hands, wishing for the grips on his Harley and the comforting freedom that came along with it.

He said nothing.

Whatever fate awaited him and Trinity today, he'd committed to it. No way to back out now. The assault rifle Oleg had given him waited in the trunk of the car.

A loud engine roared beside the Audi, and he glanced right to see Opie riding alongside. Opie peered in the window, just making sure the Russians hadn't decided to put a bullet in Jax's head now that they had him in the car. Jax nodded once and Opie dropped back behind the Audi to ride side by side with Chibs. The stitches Rollie had put in Opie's side seemed to be doing the job, keeping the graze along his ribs closed, and his color had improved. He'd be in pain, but he'd manage.

"Your men look out for you," Oleg said.

"Not my men," Jax corrected. "They're my brothers."

Ilia glanced at him but then returned his focus to the road ahead. Jax thought he could practically hear Oleg thinking in the backseat.

"I understand," Oleg said at last. "It is the same with us."

Luka scoffed and started to say something. Oleg struck him in the head with the butt of his pistol, and Luka grunted, almost whining, then fell silent.

The Audi's tires seemed strangely loud on the road. The morning sun blazed down, baking the hood of the car and the tinted glass windshield, and Jax knew the day would be a scorcher. Why a girl from Belfast would think she could find happiness in Nevada, he had no idea.

In his pocket, his cell phone buzzed. As he reached to retrieve it, he realized it wasn't his phone at all. He carried his in another pocket; this one belonged to Luka.

The text message came from someone called VK. Two words: *Check in.*

"Your friend Krupin wants you to check in," Jax said.

They kept driving. Oleg forced directions out of Luka, but there were hesitations that concerned Jax. They moved past a ranch and through a tract-housing development until they reached the outskirts of Las Vegas proper. Hotels and casinos loomed in the distance, silhouetted by stark sunlight.

"No way is Lagoshin camping out on the Strip," Jax said, glancing over his shoulder at Luka. "What are you up to, asshole?"

"Go left," Luka replied in English.

Ilia complied, and moments later they were rolling through a neighborhood of faded office buildings and auto body shops. Luka's cell buzzed again. Another text from VK: *Call in now. We're moving.*

The breath caught in Jax's throat. He drew his gun as he turned on the seat. Oleg glanced up in alarm and Ilia twitched at the steering wheel, but by then Jax already had his gun aimed at Luka.

"What are you doing, Jax?" Oleg asked warily.

Jax ignored him, focused on Luka. "Krupin says they're 'moving.' Where would they be moving?"

Luka smiled thinly, pure arrogance in his eyes.

Jax aimed the gun at his chest. Oleg jammed his gun in Luka's side.

"Talk to me, asshole," Jax said. "I don't need you the way these guys do."

At that, Luka's smile broadened, but still he said nothing.

Jax stiffened, thinking hard. Trying to figure out a way that this did not mean what he feared it meant. He slid back into his seat, dropped Luka's phone, and dug out his own.

"Who are you calling?" Oleg demanded, his own suspicion rising.

Jax found the contact he sought on his phone and hit CALL.

"Krupin says they're moving. What if Lagoshin got a line on where you've been holed up? Trinity's back there alone. I'm calling in some protection."

Many Russians were pale complexioned by nature. Oleg grew paler.

"She is your sister," he said. "You're not going to demand we turn around?"

Jax tightened his grip on his gun. "Would you do it?"

Oleg pressed his lips into a thin line. He loved her, but there was nothing he could do, and nothing he could say.

The phone kept ringing. Jax listened, praying that it would be picked up.

Drinkwater had been duct-taped to a chair. His arms, legs, and torso had been taped down in three different colors, and an old-fashioned paisley necktie had been used to gag him. It wouldn't have kept him from screaming, and, given time, he would've been able to get his mouth free—shout for help—so it seemed strange that whoever had done the very thorough duct-taping had chosen the tie.

Rollie stood in Drinkwater's bedroom and stared at the two bullet holes in the man's face, one in the forehead and one where his left eye ought to have been. The bullets had blown out the back of his skull.

Messy, he thought. *Why be so meticulous about binding him . . . why bother with a gag at all . . . if this was how it was going to end?*

Unless the shooter hadn't intended for it to end this way.

Which made no sense. It wasn't as if Drinkwater could have lunged at his killer—not with the duct tape strapping him to the chair.

Rollie scratched at his ample gut, then glanced around the bedroom. Whoever had killed Drinkwater, they'd gotten what they came for. The room seemed undisturbed except for the dead man and his gore. Drinkwater had answered his killer's questions.

If the killer had questions. *Maybe this was about nobody else getting the answers.* That felt right.

"Look around," Rollie told Thor. "Make it quick. The longer we stay, the more chance there is of something going wrong."

Thor started checking the pockets of jackets and searching night-table drawers. They'd left Bronson, Baghead, and the prospect at a small park down the street, and it wouldn't be long before their presence unnerved someone enough to call the PD.

Rollie bent to take a closer look at the corpse. He reached out and used a knuckle to drag down the edge of the paisley tie, still trying to work out the duct-tape question. Wherever the duct tape had come from, the killer hadn't run out of it. Two of the three rolls on the floor still had tape on them. So why choose the tie?

He heard Thor's phone buzz and glanced up.

"Just Hopper," Thor said before he answered.

Rollie went about his business, half-listening to Thor's calm responses to Hopper's report. Still focused on the tie, he opened a wardrobe and glanced inside. Jackets, suits, shoes on the bottom . . . and many, many ties. Nothing seemed out of place.

He glanced up as Thor finished the call with Hopper.

"Any leads on Jax?" Rollie asked.

Thor shook his head. "Bag talked to this cocktail waitress he used to bang at Lucky Pete's. Bartender there is Ukrainian or something, apparently knows Viktor Krupin. We should be able to track down Krupin, at least reach out to him—"

"It'd have to be damn fast to be any use to us," Rollie said, "but we'll see what he turns up."

Thor bounced from foot to foot, anxious to be leaving. Rollie felt the same—it had been risky even coming here, and now that they'd found Drinkwater dead, the potential for a murder charge weighed heavily.

"All right," he said. "Let's go."

"Where to?"

"No choice," Rollie said. "If we're gonna find Jax, we have to call our friends in Charming."

"If he's behind this, and Clay is backing him—"

"Jax and his buddies came here incognito—no cuts," Rollie said. "If he's betrayed us, there's no reason for us to think the rest of SAMCRO is involved, especially not Clay."

Rollie didn't give Thor a chance to argue. He moved swiftly out of the bedroom and into the corridor, retracing their steps.

In his pocket, his own cell phone buzzed. He thought it must be Hopper again, though it occurred to him to wonder why Hopper wouldn't just call Thor directly again.

Rollie answered. "Speak."

"It's Jax."

"Where the hell are you?" Rollie demanded.

Thor stared. "It's him?"

"Sorry to keep you waiting," Jax said.

"You owe me some answers, kid—"

"We need backup, Rollie. I hope Thor gave you that message. We need bodies, and we need guns. You know the old Wonderland Hotel in North Vegas, out west of your place?"

"Hold up a second."

"Rollie—"

"Joyce is dead. Died helping you out. I want to know—"

"Joyce was a rat," Jax said angrily.

"The fuck he was."

"Lagoshin knew where to find us. Joyce told him. Unless you want to tell me you also didn't know the guy was selling drugs at Birdland."

Rollie went silent.

"Doesn't matter now," Jax went on. "Lagoshin's crew killed him, and they'll kill the rest of us if they can. I told you they went after me and Opie the other day. We're on our way to erase Lagoshin from the picture, but I think some of his men may be headed for the Wonderland, and my sister's there alone. I need some of your guys over there, and the rest to meet up with us to take out Lagoshin."

Rollie stared at the spray pattern of blood and brain matter in the bedroom. The air-conditioning had kicked in, but still the stink made him want to retch. He tried to picture Joyce and the dead Russian out on that ranch road, tried to puzzle out how many motorcycles had been there, how it had all unfolded.

"You hearing me?" Jax asked.

"I hear you."

"Where are you now?"

"At your friend Drinkwater's house," Rollie replied.

Jax shifted the visor around to shield his eyes from the sun's glare.

"What the hell are you doing there?" he asked, glancing at the dashboard clock. Still so early. It made no sense for Rollie to be at Drinkwater's. Thor knew the name from their meet with Carney, but—

"Trying to track you down, Jax. Trying to figure out how one of my guys ended up dead in a ditch. Especially since Mr. Drinkwater's too dead to tell me anything."

Jax's mouth went dry. "You killed him?"

"Are you just screwing with me now?" Rollie snapped. "The guy's brains are all over the place. What are you *up to*, Jax?"

Numb, Jax tried to pull his thoughts together. "How did you end up there?"

"Oh, we stopped at the old Irishman's place first. He's dead, too."

Jax's thoughts spun. Who had killed Drinkwater and Carney? There could be only one answer. Just as there could be no doubt that Drinkwater had given his killers the answers they sought.

"Rollie, listen to me—"

"Oh, I'm listening, Jackson."

"Get to the Wonderland with every gun you've got! I'll call you back!"

Rollie started to argue, but Jax cut off the call. He spun to stare at Ilia: "Turn around! Do it now!"

In the backseat, Luka started to laugh behind his fresh gag. Oleg ignored him, leaning forward, alarm igniting in his eyes.

"Lagoshin knows about the hotel?" Oleg demanded.

Jax turned to stare at him, the ugliest scenarios playing out in his head. "Shit yeah he knows. Hell, they might be there already . . ."

He saw the realization in Oleg's eyes. They had left Trinity alone.

"Turn around!" Oleg snapped, and, at his command, Ilia finally did.

Car tires squealed. Oleg took out his cell and started calling Kirill and the others.

Luka lunged, slammed Oleg against the window. Wrists bound, he struggled to snatch Oleg's gun. Jax swore, bringing his own gun around, but he didn't need it. Oleg planted his feet, pistoned his legs, and drove Luka across the seat and into the opposite door. Luka's head struck the window, cracking the glass.

Oleg raised his gun and shot Luka twice in the chest, reached over to open the door, and then shoved the dying, bleeding man out onto the street as the car roared along at seventy miles per hour and more.

Luka had outlived his usefulness.

Oleg slammed the door shut and steadied himself with a deep breath. He and Jax exchanged a glance, and Jax knew, in that moment, that the two of them wanted the same thing. Lagoshin had to die, and Trinity had to live.

Rollie stood in the hall, gazing back through the door into the dead man's bedroom, cell phone dangling in his right hand. His whole body seemed to vibrate with uncertainty and indecision.

"So?" Thor asked.

"Jax and his boys are in trouble, and he expects us to be the cavalry."

Thor came to stand in front of Rollie expectantly. "You really think he's doing all of this? That all these bodies are on his head?"

Rollie stared into the bedroom, focused on the hole where Drinkwater's eye had been. "I think these guys are all dead because Jax Teller came to town looking for his sister. I'm not blaming him for that—I'd do the same for family, and so would you. But something doesn't sit right about the way Izzo described the scene out on that ranch road, and Jax isn't in a hurry to explain. Yeah, he's got other shit on his mind, but . . ."

His words trailed off. He stared at his feet a few seconds, listening to the ticking of a wall clock up at the top of the stairs ahead. The AC kicked on and cool air hummed from the vents. Rollie blinked and shook off the cloud of indecision. Whatever they were going to do, they had to get the hell out of *here*.

"Let's roll," he said.

Thor followed him down the stairs. "We're going to back him up?"

"He's VP of SAMCRO. Of course we're going to back him up," Rollie said. "But I feel like we're being played, so afterward I intend to get answers, even if I have to stomp the shit out of Jax Teller to get them."

Trinity sat on the swing set behind the Wonderland in a dirty T-shirt and a pair of black jeans. Her combat boots were comfortable enough, but too hot. She'd put them on because of the terrain and the broken glass out near the swing set, but now she wished she had something lighter.

She pushed back until she could barely touch the ground and then released, swinging forward and pumping her legs. The rusty swing squealed with each pendulous motion, but she relished the breeze on her face. The sun had come on strong this morning, and she could already tell the day would be scorching. Heat radiated up off the cracked concrete around the swing set.

Before they'd all left this morning, she'd been pissed off about being left alone. Oleg had thought she was afraid—which made no sense, given that they were the ones who had tracked down Lagoshin and were going to war. She'd had to explain to him, and not for the first time, that she just didn't like being left behind.

You're not a soldier, he'd reminded her.

I didn't prove myself at Temple's ranch? she'd demanded.

Then she had seen the pain in his face. He'd told her that he had never wanted to put her in a position where she had to take a life. *I didn't think that was the way you wanted to live,* he'd said, and then he'd asked her, politely, to stay behind.

Oleg didn't just want her to stay out of the line of fire. He didn't want her to have to kill anyone else.

She'd stayed behind.

Now that they were gone, though, she didn't mind being alone. All the anxiety and drama, the entirely rational fear that rippled beneath the skin of every one of Oleg's brothers—not to mention Oleg himself—had created a tension in her unlike anything she'd felt before. Jax's arrival had only added to the tension, happy as she'd been to see him.

Alone, she thought. *Alone feels good.*

They'll be all right. And then it will be over. No more Wonderland Hotel. Maybe no more Las Vegas. She hoped to spend time in California, see the American west coast. She spent half a dozen lovely minutes on the swing, but she could feel the way the sun had begun to bake her pale Irish skin.

Her stomach rumbled.

After breakfast, she'd decide what to do with the next few hours of her life. Trinity stood up from the swing and then froze.

Car engines rumbled out in front of the hotel. She could hear them. Car engines alone were not a surprise—during the day the road got its meager share of traffic—but these weren't passing by. They were in the parking lot.

One by one, the engines went silent. If she'd stayed on the swing with its squealing hinges for another few seconds, she'd have missed the sound entirely.

Car doors slammed.

For half a second, she let herself think that the guys had all come back, but she knew it was much too soon. It couldn't be them.

Alone, she thought again. There were plenty of guns inside the hotel, but she was in back, fooling around on the damn swing set. If she had the keys to the one remaining car, the old BMW only forty feet from her right now, she might have been able to get the jump on them, outrace them until she got somewhere they didn't dare attack her. Somewhere she'd be safe for the time being. But she didn't have the keys.

Trinity bolted for the back door of the hotel, counting her steps, telling herself that the men out front would approach slowly and cautiously and so she had time. Seconds, at least. A handful of seconds. Her heart slammed against the inside of her chest, and her thoughts went through the layout of the hotel, trying to figure out a place she could hide. They'd never planned for this. To defend an assault, yes—but she'd never be able to keep them from entering the hotel on her own. No, if they were coming in—and they *were* coming in—she needed a gun and a place to hide.

Only when she'd reached the door and ducked quietly inside, her senses attuned to the approach of the killers out front, did she realize that she'd gone the wrong direction. She could have run into the scrubland, found a place to hide herself while they searched the hotel and found nothing. If she'd had to, she could have hidden until Oleg and Kirill and Jax and the others came back—they'd have to come back eventually—but she was committed now.

A gun. A place to hide.

If only she could have heard her own thoughts over the thundering of her heart.

17

Trinity slipped through the door at the back of the lobby and dropped into a crouch, her pulse throbbing at her temples. To her right, half the lobby remained curtained off from the outside world by heavy drapes, but if she wanted to get deeper into the hotel, she had to go left—and that meant running past a stretch of windows that were uncovered. Sunlight poured in. Dust motes swam and danced in the vast shaft of light, as if drawn to it like moths to a flame.

She kept low and went left, hustled to the front desk and then dove over it, sliding on her belly. She reached down to break her fall but still thumped onto the old carpet, twisting her head so she landed on her shoulder. Her legs came down on top of her, and she spun around, back against the counter, waiting for gunshots and shattering glass.

Nothing.

"Okay, okay," she said, just to hear the whisper of her own voice.

She darted along behind the counter, trying to picture that vast front window and how far across the lobby the counter would take her—how much distance she would have to cover in the open, where they might see her. Fifteen feet, maybe, until she disappeared into the corridor. Unless they were already inside by then. She had no time to lose . . . and yet she hesitated.

Growing up, she'd heard ugly stories about assassinations and bombings and brutal beatings that had filtered into her nightmares and daydreams. The nearness of such crimes had a greater potency than lullabies and bedtime stories. Trinity had understood quite young that she would have to take care of herself. She was able, and more than willing.

But in that moment behind the counter, what haunted her was that for all the crimes and punishments that the RIRA had doled out—or that she'd heard about—the whispers about the Bratva were worse. If Lagoshin and Krupin got their hands on her, she would be used to send a message to Kirill and Oleg. Would they cut off her hands and feet and breasts? Would they set her on fire?

She exhaled, shivering with a chill that should have been impossible with the heat of the day radiating through the windows.

If she'd been Krupin's girlfriend and the situation were reversed, what would Oleg have done to her?

The question made her want to scream, but worse than that was the idea that whatever harm, whatever obscenity might be perpetrated upon her, it would be to use her as a tool, a message, an example. If she was going to die like this, she wanted it to be because of things she'd done, not whom she was sleeping with.

Keeping low, she rushed along behind the counter and then popped her head up. Through the plate-glass windows, she could see a massive black SUV and a charcoal-gray sedan, but they were off to the right. Men were standing behind them, but she was in the shadows, and she thought they might not see her. A pair of gunmen ran from the sedan to circle around the hotel. She waited, holding her breath while they passed, and then she was up and over the counter.

Trinity hit the floor in a tumble, came up on one knee and glanced at the windows again. How many cars, how many men? It didn't matter, really. The answer was *too many*.

She bolted, willing them not to see her. She expected shouting and gunshots, but then she darted into the corridor, felt the crunch of crusty old carpet under her boots, and knew she was clear.

Gun.

It was the only word in her head. Her right hand clenched and unclenched, yearning for the weight of a weapon. *Guns are hateful things,* Maureen Ashby had always said to young Trinity, *but remember, love, that bullets are like presents—better to give than receive.* It was how Maureen had justified so much of the family's violence.

Trinity reached her room, twisted the knob, slipped inside without banging the door. Her gun was where she'd left it, top shelf of the closet underneath a leather jacket she'd had no use for since they'd arrived in Vegas. Loaded, always.

She was out in the corridor in a handful of heartbeats, glancing both ways. Slipping into the hallway, she heard glass shatter in the lobby, and suddenly her options had narrowed. Lagoshin's men were coming in. They'd search the hotel. Trinity couldn't shoot her way out, which meant the only question that mattered was: Where could she hide? Where could she tuck herself away and still have an exit strategy?

Elevator shaft? The doors were wedged open, and she could get in, maybe drop down to the elevator itself, hide in the dark. But where the hell could she run from there?

Walk-in freezer in the kitchen? Dead end. As was every bathroom and guest room, all of which they'd search. Doors banged open. She heard wood splinter.

Upstairs.

She bolted past the alcove with the ice machine and a dusty-faced Coke machine. A voice shouted in Russian, profanity that she'd become more than familiar with. Trinity glanced to her left, saw the window and the tree beyond it—saw the Bratva killer beyond the tree and the way he stared. He pointed at the window, at her, shouting, and all choice had been taken from her. She ran to the z junction in the hallway, jogged right, hidden from all eyes, and then shoved through a door marked EMPLOY-EES ONLY.

Service stairs.

Exhaling, she ran, hating even the quiet scuffing of her boots on the steps. Second floor. Third floor. So much for her one asset, them not knowing she was there.

A small door—strangely small—on the third floor landing of the service stairs. She tried the latch and blinked in surprise when it opened. Gray light filtered through some kind of venting at the top of the stairwell, and a fraction of it came down inside the room on the other side of that door.

Not a room. A shaft. Service elevator.

Jamming her gun into the waistband of her jeans, Trinity climbed into that near darkness. Dusty metal rungs ran up and down the interior wall, just to her right, and she grabbed hold, reached out, and pulled the small door closed.

Up was the only option. Not a good one, but there were no good options here.

The metal rungs were cold to the touch. She moved fast, the gun jamming into her with every step. Fourth floor. Fifth floor, and it was taking too long. They'd be searching everywhere by now. Banging open doors and looking under beds.

Top of the shaft, beneath the mechanisms of the elevator and the vents that let in that dim gray light, she felt around and found a latch—another small door. She twisted it, put her weight into it, and the metal screeched as she forced it open. Blinking against the bright sunlight, she poured herself through the tiny door and found herself in a small alcove on the roof. Tucked between the elevator housing and the angled structure where the service stairs exited the roof, she was hidden from sight on three sides.

The sun had been cooking the top of the building for hours, and the heat baked up from every surface. Still, she took a moment to breathe. Hidden there, she felt as if she could just wait for help to arrive or for the intruders to give up and leave. If she hadn't been seen, she might have been able to do just that.

But she *had* been seen. They knew she was in the building, and it wouldn't be long before one of them came up to search the roof. When that happened, the alcove would not keep her hidden . . . it would keep her cornered.

She drew her gun and stepped from the alcove, glanced around and then hurried toward the front of the building.

The Wonderland Hotel varied in height from back to front. At the edge of the rearmost section, Trinity stared down along the Spanish tiles that sloped to the third floor and wondered if she could scramble down them without falling. From there, she could drop down on top of the portico breezeway at the front, where cars had once pulled up so bellmen could take their luggage. If she was quiet . . . if she was careful to wait until nobody was in sight . . . she might make it to one of their cars. Were any of the engines still running?

Don't think—move!

Carefully, she put one tentative foot on the sloping tiles, then realized that she needed to sit—to slide down instead of trying to stay on her feet. It might make more noise, but there was less chance of dying in the attempt.

"Okay," she said quietly.

Then she heard the engines. The low rumble of an approaching car. The grinding, growling roar of a couple of Harley-Davidsons.

Hope flickered inside her, and she glanced up. Four cars and two motorcycles. Her boys would be outnumbered, but they were coming. She didn't even need to warn them because they'd see the cars out front.

The service door clanged open behind her.

Trinity's heart went still. Her grip on the gun tightened and she spun around, taking aim even as she did so. The blond guy who'd come out onto the roof hadn't really expected to find her there, so he wasted a couple of seconds blinking at the sudden reality of her presence before he swung his gun toward her.

She pulled the trigger three times and managed to shoot him once, in the left leg. The sound of the bullet tearing wetly into flesh made her feel sick. The pain and the impact toppled him sideways, and he slammed to the roof with a grunt. His gun flew from his fingers and skittered a few feet from him. Wounded, trailing blood, he scrabbled toward the gun, calling her bitch, whore, and worse in his own language—why had she only learned the ugly words?

Trinity dashed toward him, gripping her gun in both hands, and aimed it at his head.

"Another inch and you die now," she said, with a ferocity she promised herself she didn't really feel. She wasn't really like that, didn't have the savagery inside that her bloodline on both sides would suggest. Just as she'd promised herself that she wouldn't really have taken out Luka's eye with a knife. *This isn't me,* she thought.

He moved and she pulled the trigger. The bullet struck the roof inches from his shoulder, threw up divots of concrete. The blond Russian hesitated, glancing at her. Trinity stepped closer.

"We're just gonna stay right here until it's over," she told him.

He sagged, seemed to give up, and then he planted his hands on the roof and swung his good leg out, struck her calves, and swept her off her feet. Trinity fell on her hip and smashed an elbow on the roof, but she did not let go of the gun. Blondie snagged her ankle, and only then did she see the knife that had appeared in his right hand.

The blade came down, and the gleaming steel bit into her left thigh.

Trinity screamed. Then she shot him in the face.

Jax clutched his cell phone. "You see this?"

Ilia responded, but Jax hadn't been speaking to the Russian behind the wheel. He had Kirill on the line, and the Bratva captain started talking fast, his clipped tones blocking out anything Ilia might have said.

"Done," Jax said, tossing the phone to the floor.

He picked up his gun as the car roared toward the Wonderland Hotel. The mountains wavered in the heat-hazed distance, but his focus was on the figures moving around the edges of the hotel. Someone darted out from behind the building, saw the cars and Harleys coming, and then vanished again. In front of the hotel, a pair of figures stood in front of the black Escalade with guns strapped across their backs, and Jax felt his insides freeze. Assault rifles. His 9mm handgun had stopping power, but not if he never got a chance to use it. And he'd never reach the fancy Russian AR that Oleg had given him before the enemy opened fire.

"Kirill says we take the back," Jax said, raising his voice to be heard over the engine's roar. "They've got the front."

Oleg slapped his hand on the driver's headrest. "You heard him. Go!"

Ilia twisted the wheel to the right, ignoring the parking lot. Ilia steered them into a delivery lane, rear wheels slewing and screeching on pavement. Jax saw movement in the backseat and glanced over to see Oleg pulling a new Kalashnikov AK-12 from under the seat. It gleamed, even newer than the one Jax had left in the trunk.

"Where the hell'd you get that?" he asked. "I didn't think they'd made more than the prototypes for it."

"This *is* a prototype," Oleg said. "Call this a field test."

The men by the Escalade opened fire. Bullets tore up the street and the burnt grass beside the hotel. Ilia and Oleg ducked, and the rear passenger window blew in, tiny bits of glass spraying all over the interior. Jax watched the other three cars race toward the hotel, the Mercedes turning into the circular drive as bullets strafed it. The RAV4 slid past. Guns thrust from windows spat bullets rapid-fire, but the RAV4 wasn't stopping or slowing. It sailed by and turned, heading for the other side of the building.

Jax worried about Chibs and Opie, glanced back and saw that they'd turned to follow him, Oleg, and Ilia. The Harleys roared up beside them, using the car as a shield. Smart. *Stay alive,* he thought.

Oleg shoved the AK-12's nose out the window and opened fire, strafing the Escalade. One of the men stood his ground and fired back, but the other ran for cover, trying to get behind the giant SUV. The Mercedes—with Gavril at the wheel and Kirill firing out the window—slammed into the man and then into the Escalade, sandwiching him between the two vehicles in a scream of metal and human anguish.

Then they were alongside the hotel and out of sight of the melee out front.

"Here we go," Ilia said, cutting the wheel to the left as they turned, skidding around the corner. The fence around the empty swimming pool loomed ahead.

"Kitchen door," Oleg said. "Close as you can."

Ilia said nothing, only nodded grimly.

Jax felt a dreadful calm descend upon him. The job was killing. The path from here to the other side of this chaos would be one of unhesitating bloodshed. He'd been down this path before.

His jaw tightened. His heart calmed. The car skidded to a halt. Jax was out the door before Ilia had a chance to throw it into park. Cold inside, he felt the sun baking his skin. The world seemed to shift into lower gear. He called for Ilia to open the trunk and was headed around the back of the car when he saw one of Lagoshin's men come around the side of the Dumpster, tall and pale with thinning hair and pockmarked skin. Jax shot him twice. The man pulled his own trigger as he went down, blowing in the Audi's windshield and putting a bullet so close to Jax that it zipped over his left shoulder.

Jax glanced down, saw the furrow in the fabric of his shirt, saw the blood welling and soaking into the fabric, and realized the furrow had been dug not just in cloth but in skin.

He bled, and he moved, running to the trunk. He jammed his handgun into his waistband and pulled the assault rifle Oleg had given him out of the trunk. Then he ran for the hotel.

Ilia and Oleg were ahead of him, yanking open the kitchen door, whose frame had already been shattered by the intruders. Motion in his peripheral vision made him glance left, and he saw Opie and Chibs running toward him, and suddenly he woke from the strange, dreamlike feeling that had enveloped him. He felt the searing pain of his wound and smelled the copper of his own blood and the smell of cordite.

"You all right?" Opie asked, in that familiar gravel voice. He'd turned a little pale, seemed to be favoring his left side where the bullet had grazed him, but it didn't appear that he'd started bleeding again.

Chibs went to the door but hesitated to follow the Russians inside, waiting for them.

Jax still felt calm, focused, but a new confidence made him exhale. He was with his brothers. They would prevail.

"Let's go," he said, suddenly hating the weight of the assault rifle. It would help even the odds, but he'd rather have a handgun any day. More precise. Less unwieldy. "Chibs, check the stairways, top to bottom. Opie and I are going room to room. Take out anyone in your way. If Trinity's alive, we're getting her out."

"What about Lagoshin?" Opie asked.

Jax nodded, remembering the beating Lagoshin had given him and the vow he'd made. "Trinity comes first. We stay alive, we can take care of that asshole later."

Boots scuffed the ground. They turned to see another Russian coming around the corner beyond the Dumpster. Opie lifted his gun but didn't need to fire. The Russian threw his arms up as bullets stitched up his back, some of Kirill's men having come around from the other side.

Jax tried not to keep count of how many men he saw go down. His side was badly outnumbered, but numbers didn't tell the whole story. Even so, he was glad to have Rollie and the SAMNOV crew on the way. He just hoped they would hurry.

Chibs led the way through the kitchen. They spotted Oleg and Ilia for a second, but then there was gunfire in the corridor ahead, and the two Russians raced headlong toward it. Jax pulled the trigger on the TsNIITochMash, and a barrage of bullets burst forth, the silencer muffling the noise. Then he ran on. He wanted to back Oleg and Ilia up, but he had other priorities.

"Go," he said to Chibs, who nodded and set off at a run, swinging right and left in search of a stairwell door.

Jax called his sister's name in the kitchen. Opie checked the walk-in cooler. Then they went into the corridor and started their search. Room to room, watching each other's backs as they listened to shouts and gunfire echoing through the hotel.

"Wonderland," Opie said, voice dripping with irony. He winced at the pain in his side but said nothing of it.

Jax didn't smile. He slammed open a bathroom door and went in, gun ahead of him, calling his sister's name in a voice that echoed back to him.

The place sounded hollow. Empty.

For the first time, he understood that she might already be dead.

18

Chibs glided along the corridor, back to the wall. He glanced into a few open doorways, turning and then moving on in fluid motion. His pulse was steady, his breathing calm. During his time as an army medic, one lieutenant had said if they'd monitored his brain waves during combat, the test would show that Chibs was asleep. "Maybe even dreaming." Every time violence erupted around him, Chibs assumed he was going to die—he just wanted to make the bastards pay before he did.

When he wasn't in the field, though . . . it was then that Chibs had trouble. Under fire, he was calm, but when things were quiet, he could feel old anger simmering inside him. Even now, years later, he spent most days with an electric tension buzzing along his spine. He'd been a man without a country, and the brothers of SAMCRO had opened their arms to him. Without SAMCRO, he had nothing.

Jax had made some questionable choices in the past few days, but Chibs had Jax's back no matter what, partly because they were both SAMCRO and he loved the man, and partly because he knew that if Trinity was his sister, he'd have made the very same decisions.

Chibs stopped at the elevator, punched the button to see if it was working. The button didn't light up, and he put his ear to the metal door. No hum. Boots pounded somewhere upstairs. Gunfire came from the front of the hotel.

"Behind you," came a low growl.

Chibs glanced back. Opie and Jax had turned the corner and were following him at a distance.

Someone swore in Russian. Chibs whipped around, saw the man who'd come into the hall up ahead, and took aim. He squeezed off two rounds. One caught the Russian in the arm, just a graze, but the man dove around a turn in the corridor ahead.

"Go, go!" Jax snapped.

Chibs glanced up, saw the stairwell door to his left, and pushed through. Jax had given him one job, and he intended to do it. As the door swung shut, Chibs glanced back into the hall and saw Opie thundering along with his gun, taking aim. Opie fired, and someone swore. Then the door clicked home, and Chibs was alone.

On the stairs, the violence sounded muffled, almost distant. Chibs was dead calm. He hustled up the steps, watching and listening for the presence of Lagoshin's men. Halfway between the third and fourth floor, he paused and listened to the way his heartbeat thumped inside his head. He might be calm under fire, but he hadn't gotten any younger these past few years. Running up multiple flights of stairs forced him to catch his breath.

The stairwell had a chalky, dusty smell, with dampness underneath it, like something had crawled behind the wall months ago and died.

Chibs heard a scuff on the stairs above, just around the corner. A huff of breath, followed by a quiet, very human sound. He thought it was the sound of despair.

Gun leveled, he turned the corner. "Not a whisper," he growled, finger applying pressured to the trigger.

Trinity sat on the steps, tightening a torn and bloody swatch of a man's shirt around her leg. She bared her teeth at him in obvious pain.

"You try doin' this and not lettin' out a squeak here and there," she snarled.

"Jesus," Chibs whispered, and it was at least half a prayer.

Gun still out, he went and sat beside her on the steps, got one arm behind her back, and lifted her up so that she stood on one leg and leaned against him.

"Do your best, darlin'," he said, glancing up at the fourth-floor landing and down at the third. "We can't stay here."

A sheen of sweat coated Trinity's lightly sunburned skin. She breathed slowly and evenly, pain written on her face as Chibs helped her descend one step at a time.

Below, someone came through the door at the second-floor landing. Chibs froze, but the sudden halt set Trinity off balance, and he had to compensate, shifting to catch her. She put weight on her injured leg and hissed through her teeth. Not much noise . . . but enough.

"Yakim?"

The voice brushed the concrete walls, rising up to Chibs and Trinity. They stood paralyzed, not breathing. *Go away,* Chibs thought. Instead, the man on the second-floor landing called out in Russian, alerting others that someone was on the stairs.

Chibs cursed under his breath and jammed his gun into his belt. He lifted Trinity into his arms and clomped heavily down the steps. She swore at him but didn't try to fight loose. The man on the second-floor landing shouted again for backup and then started up toward them. Chibs glanced down as he reached the door into the third-floor corridor and spotted the goateed man below, eyes peeking up in the gap between flights of stairs.

The barrel of the man's gun winked at him. Gunshots echoed painfully in the stairwell, and a bullet chipped at the concrete over Chibs's head.

"The door!" Trinity snapped.

"I'm trying!"

Chibs bumped her against the wall and door frame, and she cried out, but he managed to get his hand on the knob, drag the door open, and lug her through. He started moving, but she was no slight wisp of a girl, and she knew it.

"Put me down! I can walk!"

He didn't argue, but when he tilted her onto her feet, he made sure to support her. They moved together, rushing along the corridor with its stained carpets and missing ceiling panels. The Russian stepped out into the hallway, only moments behind them.

Chibs let go of Trinity and drew his gun, turning in one smooth motion. The Russian had an assault rifle. When he pulled the trigger, bullets punched the carpet and the walls in an arc that would have cut them in half if Chibs hadn't shot him three times. The third bullet went through the man's throat—no more shouting for help. He opened his mouth and a wet, gurgling noise spilled out.

"Move!" Chibs shouted at Trinity.

She hobbled onward while Chibs raced back and tore the assault rifle from the man's hands as his throat and chest wounds pumped blood all over the floor. Chibs glanced up at the sound of heavy footfalls from behind the stairwell door and knew that Yakim and others had come as reinforcements.

"Get to cover!" he shouted.

Trinity put weight on that leg again, then stumbled against the wall and slid along it, using it to keep herself vaguely upright. Chibs ran past her as the stairwell door opened behind them. He tried the door to the next guest room, found it locked, and kicked it in just as Trinity caught up, trailing blood that added crimson to the other stains on the carpet. He took her hand and guided her inside, and she staggered toward the dusty bed as he ducked back into the corridor and pulled the trigger on his appropriated assault rifle.

Yakim took a bullet to the knee and went down in a screaming flail, but there were two guys behind him who opened fire. Chibs ducked back inside, then poked his head out again and let off another short burst from the assault rifle.

Grim-hearted but once more strangely calm, he pressed his back against the inside of the door frame. Bullets cut through the wall, and he dropped to a crouch. Trinity scrambled across the floor to lean against the wall nearby. She held out a hand, and Chibs handed her his pistol, only a few rounds remaining in the magazine.

"Help is coming," Chibs said.

19

The SAMNOV tore along the pavement toward the Wonder-land Hotel, tires throwing up a cloud of dust and righteous fury. Rollie rode in the lead, an icy ball of dread and suspicion heavy in his gut. He'd known Jax's father, J. T., and though the man had been arrogant as hell, he'd also been a man of honor. Death had come for him far too young. Too young to have had the proper influence on his son. That remained to be seen.

Hopper rode up on his left, gesturing toward the hotel. Rollie had been so wrapped up in his thoughts that he'd stopped paying attention to anything but the heat lines rising from the pavement ahead. They were still half a mile from the hotel, but now that Hopper'd drawn his attention to it, Rollie saw the many vehicles parked out front.

Slower than before, he rode toward the hotel with the eight members of SAMNOV who'd been close enough to respond to his summons. Hopper and Baghead, Antonio and Thor, Clean and Bronson, Ugly Jim and Mikey the Prospect. Nine guys—that was what SAMNOV could muster. Enough to cause problems.

Gunfire cracked the air. A gunman patrolled the roof. Two men ran around the perimeter, and one of them took shots at the guy on the roof, hoping to get in a lucky shot.

Rollie pulled his bike onto the dirt shoulder, engine growling as it idled. Thor drew up next to him on one side, and Hopper on the other, while the rest of his club halted behind them, waiting.

"What now?" Thor asked. "You're not going to get any answers from Jax in the middle of this shit."

Rollie dragged his goggles up and squinted at Thor in the glare of the sun. "Now we back him up. You think I'd leave our brothers in the middle of a crisis?"

Thor smiled thinly, ready for a fight.

"What about the Russians?" Hopper asked. "How do we know which ones are on our side and which ones are with Jax?"

Rollie thought about that a second, staring at the hotel. Then he dragged his goggles down, fitting them carefully over his eyes. He turned and raised his voice, making sure the rest of his men could hear him.

"Hard and fast!" he barked. "Take out anyone who takes a shot at you. If we get any friendly-fire killings in here, it's damn well not gonna be one of us!"

He twisted the throttle, and the rear wheel tore up the dirt shoulder.

Cavalry's coming, Jackson, Rollie thought. *For better or worse.*

Jax and Opie raced through the lobby, encountering nothing but sunlight and shattered glass. Opie turned left, and Jax turned right, taking aim through broken windows in case some of Lagoshin's men had gone back inside. Jax felt as if he skated along the surface of a death that yawned wide beneath him, but he and Opie were in the flow now, and there was no time for second guesses.

Gunfire drew them to the west wing of the hotel, which had a couple of floors of guest rooms on top of a trio of ballrooms, two on the first floor and one off the mezzanine.

Jax put his back to the wall, motioned for Opie to halt. On the wide steps up to the mezzanine, Oleg and Vlad crouched behind marble balusters, shooting through the openings at the double doors of a first-floor ballroom. Jax caught a glimpse of a short gunman just inside the ballroom, saw the oily sheen of his skin and the dead fish eyes and recognized Viktor Krupin instantly. The gunshot wound in his shoulder had to hurt like hell, but it hadn't slowed him down.

He swung around the corner and fired a burst from the TsNIITochMash. One of the bullets brushed by Krupin's face close enough to dry his sweat, and the Russian dodged back into the ballroom.

Jax ran down the hall, TsNIITochMash at the ready. Opie shouted angrily at him for breaking cover but followed anyway. Oleg and Vlad saw them coming and stood, moving down the stairs, covering the ballroom's doors. One of Lagoshin's men showed himself, ducking low as he fired a shot at Jax and Opie. All four men returned fire, and at least two of the bullets struck home. The guy slammed against the door frame and then slid back into the room, leaving a wide smear of blood on the frame and wall.

Alive or dead? Jax wondered. *Probably dead.*

"How many more?" Opie asked.

"At least three," Vlad said.

With Jax and Opie on one side and Oleg and Vlad on the other, the men inside the ballroom were pinned down unless they chose another exit. If they came out these doors, they would be in the middle of a cross fire.

"We've got to get to Trinity," Oleg said desperately, glancing back up the stairs toward the mezzanine.

Jax froze. "Where?"

"Follow me." Oleg moved back to the steps, glancing at Vlad. "Kill them if you can."

Vlad nodded, smiling. "Send help."

Oleg did not reply. Jax saw him moving toward the steps and glanced at Opie, who only nodded.

"Go," Opie told him.

Jax didn't hesitate. He raced across the killing floor, the space between Opie and Vlad where the Russians in the ballroom would have a clear shot at him from inside. He held his assault rifle ready, caught a glimpse of Krupin, but the man pulled back out of sight, perhaps remembering the breeze on his nose from Jax's bullet.

Then he was racing up the stairs after Oleg. When he hit the mezzanine, he saw that Oleg had stopped to wait for him in front of a floor-to-ceiling window that looked out at the back of the hotel, toward the empty swimming pool and the overgrown back lot. Oleg pointed out the window, and Jax glanced across the lot. From that window, they had a clear view from the west wing to east. At first he saw nothing, but then he spotted movement in a guest room window, one floor up and across from them. A flash of strawberry blond hair and then a dark figure, a broad man whose silhouette Jax knew immediately—Chibs.

The sound of gunfire had punctuated every moment since their arrival—some near and some distant—but he felt sure some of it was coming from that guest room on the third floor of the east wing.

"Fastest way," Jax said.

Oleg darted back along the balcony portion of the mezzanine. Down below, he spotted Opie and Vlad, heard Opie shouting for Krupin and his men to throw out their guns and he'd let them live. Then Oleg reached a fire door, and Jax followed him through it. They hustled up the steps to the third floor, opened the door, and stepped into the corridor there.

Jax glanced right and left, oriented himself, and ran to the right without waiting for Oleg. There were guest rooms here, two floors above the lobby. *Stay alive,* he thought, mentally commanding both Trinity and Chibs.

A fire door blocked the other end of the corridor—an entrance into the east wing—and he and Oleg hurtled toward it.

Lagoshin spat curses as he erupted from an open guest room door, crashed into Jax, and slammed him into the peeling wallpaper on the opposite side of the hall. The TsNIITochMash flew from Jax's grip and skidded along the carpet, far out of reach. Jax still had the bruises to remind him of the last time he'd met the massive Russian, and he didn't want a repeat. He tried to twist free, but Lagoshin got a hand on his throat, smashed his head against the wall, and started to lift him off the ground. Jax's back slid up the wallpaper, and his sneakers left the carpet.

Oleg shouted at them and raised his assault rifle, and one of Lagoshin's men emerged from the guest room. The barrel of his handgun gleamed in the dusty daylight. Jax tried to shout Oleg's name, but the Russian fired. The bullet ripped through Oleg's gut and then lodged in the wall. Blood sprayed as Oleg went down. On the ground, he raised his AR-12 and fired, killing the man who'd shot him.

Then he bled. He tried to aim his AR-12, but if he pulled the trigger he might kill both Lagoshin and Jax. Wounded, hands shaking, Oleg pulled the trigger anyway. Three shots, and then he clicked onto an empty magazine. He'd be no help.

Jax wheezed, and his chest burned. As Lagoshin held him aloft, he managed to yank out his Glock, brought it around, and jammed it against the big bastard's chest. Lagoshin grabbed his wrist and twisted, ripped the handgun from his grasp.

"Teller," Lagoshin said, buckshot scars on his face gleaming.

Jax's eyes widened, but he shouldn't have been surprised. Of course Joyce had eventually revealed his identity to the Bratva.

"You've been foolish. You killed Putlova, but I didn't care about that. He was an arrogant bastard. Now I kill you. I kill Sokolov and his men. No more gun business for the Sons of Anarchy."

Black spots at the corners of his eyes, losing air and on the verge of losing consciousness, Jax pressed his heels against the wall behind him. Fueled by rage and desperation, he brought his feet even higher and pushed hard, pistoned off the wall, and forced Lagoshin backward. The Russian lost his grip on Jax's throat, and Jax sucked in a ragged gasp of air as he hit the carpet on one knee.

Lagoshin barked Russian profanities and bent to reach for him. Jax dropped onto his side and whipped both legs around, knocking Lagoshin's feet out from under him. Lagoshin fell hard, his head striking the wall, and landed on the carpet with a thunderous crash. Jax stood as Lagoshin tried to rise, disoriented.

He kicked Lagoshin hard in the temple, then delivered a follow-up to his mouth, but he said nothing. Jax had no interest in taunting Lagoshin. The huge man groaned, then shook himself like a wet dog and growled as he rose to his hands and knees. Jax glanced at the handgun that Lagoshin had torn from his grip. Just beyond its place on the carpet, Oleg sat against the wall with his hands pressed hard to the wound in his abdomen. His eyes were open, but he looked pale, his face slack.

"Kill him," Oleg rasped, blood bubbling on his lips.

Jax aimed another kick at Lagoshin's skull. Even as he did, the big Russian launched himself upward, hurling himself from hands and knees into a battering ram. He tackled Jax, slammed him to the carpet and straddled him, backhanded him twice and wrapped his huge hands around Jax's throat and began to squeeze. The pressure forced a strangled grunt out of him, the last of his air. The pressure made Jax cry out in rage and pain.

In his mind, he saw the faces of his sons. Of Tara and of his mother. Somewhere nearby, Trinity and Chibs were in trouble, but he realized he was not going to be able to help them.

***

Trinity had fooled herself into thinking they could escape through the window. She'd picked up a chair and slammed it against the glass. If the pool had been full, maybe they'd have been able to make the jump, but they were thirty or forty feet above the rear parking lot. If the fall didn't kill them, it would mess them up badly enough that they'd be lying there broken and bleeding until Lagoshin's men came and finished the job. She'd given up smashing the chair against the window after the third attempt. The glass had cracked, but there seemed little point.

Only then had she seen the door to the connecting guest room. She'd unlocked and opened the door, but of course there was one on the other side—one that could only be unlocked from the adjoining room.

"Chibs!" she called.

He had shoved the dusty, stained mattress off the box spring and put it against the wall, an added layer for the Russians' bullets to pass through. Now he glanced out the door, assault rifle clutched in both hands.

"I can do this all day," he shouted to them. "You want us, you're gonna have to come in after us!"

"Chibs!" Trinity snapped.

He whipped around to glare at her. She pushed the floor lamp back so he had a clear view of the connecting door and pointed to it. Holding his gun, she mimed shooting at the lock, and he nodded, a mischievous light in his eyes.

Chibs held up his hand, palm flat, halting her. She frowned, and he sketched his fingers at the air, indicating that she should go out through that room and into the corridor. It took her a moment to realize what he wanted, and when she did, she thought there might have been a look of mischief in her own eyes as well. She relished the moment. Any second that passed with her feeling something other than fear was something to cherish.

She gestured toward Chibs.

He thrust his assault rifle out into the corridor and fired blindly in the direction of their attackers. With the gunfire as cover, she shot out the lock, blowing a hole in metal and wood, tearing the mechanism in two.

The door swung inward. She didn't even glance at Chibs as she rushed into the next room, spotted the same dusty bed, the same dust motes dancing in the sunlight streaming through the windows, the same sad, faded artwork on the walls. She ran to the door, hauled it open, and ducked into the hall. The Russians were twenty feet along the corridor, ducked into the recessed doorway of a guest room and so laser-focused on the space where they expected to see Chibs firing at them that it was a couple of seconds before one of them noticed her.

Trinity didn't try to aim. She lifted the gun and fired its last two bullets, then ducked back into the room and threw herself onto the floor.

Bullets tore up the open doorway, splintered wood and drywall flying.

More gunfire, but echoing now from the next room as much as it was out in the corridor. She heard a cry of pain, a terrible grunt, and then the wet, heavy sound of bodies toppling to the floor. Trinity had provided a distraction, and Chibs had taken full advantage of it.

"Clear!" he called from the corridor.

She lurched to her feet and out into the hall, gun left on the floor, forgotten.

In the hall, Chibs relieved the dead men of their weapons. He handed her a sleek assault rifle. The gun felt heavier than anything she had ever carried in her life.

You're alive, she reminded herself, and the burden lightened a bit. But only a bit.

Chibs grabbed her arm and gave her a little shake. Trinity snapped her gaze up to stare at him.

"You with me, girl? I need you focused. We're not out o' this yet."

Trinity stared at the dead men. "I'm with you."

"Quickest way down'll be the stairs," Chibs said. "Likely to be some more of these bastards in our path, but my job is to get you out of here."

"I'm not leavin' without Oleg," she said coldly.

He hesitated, and she could almost see him weighing his options. "We have no way of knowin' where they are. Best thing we can do for them is keep the exits clear."

Rollie stood in the lobby, head cocked as he listened to the sounds of gunfire. Baghead and Mikey the Prospect were with him—he'd sent the rest of them off in different directions to do what they could—but now he hesitated.

"Which way?" Mikey asked.

Good question, Rollie thought. They could just hold the lobby, but he wanted to get to Jax before the Bratva did. Like any brotherhood, they might fight among themselves, but if an outsider came after one of them, they circled the wagons. Rollie would give up his life for that principle.

"Front window!" Baghead snapped.

Rollie turned, sweeping his gun hand up and around to take aim at the shattered, jagged remains of the plate-glass windows. He spotted a pair of stone-faced killers just outside, gray in the shadow of the hotel. One wore a white tank, and his arms were wreathed with tattoos. The other wore a black suit and tie.

Mikey the Prospect took a single shot that snapped off a shard jutting from the window frame. The tattooed Russian spun out of view, no longer framed by the window.

"Mikey, knock that shit off!" Rollie shouted, as he and Baghead moved up on either side of the kid. *Friggin' prospects*. Even Bag hadn't forgotten his orders so fast.

The black-suited Russian put his hands up but didn't drop his gun. "You are Jax Teller's men?"

Rollie winced. He was president of SAMNOV, and Jax was VP up in Charming. He sure as hell wasn't one of Jax's men.

"We're with him, yeah," he said.

The Russian lowered his hands. Rollie, Bag, and Mikey covered him. "Then we are on the same side," black suit said. "I am Kirill Sokolov."

"Sokolov," Rollie replied. "The man who would be king."

The Russian grinned. "If you say so."

"All right, then," Rollie said, lowering his gun. "Let's go get you a crown."

Opie popped a magazine out of his gun and dug a fresh one from his pocket. The bullet graze on his side had started to seep blood through Rollie's stitches. The wound would stay closed—wasn't even that serious—but he had to be careful not to tear it open completely, or blood loss could take him out of the fight.

He glanced at Vlad. "I'm out of ammo after this. We keep dicking around out here, and they'll outlast us."

Vlad stared at him as if he'd grown a second head. "You want to rush them? We have them pinned down. If we wait, others will come, and we will have greater numbers. They will have to surrender."

"You know these guys," Opie said, frowning at him. "You think they're gonna surrender? We need to finish this so we can help Jax and your guys with the rest."

Vlad rose up from behind the marble stairs outside the ballroom and took two shots at the open doors, just to remind Krupin and the others that they were still there. Opie slammed home his replacement magazine and chambered a round.

"There are two of us and at least three or four in there," Vlad said. "I don't like the odds."

Opie shot him a withering look. "Neither do I."

Vlad exhaled, lowered his head, and then laughed softly. "All right. We go on three. One . . ."

"Two," Opie said.

He snapped his head up at the sound of quick, light footfalls along the corridor down below. On the grand staircase, he and Vlad swiveled to aim at the advancing figures, only to exhale when they identified the new arrivals. Opie didn't know Rollie or Baghead well, and he didn't even remember the prospect's name, but he saw their cuts and the club insignia on those vests, and the desperation he'd felt a moment before left him. He imagined Vlad felt the same way seeing Kirill and the other Russian there. Five men. Five guns, including two assault rifles.

Opie and Vlad smiled at one another and finished the count.

"Three."

They rushed down the steps, moved sidelong toward the open ballroom doors. Opie waved to the others, signaled them to approach the other set of doors—which remained closed. Kirill went first, flung open the doors, and rushed inside, shooting as he moved, fearless and a little mad, the way anyone who wanted the job he wanted had to be. Opie caught a glimpse of Rollie following him, and then he and Vlad were bursting in through the other doors.

Gunfire tore up the ballroom floor and walls.

Opie spotted Krupin toward the back, on the far side of the dance floor, where a large section of wall had been paneled in mirrored glass. He strode toward Krupin, images in his head of their first meeting, of the gleeful, arrogant sadism of the beady-eyed little man. Those eyes had fear in them now, and he felt as if a vengeful flame ignited inside him. Opie had tried to put the violence and bloodshed of this life behind him once, but in moments like this he doubted such a thing could be possible. He yearned for a peaceful life, but he would not turn his back on his responsibilities to his brothers.

Krupin's right arm hung limply, blood soaking through his shirt from the gunshot wound of the night before. Opie shot Krupin four times, bullets ripping through him, shattering the mirrors on the wall behind him. Blood-spattered shards crashed down on top of the dying man, some reflecting Krupin's shock and pain and some showing Opie a reflection of his own grim features. As the gunfire ceased, only soft echoes remaining in the ballroom, he turned away. He hadn't liked the look of his eyes in that reflection. He would have expected to see a killer's eyes, but all he saw in those mirror shards was pain.

Black sunbursts of oxygen deprivation blossomed in Jax's eyes. His legs pounded the floor, and he smashed his fists into Lagoshin's side. He tried to force the monster's arms away, but Lagoshin's size and weight overwhelmed him. In his fury, the Russian felt none of Jax's blows. In the rush of imminent death, Jax could no longer feel any of his own injuries, only those hands around his throat and the burning hollow in his lungs.

Lagoshin looked down on him and grinned. He whispered something in Russian that Jax would never understand.

A fresh wave of rage flowed over Jax, one last burst of strength, and he slammed his fists into Lagoshin's sides, already thinking ahead to his next move—his last move. He had to reach the enormous bastard's eyes.

Tensed, about to thrust his arms up inside Lagoshin's reach, he punched one last time . . . and realized that his left fist had struck something at the Russian's side that shouldn't have been there. In the fog his thoughts had become, it took him a precious moment to realize it was a sheath. A handle jutted from it.

Lagoshin had a knife.

Desperate, lungs screaming for air, Jax drove his fist into the Russian's side one final time, but now his fingers closed on the handle of the knife, and he drew it out. In his triumph, Lagoshin didn't notice until the blade punched through his right side. Weakened, Jax only had so much strength, but he had enough to drive the blade in and *twist*. He hacked tough muscle, split skin.

Lagoshin roared and lurched off him, scrambling backward in a crouch until he hit the corridor wall. Pain contorted his face as he looked down along his side and saw what Jax had done—saw the knife handle jutting from his side.

Drawing in ragged breaths, fighting back the blackness in his peripheral vision, Jax crawled along the carpet to the opposite wall and used it to leverage himself upward. Leaning against the wall, he reached deeper . . . breathed deeper . . . and found a determination that his body lacked.

Jax took a deep breath that seared his throat and stepped away from the wall. Lagoshin reached down and ripped the knife from his own side. Blood poured from the wound, painting the carpet and then running in a steady stream that soaked into his pants. Eyes bright with murder, Lagoshin stepped toward him. Jax punched him in the throat. Wheezing, sucking in air, Lagoshin staggered backward. Jax went to follow, but the Russian swiped the blade across the space between them and tagged Jax on the arm, a thin red line burning against his left tricep. A shallow cut, but the knife would do much worse.

"I will enjoy killing your sister," Lagoshin said.

Twin gunshots exploded in the hallway. Twin holes appeared in Lagoshin's torso. He took a single step backward, blinked, stared at Jax and then down at the rose-red patches blossoming on his chest . . . and then he fell to his knees. A long moan came from his throat, and then he slid down to lay on his side as if he had simply decided the time had come to sleep.

Jax staggered backward a step, staring at the dead Russian. Slowly, he turned to see Oleg lying on his side on the bloody carpet with a 9mm pistol in one hand and the other pressed against his abdomen, his shirt soaked in blood. The smell of blood filled the corridor—his and Oleg's and Lagoshin's mixing together into a metallic, copper cloud—and he forced himself to ignore his injuries. He walked to Lagoshin and stepped on the Russian's wrist, tore the knife from his grip and tossed it away.

"He's dead," Oleg said, his voice a groan.

Jax turned to see Oleg trying to force himself into a sitting position again, and failing. He lurched over to Oleg and knelt beside him. Gutshot, blood still foaming from the corners of his mouth, he was close to death.

"Thank you, man. Truly," Jax said. "You saved my life just now."

Oleg gripped his arm, staring at him with the dark urgency of words he did not have the strength to speak.

Then his gaze went dull and his grip slackened, and he was gone.

Jax sat down to rest beside the dead man.

His eyes closed.

Jackie. Wake up, brother.

It might have been minutes later, or only seconds, when he heard the quiet burr of Chibs's voice, and he opened his eyes again. Jax blinked to clear his vision, weak from blood loss, exhaustion, and the beating he'd taken. Chibs knelt to his right, a hand on his shoulder, shaking him awake. To his left, Trinity stood staring down at the pale corpse of the man she'd loved and at the pool of blood that surrounded him where he sat against the wall. She cried silently, mute with grief. For long moments, it was as if she didn't even realize that Chibs and Jax were there in the corridor with her. Then a dark, familiar anger stole over her face, and she glanced at the gun in Jax's hand, then over at Lagoshin and the bullet wounds in his torso. He hadn't been able to save Oleg, but he had taken vengeance for her.

It was cold comfort, but it was all he had to offer.

20

Trinity spit on Lagoshin's corpse.

She wiped furiously at her eyes, hating every tear that fell. Death had been no stranger to her life, but when she had lost people she loved, it had been at a distance. The presence of Oleg's body, the way his mouth hung open as if he might be just about to speak . . . the dull sheen of his dark eyes . . . it carved a hole in her chest.

"Jesus," she whispered, the closest thing to a real prayer she had uttered in years.

Chibs helped Jax to his feet. Trinity went to her brother, and he opened his arms to her, pulled her into a bloody embrace. Her tears had dried, but grief poured from her and he held her tightly, absorbing it all.

She took a deep breath and stood back from him. When he took her by the arm, she saw a pain in his eyes that reflected her own, and she loved him for it. They walked away together, Chibs in the lead with his gun drawn, leaving the dead behind.

They made their way to the steps that passed the ballroom and then down the sweeping, grand staircase. Chibs kept a wary eye on the bodies they found along the way. Pyotr lay sprawled on the stairs. At the bottom, just outside the first-floor ballroom, Vlad lay halfway through the doors with a bullet hole in his forehead. Trinity turned away, unwilling to see the gray and crimson matter that decorated the door behind him.

"You smell that?" Chibs asked as they came around the corner into the hall leading to the lobby.

Trinity had lowered her gaze, staring at the carpet as she walked. Now she glanced up and sniffed the air. She saw Jax nod, knew he smelled it, too.

Gasoline.

They walked into the lobby, found it full of dead men, but there were many still alive, too. Timur and Gavril had fetched full gas cans from the trunks of the cars out in the parking lot and were spilling gasoline all around the corners of the lobby. On the other end of the room, Ilia was doing the same. Opie stood by the front doors, watching the street impatiently for any sign of the police. A heavy, bearded man in a Sons of Anarchy cut turned to see Trinity, Jax, and Chibs entering and rushed toward them.

"Son of a bitch," the big biker said. "We figured you for dead!"

"Rollie," Jax rasped, clearing his throat.

Then Opie was there, a strangely calm presence, like an oak tree had just grown up beside them. He took in Jax's injuries and the grief on Trinity's face, and she could see that he understood immediately. A ripple of regret passed over his features as if he understood her sorrow, though she knew she might only have imagined it.

"Antonio went looking for you," Opie said, glancing from Jax to Chibs.

"We saw him," Chibs replied, turning to Rollie. "He's not coming."

"Aw, shit," Rollie said, and then he shot Jax a blazing glare. "You've got a lot to answer for."

Despite his injuries, Jax stood a little taller. "I'm sorry about Antonio—"

"And Mikey."

"And Mikey," Jax echoed. "I'm grateful to you for backing us up. Could be we'd all be dead if you hadn't shown up when you did. But if you want someone to blame, Lagoshin is upstairs with a couple of bullets in him. He's the asshole responsible for all of this."

Rollie's eyes narrowed. Trinity could see that he didn't entirely believe Jax.

Then she heard her name and looked up to see Kirill entering the lobby from the opposite end. His voice was hopeful until she met his gaze. What he saw in her eyes stopped him in his tracks.

He swore in Russian, staring at the floor for a moment before glancing at the ceiling. At heaven. His lips moved silently, and she wondered if he was cursing God or talking to Oleg's spirit, making some promise of revenge. None of it mattered. With Lagoshin dead, the only thing any of them could do was survive.

Several other members of the Sons of Anarchy came into the lobby behind Kirill. Trinity looked beyond them, but that seemed to be the last of the survivors of the massacre at the Wonderland Hotel.

"No sign of the cops yet," one of the bikers said.

"They'll be here," Rollie replied. "We need to move."

Trinity felt numb as she walked to Kirill. He stiffened as she slid her arms around him, leaned her head against his chest. After a moment, she felt his body relax, any resentment he'd felt toward her forgotten. They would both live through the day—Kirill would be captain of the Bratva in this part of the country, at least for a while—but it didn't feel to Trinity as if either of them had won. Not even a little.

"We have to take Oleg out of here," she said quietly.

Kirill stepped back, breaking her embrace. His expression had turned back to its usual stone. "No time."

"But Oleg—"

"What of Pyotr and Sacha and Vlad? Should we leave them to the fire?"

Trinity flinched.

"We must go now!" Timur called.

Kirill moved around her as if she meant nothing to him, and she supposed that compared to what he had lost today, that much was true. They weren't friends, and with Oleg dead they certainly weren't family. Still, she felt as if she was a part of this brotherhood—their sister—whether they returned the feeling or not. She owed Oleg that.

"Trinity, let's go," Jax said, and his voice got her moving.

When she walked to him, he took her by the arm, and the two of them followed Opie, Chibs, and the rest outside. Some went out the back door, where the cars were waiting, and others used the front.

"Let it burn," Kirill said.

Trinity turned to see Gavril snap open an old metal lighter, flicking the thumbwheel to summon the flame. He tossed it through the open door, and it slid along the floor until the flame reached the spilled gasoline. The curtains now on fire, their flame rippled upward, racing along the floor and up the walls, spreading out the doors on either side of the lobby. In minutes, the main body of the hotel would be engulfed.

Jax looked at Kirill. "We good?"

Kirill paused a moment before nodding. "We are."

Jax took Trinity's hand to lead her toward his motorcycle, but she hesitated, turning to look at Kirill and Gavril and the others.

Kirill hesitated. "You're welcome with us, Trinity," he said, but she wasn't sure that she believed him.

Jax squeezed her hand. "She needs her family now."

Trinity shot him a hard look and pulled away. "Don't tell me what I need."

Jax held up his hands in surrender and she saw how much blood had soaked into his clothes, saw his injuries with fresh eyes and the way he wavered on his feet. He'd come for her, searched for her, and when he could have walked away, he had fought to the death at Oleg's side. It could have gone the other way, with Jax dead and Oleg alive. He'd risked that for her.

"Trinity," Opie said, and she glanced at him. Despite his size and his intimidating appearance, he had a gentle kindness about him.

For a moment, she'd been unsure how she defined her own family. Now she turned to Kirill. He saw her decision written on her face and nodded, encouraging her. She smiled thinly—sadly—to thank him and to let him know they would mourn together, even though they would be apart.

Behind them, the Wonderland Hotel burned.

Cars came out from behind the hotel and skidded into the street, tearing off into the distance.

Trinity turned to Jax. "What are you waitin' for? I don't want to go to jail."

He smiled, wincing at the pain in his swollen face, split lip leaking blood.

They walked to his motorcycle together, climbed aboard, and joined the exodus. As they rode away, she said a silent farewell to Oleg in her heart, hoping the fire reached him before his body could be carted off by the coroner. Given the choice, he'd rather have burned with his brothers.

Trinity held tightly to Jax's back as he twisted the throttle and they flew along a back road, toward the red hills in the distance.

Rollie rarely tended bar at the Tombstone anymore, but that afternoon he doled out beers and poured shots of whiskey. Earlier in the day, he had been in the back with the others. Numb and grieving, they'd doctored each other's wounds. Bloody clothes had been burned in a barrel in the back lot. They'd showered and changed, punched walls and said prayers to a God none of them was sure would be listening.

Thor was in the kitchen cooking. Baghead and Clean were in back with Trinity and the boys from Charming, and Rollie was out here wiping the counter and trying to wrap his mind around it all. Maybe it wasn't fair for him to blame Jax for everything that had happened—maybe the kid's story about Joyce's murder out on that ranch road was true—but Rollie couldn't help it. He needed somewhere to aim his rage.

But when Jax walked out from the back of the bar in a clean T-shirt and jeans, his face swollen from the beatings Lagoshin had given him but otherwise all right, Rollie took a deep breath and swallowed his bitterness before turning to face him.

"You all set?" he asked.

Jax slid onto a stool, wincing in pain. "Trinity's on a ten o'clock flight. Couple of hours, and we'll be out of here." He cocked his head, studying Rollie. "Unless you want us to go now."

Rollie considered it. Pressed his lips together to fight back the words he really wanted to say. When he exhaled again, some of his fury eased.

"Take the time you need. But I won't be sorry to see the back of you."

"I just came out here to tell you I owe you," Jax said, his voice still a rasp. The bruises on his throat showed just how close Lagoshin had come to strangling him.

"Damn right you do," Rollie said. "Things go along pretty quietly here as a rule. Then you roll into town and I've got three dead brothers."

His anger simmered, and he stared expectantly at Jax.

"She's my sister, Rollie," Jax said. "What would you have done?"

Rollie didn't have an answer to that. He shook his head and grabbed a bottle of Jack Daniels, poured himself a shot, and tossed it back. He didn't offer one to Jax.

"Eat your fries," Jax said. "I'll see you before we go."

When Jax had retreated into the back room again, Rollie noticed that Thor had remained at the bar instead of returning to the kitchen.

"Something you wanna say?" he asked.

Thor stared at the door Jax had gone through. "Not really. I like him well enough. I just still get a feeling there's something hinky about his version of what went down with Joyce last night."

Rollie picked up another shot glass, filled it, and slid it down to Thor. "Me too," he said. "But it's just a feeling, and I'm not gonna stir up shit with the mother charter based on that. Weird thing is that I always liked Jax, but it's like he's not the same guy I used to know."

Thor downed his whiskey and banged the shot glass down on the bar. He wiped the back of his hand across his mouth.

"Is anyone?"

When Jax kissed Trinity good-bye at the airport, he still had Oleg's blood under his fingernails. He'd scrubbed himself as well as he could in the shower, but he just couldn't get it all off.

"Oleg saved my life," he said.

Trinity visibly trembled, swallowing her grief. "He was a good man."

"He was," Jax agreed.

"And now my mum gets her wish."

Jax shook his head. "This isn't what she wanted."

"Listen you," she said, holding his hands in her own, sorrow-filled eyes locked on his. "We're gonna keep in touch now. It was peculiar before, I know, for all sorts of reasons. But I could get used to the idea of havin' a brother."

CHRISTOPHER GOLDEN

Jax smiled. "We'll keep in touch," he promised. "Starting with you calling to let me know you got home all right."

People streamed around them, most trailing wheeled luggage or toting little children and ignoring the small island made up of Jax, Trinity, Opie, and Chibs. Announcements came overhead. Travelers hustled toward the lengthy security line, talking on cell phones and checking the time, worried they might miss their planes.

"You should go," Jax said.

Trinity's smile was cracked porcelain. Perfect and smooth and beautiful but betraying fractures that could be sealed but never healed.

She kissed Opie and Chibs, both of whom spoke soft farewells, and then she hugged Jax, and he held her tightly, flushed with guilt. If he'd had it to do all over again, he would still have Oleg's blood under his fingernails. Yes, he'd made Maureen Ashby a promise, but sending Trinity home was about more than that. If she'd stayed with Oleg, it would have just been a matter of time before she'd ended up dead or as a pawn in some negotiation between the Russians and SAMCRO, and he couldn't risk either. By protecting Trinity, he'd also protected the club.

"Tell your mother she owes me one," Jax said, making a joke of it, though he meant every word.

"I'll pass it on," Trinity replied.

Opie had been holding the new bag containing a couple of changes of clothes and some toiletries they'd bought for her before coming to the airport, just to make sure Trinity didn't draw any special attention at security. Her belongings had been seized by the police when the fire at Wonderland had been put out. Izzo had done the club one last favor by getting his hands on Trinity's passport. When Opie held the new bag out, Trinity took it and slipped it over her shoulder. There were no more words. She raised her hand in something close to a wave, then turned and joined the queue. Jax, Opie, and Chibs waited until she had passed through security and moved deeper into the terminal, out of sight. Only when there was nothing more they could do to ensure she boarded the flight to Belfast did they at last turn and leave the airport.

Though night had fallen, the day's heat remained. As they walked to the lot where they'd parked their bikes, the air, so dry it stole the spit from their mouths, baked them. Jax straddled his bike, kick-started the engine, and minutes later they were riding northwest, tearing along the nighttime road and leaving the lights of Las Vegas and the deeds done there behind. Jax thought of Tara and his boys, and his heart swelled, making him give the throttle an extra twist. He thought of his mother and Clay and the delicate balance of power he'd left behind in Charming. They could get through it all, he knew. SAMCRO would survive, and in time the club would thrive.

Someday his father's dream of making the club legit—of getting out of all illegal business—would come true. Jax would take Tara and his boys and start a new life. All of that waited for him in Charming—a peaceful future, a new beginning.

Oleg had saved his life—the blood under Jax's fingernails was his. But there was other blood on his hands, invisible but there nevertheless. The blood of hard decisions.

As he rode, he wondered what his father would make of the man he'd become. The question haunted him.

Jax sped up, his Harley knifing through the night-black desert, but he could not escape his ghosts. They rode with him.